The Trinity Knot

H R Conklin

Celtic Magic

Book 1

Dedicated to my father,
Saxon William Roe
1946-2014
He taught me to never give up.

Celtic Magic

Be wary the gifts the faeries may give,

We know not how they influence the life we live.

The Trinity Knot

Summer is for warmth and growth

A new understanding of what family means

A song of possibilities for what we can do

Reality expands and our soul sings.

THE PRIZE

Isle of Skye, Scotland
late 1600s

Mairi MacCrimmon raced across the moor through the thick heather, becoming hopelessly lost in the dense fog that had suddenly risen out of the numerous burns and glens, making it nearly impossible to see even a foot ahead of her. She ducked under the low branches of a grove of oak trees, narrowly missing hitting her head, though not avoiding tripping on her dress. She only just managed to roll onto her back as she went down, succeeding in safely tucking the precious silver faerie chanter against her chest. Lying in the muck of leaves and mud, already becoming drenched through from the soup-like fog, she stayed as still as possible, listening. *How close are they?*

Too close for comfort, she could hear the howling and whining of the hundreds of hounds that belonged to not only her own MacCrimmon clansmen, but also their allies, the MacLeods. They had been released to find her, as if she were a frightened rabbit to be caught and killed during the hunting games of Lughnasadh. *Och! I am a frightened rabbit.* Even worse, based on the sounds and calls of the rowdy bunch chasing after her, she was sure the MacDonalds were intending to find her, too. She had truly stirred up the beehive this time.

Attempting to catch her breath and calm her nerves, breathing in the reassuring smell of wet leaves and soil that she hoped would mask her own scent, Mairi stood up, stumbling through the grove in search of a hiding place. She was pretty sure that never in her or even her grandmother's lifetime had all three clans been on the same end of a chase. Of course, it was more of a race, and there was a very special prize at the end of it.

Leaning against the thick trunk of an oak tree for reassurance as she got her bearings straight, she traced her delicate fingers along the beautiful faerie designs etched into the surface of the silver faerie chanter, feebly trying to cover the holes with her small fingers. She wasn't even one of the faerie line of clansmen, yet she could feel the power of the faerie magic vibrating throughout the instrument piece. It pulsed with a vitality all its own, and it tugged at her, begging to be held, to be owned.

She hadn't meant to so obviously steal it. She'd been listening to the clansmen talk the night before as she'd helped serve the mead at this year's Celebration of Lughnasadh, and a rowdy bunch of MacLeod's began bragging about a family tale, telling how their ancestors had taken a faerie chanter off the bagpipes of a MacDonald piper centuries ago. With this chanter, obviously charmed by the Fair Folk evidenced by the never tarnishing faerie silver, the MacCrimmon pipers, allies to the MacLeods, had managed to win the title of Chief Piper at the annual Bagpipe Competition every year since. But Mairi's sense of justice at the thought of thievery and cheating had gnawed at her all night. She felt it was her duty to return the chanter to the rightful owners.

The new day dawned, and as Mairi arrived to clear last night's mugs and help her clan brothers dress for the competition by pinning on their ornaments and buckling their shoes, she saw it. The chanter! Lying on a chair as if it was an ordinary chanter, but it wasn't. She would have known it wasn't ordinary even if she hadn't overheard the clansmen talking. The silver metal was etched with the most intricate carvings that only one of the Fair Folk could have possibly put there.

Something in her broke, and she had to have it. Looking around at the still snoring men, she pulled the chanter, carefully, quickly from the rest of the bagpipes it was attached to. Taking the whole pipes was out of the question as they were way too heavy and difficult to hide if she was going to return it to the rightful owners. At least, she thought that was what she meant to do. But now, she wasn't sure what she could do, because she'd been seen as she snuck away. It was breaking clan rules, a woman daring to touch the bagpipes, even if it was only the chanter, the seemingly innocuous part with the finger holes. It was double the trouble for being a faerie chanter, as well.

The men shouting at her had alerted the clans, and she'd run from the castle, darting in and out of the oak trees that grew here and there along the edge of the moor, losing them as they tripped over each other in their hung-over stupors. She'd headed for the Faerie Grove to gain the aid of the faeries themselves. But now that plan appeared foolish, and simply escaping alive seemed impossible. Thankfully the dense fog had sprung up as if from nowhere.

SNAP! She froze as she heard a branch break nearby as a foot came down hard on it. Shaking off her fear for the moment, she dropped to her knees and began scurrying as quickly as she could, wriggling into the small gap she luckily located at the base of an oak tree as she scrabbled around. Grateful she was one of the more petite Scottish women, she swallowed against the bile rising in her throat. *Please Aife, protect me,* she prayed to the Goddess. *Please let it be my true love, let it be Liam MacLeod.* She thought, momentarily, of her Liam. He was a distant relation of the current MacLeod clan chief. Would even he be able to save her, druid or not?

Oh Lugh! To be safe she called on the God, too, in whose honor the Summer Games were being held. *Don't let it be Ian MacDonald,* she added, as images of the broad shouldered, redheaded druid with the cruel smile danced across her memory. If he captured her, Ian would as soon shave her head and strip her naked in front of all the clans, rather than put her in jail to rot, jail being the kinder option. She'd seen this very thing happen to another girl, and the girl had been a MacDonald just like him. The girl's crime, denying Ian marriage though her father had made the offer. Mairi shuddered. She couldn't fathom what he would do to a MacCrimmon like her.

She tensed her body, trying to still her breath to near nothing, as she waited. The fog lifted a little outside her tiny sanctuary as a man's foot enclosed in a druid's sandal stepped into her view. She stuffed a fist into her mouth to stop herself from letting out a scream, her other hand gripping the chanter tight.

A man's deep voice spoke to her in Gaelic, "Mairi, I know you're in there. Come out now."

SPRING BREAK

San Diego, California
March, present year

Mairi MacDonald grabbed her favorite sunshine yellow 5'10" keel fin Skip Frye fish surfboard, her birthday present from her dad last year. She felt the warm sand granules sink beneath her bare feet as she ran across the beach behind her dad, reveling in the heat of the morning sun beating on her back, soaking through the full suit necessary this time of year. She squealed a little as her toes met the first onslaught of ice cold salt water, splashing her way into the depths of the Pacific Ocean.

Diving under the first set of waves, red curls slicking back like satin ribbon under the turquoise water, body forming to the sleek length of fiberglass beneath her abdomen, she grinned at the sheer delight she always felt as she became one with the underwater world. Breaking through the surface, shaking the salt water out of her eyes, Mairi imagined she must look like a seal bobbing up from below.

Paddling hard, cupped hands digging deep to get the most forward momentum as she strived to keep up with her dad, she chanced a glance over her shoulder. Giving her younger brother, Jamie the thumbs up as he battled water to catch her, Mairi glimpsed their mother on the beach spreading a blanket and setting up their space. Mairi turned in time to see another wave coming her way and she again grabbed her board, pushing the nose under the wave to duck dive beneath the swell.

Surfacing on the other side, she was surprised to see her dad was only a couple of feet ahead. *He must be waiting for me,* she thought. She shouted to him, "Slowing down, old man?" He turned to look at her and for an instant Mairi caught a look of incomprehensible pain. "Are you alright, dad?" she asked, confused by the expression she'd never seen on her happy-go-lucky dad's face.

His expression quickly switched to his customary grin, "Yeah! Everything's great! I just wanted to give you a fighting chance." He laughed and splashed at her with a swooping arc of water sent her way by his powerful forearm.

Reassured, Mairi renewed her efforts to catch him, and they soon found themselves in the outside, grabbing their place in the lineup near the OB Pier. They turned and sat up, feet trailing in the water on either side of their boards, and in unison cheered Jamie on as he pushed his way through the final wave to the outside to join them.

I don't think it can get any better than this, Mairi thought, stoked on the prospect of a whole day of surfing and hanging out at the beach. *I'm glad we decided to stay home for Spring Break this year, even if I do miss our usual spring trip to Baja.* When her parents had initially presented the idea of a "staycation" to Mairi and her brother, they weren't too happy about it, but daily trips to the beaches near their home were proving to be a good plan.

An hour later, as Mairi paddled back out from a failed wave, the sun overheating her back as it reached its apex in the sky, her father shouted, "Mairi! Go for this one. Ride it in and we'll eat lunch with your mom."

Mairi nodded to her dad and turned to begin paddling, lining her board up with the pace of the oncoming swell of rising water coming her way. Just as she felt the front of her board get lifted up and move as one with the swell, Mairi jumped to her feet and maneuvered her board to shoot right, positioning herself in the barrel of the wave.

Dragging her fingertips along the wall of water cascading up and over her head, basking in the green light surrounding her, she shouted her sheer joy as she shot out into the sunlight. She had time to take in the crowded beach full of a rainbow of shade umbrellas as she rode the wave all the way in. As the beach came closer, she dropped to her knees and slid off her board, letting the shrinking wave roll to shore ahead of her.

Her brother ran in from where he'd already joined their mom on the beach, grabbing her board and high-fiving her. "That was sick, Mairi! Have you gotten a wave that good before?"

Mairi shook her head, as much to get the salt water out of her hair as to answer her brother. It had definitely been her best ride to date.

"Nice job, Mairi," her dad said as he came up behind her and draped his arm over her shoulders, beaming with his pride in his daughter's ability.

Her mother came up to her also smiling, offering a towel. "That was amazing! Wave of the day! I caught most of it on video! I'll show you at home."

Her mother turned, peach-floral beach wrap fluttering in the slight breeze blowing off shore as she handed out sandwiches. "Here Jamie, your favorite, tuna fish. Aiden, you have to eat. At least try." Mairi watched her mother firmly push a sandwich into her dad's hand. She realized her dad did seem really skinny lately.

"Thanks, Shaylee," Aiden replied. Mairi watched as her dad kissed her mom gently on the forehead. She turned quickly away, embarrassed by her parents' public display of affection. *I should be stoked they so obviously love each other, unlike so many of my friend's parents who have divorced,* Mairi chastised herself as she wrestled with her wet suit. Finally stripped down to her bikini, she grabbed the cucumber and cream cheese sandwich her mom had made especially for her. Tuna turned her stomach ever since the time she'd gotten the flu and thrown it up all over her bed.

Sitting on her towel in the warm sun, Mairi smiled at her family happily munching on their food. They were all three blondes, with varying shades of tan skin. Wrapping the ends of her long red hair around her pale pointer finger, she couldn't help but wonder if she was adopted. Other than sharing a love of surfing and camping with them, she felt like an oddball simply because she looked so different. Having been assured numerous times she wasn't adopted, Mairi let the thought drift away as she saw her dad grimace in pain.

"What's wrong?" her mother asked, obvious worry written all over her face.

"Nothing," Aiden said, gripping his side. Mairi caught her breath, but let it out as her dad looked towards her and smiled gently. "It's just that thing that keeps happening. I'm sure I simply need to exercise or something."

"Did you make the appointment with Kaiser Hospital, like you promised?" her mother pressed. Mairi looked in her brother's direction, shrugging her shoulder as she perceived his alarm. "Old people," she muttered, for her own reassurance as much as his.

"Yes!" Her dad gasped. "Yes, of course. It's on Monday. My appointment is first thing in the morning. I'm just so tired, going to take a nap now."

Mairi's phone buzzed as her dad lay down. Seeing it was her friend texting about their plans later that day, Mairi pushed the conversation aside for the time being. *After all, parents* are *old. They're bound to have problems,* she decided, happy instead to help her friend choose which movie they'd see later and forget the woes of adulthood. She was just questioning which movie her friend had in mind when she heard an odd sound coming from her dad. She looked over at him, and saw he was lying on his side, gasping for breath.

"Dad?" she called out. When he didn't answer, not even a grumble, she scooted over to him. She grabbed his shoulder and shook him. "Dad?"

He didn't respond.

"Dad!" Mairi dropped her phone and began shaking him roughly, shouting, "Dad, wake up!"

He gasped again.

"Mom! Mom!" she shrieked. "Something's wrong with Dad!" Her mom and brother skidded in behind her. Mairi could feel he was struggling to breathe, a terrible rattling sound coming from his chest. "What's wrong with him? We have to help him!" Tears ran down her face. "Help him!!"

FOLK LORE
Southern California
May 28th, present year

Danny MacDonald stood in the gray mist of the cold day. *May gray...at least this means June won't be gloomy,* he thought of the saying locals always said of the fog that often rolled in this time of year. *It fits the setting,* he decided, looking around at the cemetery full of people in mourning. His gaze followed the train of sad visitors making their way to his family as they sat around the engraved plaque sunk into the ground next to a small hole. The plaque read:

AIDEN MACDONALD
LOVING HUSBAND, FATHER AND SON

Danny wished it also said *uncle* because his Uncle Aiden had always treated him like a son, since his own father had skipped out when Danny was only two. *How two brothers can be so different is beyond me,* he thought, thinking of his tense and angry dad next to the joyous demeanor of his Uncle Aiden.

Shaking his head, Danny glanced over at his cousins,

Mairi and Jamie, sitting between their mother, his Aunt Shaylee, and their mutual Granny Kate. Red-headed Mairi stood out like a flame beside her blonde mother and brother, and their gray-haired granny. Aunt Shaylee and Granny Kate held handkerchiefs to their tear-drowned eyes, though Granny sat ramrod straight, bearing her grief with a matriarch's dignity, juxtaposed to his aunt's loud sobbing. Jamie sat with big eyes staring in horror at the hole as the druid-like priest, a member of the Unitarian Church, carefully lowered in the small wooden urn.

I wonder why Uncle Aiden wanted to be cremated? Granny Kate had wanted him to have a grave next to her own husband's so burying the ashes had been their compromise. Danny had never given much thought to what happened to his family after they died, Uncle Aiden being the first for him to witness, and he wondered vaguely about the grandfather who had died even before Uncle Aiden had been born. Danny had never heard much about his grandfather, only that he'd been in a war and died fairly young.

Looking up again from the dark hole, his cousin Mairi caught his attention. *She looks...* Danny struggled to describe her demeanor. She wasn't crying at all, and she wasn't shocked, that he could see, but *...angry. She looks really angry,* Danny decided, her red air seeming to almost spark like a firework. *Maybe I'd be angry, too. This happened to them so unexpectedly, from out of the blue.*

Danny's thoughts were interrupted as everyone in the group turned in unison towards the entrance of the cemetery as a haunting melody floated their direction. Danny heard it, too. *It's 'Danny Boy',* he realized. It was his favorite song, the one he'd been named for, in fact. He quietly sang the refrain, "Danny boy, oh Danny boy. The pipes, the pipes are calling, from glen to glen and down the mountainside." It was an evocative song, one about a soldier being called by death. He wasn't exactly sure why he'd been named for it, considering how his grandfather had died, but Danny loved the song all the same.

Standing to get a better look at who was playing the bagpipes, he saw an elderly man slowly making his way up the pathway towards their group, and as he passed beside him, Danny gasped with disbelief. He was a tall, thin man with long white hair, dressed head to toe in traditional Scottish garb. He wore a plaid kilt hanging to his knees, a Renaissance style shirt complete with billowing sleeves and laces crisscrossed at his chest. But it wasn't the clothing that caught Danny's attention, though he relished anything traditionally Celtic. It wasn't even the impeccable playing of the song on the bagpipes, and the deft way the man's fingers flew over the chanter. It was the actual chanter that mesmerized Danny, for it was a silver chanter carved with Celtic Knots, and shining in an unearthly way despite the heavy gray mist. If asked under oath, Danny would have sworn that the chanter itself pulled at him, creating a longing in him not explained by any modern science. He couldn't wait to escape the crowd and return to his Granny's house in order to do a little research and find out if this was the chanter he believed it to be.

Danny had left the funeral as soon as he saw the piper say good-bye to his granny and his aunt. Now he searched desperately through the piles of dusty boxes full of old books, diaries, Little League trophies, and other random stuff his mother had saved in his granny's attic as he grew out of childhood. He watched as his souvenir baseball rolled out of his lucky pitcher's glove, thumped loudly on the unpolished wood floor, and finally stopped under the filthy attic window.

He froze, listening for any sign that he'd alerted the funeral party going on down below that he'd escaped to the attic. When he didn't hear anything to cause him concern, he turned back to his search.

It's got to be here somewhere, he thought, returning his attention to the piles next to him as he kneeled on the dusty floor. He only needed to see the picture again to be sure it was the right one!

In his frustration, he knocked over a pile of documents about his clan's family lore that he'd photocopied from the library for his report in junior high school. It was the final push he had needed in deciding what his life's work would be, though he'd only been 12 at the time. He'd fancied himself a famous discoverer of ancient Celtic artifacts, a Scottish Indiana Jones. So now he was a senior in high school with dreams of studying art history and historical folklore, which included a minor in cultural music, at UCLA next year. He realized he might also need to study archaeology, but he had a few years to fully declare his major. As he rummaged through the toppled pile of papers, a corner of the picture he was looking for peeked out from the landslide.

Swiping his slightly long, strawberry-blonde hair out of his eyes, Danny pulled out the copy of a 15th century drawing of a set of bagpipes said to have belonged to the MacCrimmon clan, the most renowned bagpipers in Scottish history. It was said that they got their powerful talent from a silver chanter that was given to them by the faeries. Danny knew better. He knew the real story was that the chanter had been given to his clan, the MacDonalds, and had been stolen from them by first the MacLeods and then the MacCrimmons. The last trace seen of it had been in the 16th century.

Gripping the paper with the drawing of the chanter on it, he headed downstairs. He made his way through the mass of black clad visitors. *Uncle Aiden sure did know a lot of people. And of course, every one of his friends showed up to pay their respect. He was the nicest guy to everyone.*

Danny hesitated at the door, hand resting on the doorknob. *Should I say goodbye to my cousins?* A cursory look around the room told him his aunt and cousins wouldn't notice he'd left. He would have liked to have spoken to the bagpiper, found out who he was, but the piper had disappeared right away, never showing up at the funeral party. Glancing at his watch, Danny realized he needed to hurry, and headed outside to his beat up, piece of junk car.

Taking the onramp to the 5 North freeway, facing hours of slow traffic ahead of him, engine sputtering like it might not make it another foot, he put his favorite Celtic CD, The Wicked Tinkers, in the ancient CD-player. They always cheered him up, no matter how down he was. Punching in "*Ramblin Rover*," he let his mind drift to his childhood.

As a little boy, he'd grown up listening to his clan's lore as told to him by his Granny Kate. Tales of magic bagpipes, highland skirmishes, and faerie blessings or curses, depending on the story, had filled his bedtime routines. Every time she babysat him while his mother worked, Granny Kate would tell him these tales. No one believed them, of course. Who would? They were full of magic and other fanciful nonsense. Though there were times when he thought his Granny might actually believe. There was something in the way she told the tales with such authenticity.

It was enough to send him searching through library archives, children's books, and asking at museums to give Danny confidence in their historical importance. Danny decided to study folklore and its influences on people throughout history. He never intended to fall into believing any of it as truth, just as a truth the ancient people would have put their faith in.

Of course, he'd heard of the Faerie Flag of the MacLeod clan, one of the only artifacts founded in faerie tales known to actually exist. They had a family tale passed down for generations surrounding this supposed Faerie Flag and the MacLeod's kept it on display in their clan castle, Dunvegan Castle, on the Isle of Skye. This had given him an idea and so he'd developed a plan. He would search the world, like Indiana Jones did in the movies, for the actual missing Celtic artifacts in conjunction with the folklore he was studying.

Danny made the turn onto Interstate 405 North and his head started to throb. Attempting to alleviate the pain, he switched CDs to the mellower sounds of The Chieftains with Van Morrison singing *"Carrikfergus,"* causing a lump to rise in his throat as he was once again reminded of his uncle. Fumbling with the CDs, he wished for the millionth time he could afford an iPod, *and a better car if I'm going to begin wishing now,* he laughed at himself.

A part of him worried that all this studying would mean he wouldn't make a name for himself for several years still. This gnawed at him because he desperately wanted to show his father that he could be successful in spite of a rough childhood. His father had been absent most of his life, so he could make his fortune building pipelines for the oil industry without the "burden of a family." *How did my dad turn out so different from his easy-going, family loving brother? I wish Uncle Aiden had been my dad.* Danny shook his head. He'd never understood his own father.

But now he'd been given this extraordinary opportunity to show his dad. *I've seen the silver faerie chanter! The very one that was in all of the folklore, I'm sure of it!*

Suddenly, all of his doubt dropped away. This had to be the fabled faerie chanter, and it belonged in *his* family, the MacDonalds. Danny realized he wanted this chanter more than he had ever wanted anything in his lifetime. If only he hadn't hesitated. *I should have been just like Indiana Jones and taken it right then and there.*

Danny shook his head as he pulled up to his apartment, his car heaving a grateful sigh as he turned off the ignition. Picking up the picture of the chanter from the passenger seat, he exited the car. He had promised his mother he'd be home from the funeral before dark. She'd never been close to his dad's family, but she hadn't stopped him from showing his respects.

As Danny walked into the apartment, he decided that he'd call his Granny Kate after school the next day and find out what she knew. He could still feel a residual tingle from the chanter's power as it had pulled on him at the funeral and he determined he would stop at nothing to get his hands on it. He would make a name for himself and show his dad.

LOST

San Diego, California
June 23rd, present year

"It's been in our family for centuries," Shaylee groaned.

Mairi leaned on the doorframe as she watched her mother frantically look for the necklace under her bed.

"Are you sure you don't know where it is?" Shaylee asked, desperation breaking her voice. She sat back on her heels as she wiped her forehead, a streak of dirt from gardening the day before replacing the trail of sweat.

Mairi shrugged, "I already told you I don't, Mom. We're going to be late." Turning on her heel, she stalked to the car as she reached into her pocket, past the purple velvet pouch inside which lay the necklace, and pulled out her cell phone.

'Ugh my mom's so unfair. I can't believe she's still making me go,' she texted her friend.

Jamie was already waiting in the car, appearing to be oblivious to the tension between Mairi and their mom, his nose stuck in the first few pages of what could only be the world's longest novel, the complete trilogy of *Lord of the Rings*. Mairi rolled her eyes, wondering how she and her brother could be from the same parents and yet be so different. The only things they really had in common were trips to Baja and surfing.

Mairi climbed into the front seat, tossing her backpack behind her without looking.

"Hey! You hit me!" Her brother whined at her. "Geez! Why are you always so worked up?" Jamie grumbled, returning to his book.

She considered flinging a retort at him, but chose to shrug him off, muttering a half-hearted "sorry." She didn't feel like fighting with everyone that morning. After all, she wasn't actually mad at her brother, although he could have backed her up last night when she was giving it one last shot to try and convince their mom to let them stay home for the summer. *He didn't have to say that he thought going to Granda's property sounded like fun. It's almost like he wants to go.*

"Mairi!" Shaylee shouted from the front door, hands on her hips. Mairi hated her name, due to too many insulting nicknames in elementary school, such as Hairy Mairi and Mary, Mary Quite Contrary. Neither filled her with good memories. Sure, her mom had spelled it unique, in that weird way Californians always do, but it didn't change the fact that it was just "Mary." So boring!

"Mairi! You left the door wide open and Peaches got out. Now I have to look for her after I drop you off at the bus station, and I still have my lesson plans to prep." Her mom stood on the front porch of their house, looking a complete wreck, dressed in the same clothes she'd been wearing for the past week: filthy black leggings and one of her dad's old t-shirts, the one that ironically declared "Stay calm and carry on." Mairi wondered if she would even bother to change her clothes when she started teaching again.

But Mairi remained silent. She hadn't meant to leave the door open. She loved Peaches. She'd rescued the cat from a Baja shelter with her dad on her 15th birthday in April, his last present to her. She wouldn't put the cat in danger on purpose. Add this to the long list of things she had done wrong since losing her dad. Mairi shoved her headphones into her ears and pretended she hadn't heard. *Mom will find Peaches. I know she will. Besides, we let her out all the time when we're home for the day. She'll survive a few hours while mom's gone.*

Mairi peeked out from behind her fall of unruly curls as her mom climbed into the driver's side seat, taking in the greasy hair and the tear-stained face. She could hardly see the once vibrant flowery woman her mom had been before cancer had suddenly taken Mairi's dad. She watched as her mom's Birkenstock-enclosed foot pushed on the brake and she turned the key, the car roaring to life. Other than the sounds of the car motor accelerating to pass other cars on Interstate 8 as they made their way to the downtown bus station, the car remained thick with silence. Her mom was deep in thought about who knows what, and Jamie was engrossed in his novel. Mairi pretended to listen to her music, unable to keep her thoughts at bay, trying in vain to stop feeling.

Why did dad die? She'd asked herself this same question every day since that final fatal day in May, like a broken mantra. Many other questions always followed, no matter how hard Mairi tried to squelch them and goodness knew she'd tried. *How come mom didn't tell me he was sick? Why wait until the last week of his life? She says she only knew for the month before, and that the doctors thought he'd have a few more months, at least. She said it was dad's wish not to ruin my birthday.* A pang of guilt at the thought of her ailing dad using precious energy worrying about how she would feel hit her like a dart hitting a bull's eye. *But I only had a week to say good-bye! Why didn't mom tell me? Why didn't dad let me have more time?*

Mairi searched for a song on her phone that would make her stop thinking about her dad, thumbing madly through her list of Nirvana, Blink 182, and other bands. It didn't really matter what song she picked. They never quieted her mind. Her music style had become progressively louder and more unruly as she desperately searched for something to still the anger and sorrow inside. She finally settled on Metallica's "Enter Sandman" and crossed her fingers it would help.

I have nothing without my dad! With him I had adventure, surfing and camping. Mom never did anything fun with us. She just did whatever dad did. She only ever expected us to read books and explore the canyon behind our house. That's fine for Jamie, but me? It's like she never even tried to get to know me, and now she's all I've got, yelling at me to get off my phone and crying all the time about dad.

Mairi sniffed the air, pungent with the sweat of her mom's unwashed body and clothes. *Would it hurt her to take a shower? Jeez!* Bunching up her sweatshirt sleeve to cover her nose, Mairi quickly shoved the idea of how much she herself wanted to never get out of bed in the morning, never change her clothes again, hide from the world that now no longer seemed to matter without her dad in it. But she couldn't do that. She glanced back at her brother. *There's only room for one depressed person in this family. Someone has to take care of my brother and she sure isn't doing a very good job.*

Mairi knew this was probably exactly why she and Jamie were being sent away, to stay with their estranged grandfather. They had never stayed with him before, and had only just met him last spring at their Dad's funeral. He had shown up unexpectedly, at least as far as Mairi knew. In the sea of black-clad guests, he'd stood out like a Beyoncé fan at a Kanye West concert. He'd worn traditional Scottish garb and was playing an eerie tune on the Highland Bagpipe.

Her mom had seemed genuinely surprised he was there, and Mairi never got more than a "This is my Da, your Granda" as an explanation. She wasn't even sure why he was "Granda" and not 'grandpa' like all her friends called theirs. He'd played a melancholic tune at her Dad's graveside, and then disappeared by the time all the guests had climbed into their cars and gone home.

Before that encounter she'd always assumed he was a real jerk and that was why they had no contact other than the occasional gift in the mail, absent of any card or letter. *But that can't be the case. He seemed all right at the funeral. Would mom really send us to stay with a complete stranger if he was a creep?*

THE NECKLACE

Hwy 101 California
June 23rd, present year

More than half a day later, Mairi sat back against the high-backed seat with a sigh, settled in for the long bus ride up the state from San Diego to some little nowhere town in Northern California with her brother. Outside she could see row upon row of grapevines as the sun shone down on mountains and vineyards alike. For hours, there had been nothing to look at except for rolling hills of dry grass. Even the stench of the cattle ranch had been a welcome change from the dreariness of the plain landscape the Central Valley had to offer. Now they were traveling through the vineyards north of San Francisco on their way to their Granda's. *I might as well be taking a bus ride to prison. I can't believe I have to spend nearly two months away from my home!*

Mairi sighed again. *It's so unfair! Just when the best part of the year, summer, has begun, we have to leave.* No long days at the beach, lying on towels drinking cold sodas, surfing in the warm Pacific Ocean. No nights at the mall, shopping and watching movies. Not even long mornings lazily surfing the web and chatting with friends. Not that Mairi was even sure she'd want to go do all those things this summer, not after losing her dad, but having that choice taken away from her made her want to hurt her mom.

"Get it together so we can stay home," Mairi had shouted at her the night before. "Don't make us lose our home and our friends on top of losing Dad!"

It hadn't helped. Her mom had shaken her head and collapsed onto the couch.

"I can't, Mairi, I just can't," she'd whispered through her sobs.

Mairi had stood over her mom for what felt like hours before stomping to her room. "Then I guess we're losing you, too!" she'd shouted over her shoulder before slamming the door behind her.

Before that argument had ended the evening, before Mairi had snuck into her mom's room intending one more time to demand her mom listen to reason only to find it empty and the mysterious family necklace lying unguarded on her dresser, her mom had tried to prepare her for life at their Granda's house. She'd dropped the final blow, warning her there would be no Internet connection at Granda's.

Was he from the Dark Ages? Everyone has Internet connection! They weren't even guaranteed any cell phone reception. Mom said it would be sketchy at best. *How am I going to keep in touch with my friends? How am I going to check in with Mom? This summer is definitely going to be dreadful.*

"Dad, why did you have to die?" Mairi asked yet again, whispering the question to the passing cars on Highway 101, knowing there would never be a satisfactory answer. What had she done to deserve such a terrible fate? Her dad had been so healthy last summer, taking her and

Jamie to the beach every day, teaching them to surf. Going on trips to Baja, hiking the mountains, soaking in hot springs, and surfing the warm waters off the Baja coast. Mairi's heart ached from the hole created by the loss of her dad. She shook her head to chase the thoughts away. She didn't even like to think about it, because if she didn't think about it, she could almost convince herself he was on a surf trip and he'd be home any day.

Holding up her cell phone, Mairi tried again to send her mom a text to ask about Peaches. *Still no connection!* There hadn't been any service since crossing the Golden Gate Bridge and continuing North. Clenching her fists, Mairi tried once more to understand why she was heading to Northern California. She knew her Mom had to work twice as hard to make ends meet now that her Dad was gone. She'd gotten a job teaching gardening and herbal classes at the local junior colleges and summer session started this week. She also would be putting in gardens as a Master Gardener with her own private business on the weekends. Plus, she already had her own business of treating people with Ayurveda Medicine out of her home. Her mom barely had time to take Mairi and Jamie to and from school and certainly had no time for them this summer. But Mairi didn't need taking care of. She was plenty old enough to take care of herself. Instead, she was being shipped off to the first available relative. *It's probably really because Mom can barely take care of herself, let alone take care of Jamie. She leaves that to me.* Mairi sighed again, trying unsuccessfully to turn it into deep breaths like her friend, whose mom was a yoga instructor, had suggested. *Mom is such a mess!* she silently screamed, and sighed a third time.

I wish Granny Kate had stayed around to help. Granny Kate, her dad's mom, had been no help, running off on some world trip the day after the funeral. *Then we could have at least stayed in San Diego this summer.*

Mairi fiddled with the necklace still in her pocket. Feeling its shape through the velvet pouch she wondered why her mom had told her to never ever touch it. *What will happen if I do? Will I get some sort of metal poisoning? Or is Mom just paranoid I'll lose it?* That was probably it, since her mom didn't seem to trust her. Truthfully, she wasn't certain what to do with the necklace now, not having stolen anything before in the 15 years she'd been alive.

Mairi shifted her body uncomfortably. *Great!* Her brother had dozed off with his head on her shoulder, his massive novel lay open in his lap, and now she had to use the restroom. Carefully pushing his head off her, she slid out from under his weight then gently lowered his head to the seat. Even as his sister, she had to admit he was more handsome than the average boy. Her heart clenched, and she quickly looked away. With his blonde wavy hair, blue eyes, dark eyelashes, and golden California tan, he looked just like their dad. Some days it was almost painful to look at him. She wondered if Jamie realized their similarity. *Maybe this is why mom is sending us away!* Mairi was struck with the sudden thought, stiffening for a moment in her attempt to slip out of her seat. *That's so wrong, it can't be true*, she decided.

Stepping over her backpack full of snacks she didn't feel like eating and a book she doubted she'd ever read, she realized that in just two years, Jamie would be at her same school and they might even be in the same classes. She knew Jamie would break many hearts in high school, if he could get his nose out of a book long enough to notice the girls. The thought sent a shudder through her. *Ugh! My baby brother dating* . . . Mairi shook off the horrific thought and carefully made her way down the aisle, swaying with the slight rocking motion of the bus.

Mairi finally reached the bathroom and slid into the tiny cubicle. The bus hit a pothole and knocked her against the sink. "Oh!" She let out a scream, slapping the rim of the sink in frustration. How she missed her cozy little house already. It wasn't very big, her bedroom barely had space to have a friend sleep over, but it was homey. It always smelled of lavender from their garden, and before Dad died, Mom would bake cookies and homemade bread. She realized even the bathroom wasn't so bad, now that she'd been confined to using this itty-bitty restroom for the past 14 hours.

Washing her hands in the cold water, she caught a glimpse of herself in the mirror. *I should probably wear make-up,* she thought as she splashed water on her pale white skin, freckled by the same intense sun that turned Jamie's skin golden. *At least, now that Dad's gone.* She had finished the thought before she could stop herself. It was the truth, though. She had never bothered before because she knew it would just smear in the ocean when she went surfing before or after school with her dad. Without him, she might never bother to surf again.

Sighing, she forced her thoughts back to safer ground. *I'm definitely not a California babe.* Her only redeeming quality was her green eyes, like her mom's. "Green like a still pool in a deep wood," her dad always told her. He used to call her his Celtic Princess when she was little. Tensing with the memory, she realized that no thoughts were safe. She clenched her fists hoping the pain of her nails digging into her skin would make her forget her dad for the moment.

Not sure she was truly ready to turn to self-mutilation, Mairi slowly uncurled her fists and pulled her hair up into a loose bun piled high on her head, hoping to tame the unruly red curls. Taunts of "Ronald MacDonald" echoed in her mind. She groaned. It never looked like the other girls at school, the ones with the perfectly tousled hair, the kind of hairstyles that said they'd been surfing that morning before school, but everyone knew they'd really spent the entire time in front of their mirrors working on their "beach hair." She tucked a stray curl behind her ear and tried again, finger combing the lumps that sprouted unbidden along her scalp. She shrugged, muttering, "Who cares?" under her breath. She ripped the hair-tie out of her hair, automatically putting it back on her wrist, rocking with the swaying bus as she made her way back to her seat, restroom door slamming shut behind her.

The bus hit yet another nasty bump in the road and Mairi fell between two rows of nearby seats. "Doesn't he even know how to drive?" she grumbled, as she pulled herself into a sitting position. Glancing down, she saw the purple velvet bag containing the necklace had dropped on the floor. Picking it up, Mairi gripped the tiny bag in her hand and made her way back to her own seat, noticing a humming sound had started up from somewhere.

Jamie grunted when he saw her. Slipping past him to take her spot by the window, she ruffled his hair with her fingers. "Hey! Don't do that!" he griped at her. "Why do you always treat me like a little kid?"

Mairi shrugged and, ignoring him, she loosened her grip on the tiny bag in her hand. Realizing the humming sound was getting louder she looked carefully at the bag. She knew it was reckless to let Jamie see she had taken the necklace, but she really didn't care if he told on her. *Let mom come up and take it back*, she thought triumphantly. *It'd serve her right for sending us so far away. Besides,* she laughed bitterly to herself, *there's no cellular service, anyway.*

Anticipation made her fumble a bit, her hands turning clammy with perspiration. She'd never even seen the necklace up close before. Every time she'd get near her mom as she was looking at it, her mom would sort of gasp and hide it somewhere. She always looked like Mairi had caught her taking drugs, or something. *Weirdo!* Mairi thought as she caught the drawstring loops and tugged it open, sliding the contents of the bag onto her other palm. The humming grew louder. It was definitely coming from the necklace.

She flinched a little with the expectation of something dire, but when nothing happened except an electric buzz emitting from it, she shrugged. *What's the big deal? It's only a silver necklace with some sort of Celtic Knot pendant hanging from the chain.* Other than the humming sound, she wasn't at all sure what made it so special that she had never been allowed to even touch it before, let alone see it.

"Isn't that the necklace Mom was looking for?" Jamie asked her, peering over his book he'd picked up again.

"So what?" she challenged, looking him in the eye.

Before she could say more, Mairi caught a glimpse of a deer in the road through the front windows just as the bus driver veered to miss it, nearly throwing them on the floor as he swerved back into the lane, continuing their way North. Jamie grabbed her shoulder and said with a groan, "I am so tired of this bus ride. I wish we were at Granda's already!"

Mairi never had a chance to come up with a response. A strong force tugged on her body. She felt like she was being pulled into a tube, her body squeezed and elongated. *So this is what a dust bunny feels like when it's being sucked up by the vacuum cleaner,* the random thought slipping into her consciousness. Clawing for something to hold onto, anything to anchor her to the bus seat, she gasped as her hand passed right through the walls of the bus as they shimmered before her. *What is happening?* she tried to shout, but no sound left her mouth.

As if her body belonged to someone else, Mairi noted objectively that she could feel her heart start to race. *Shouldn't this hurt?* she found herself thinking. Yet it didn't, as if she was made of taffy and not flesh and bones. Then Jamie, the bus, the people around her disappeared and she was all alone, surrounded only by darkness, trapped in an endless empty tunnel. There was no air, no sounds, no taste or smell. Her body and her thoughts were all she could detect, separated as if belonging to two different people. All at once, she understood how Alice had time to recite poetry and hold conversations as she was falling down the rabbit hole. Time seemed to stand still. Then Mairi felt, or maybe she simply noticed, that her heartbeat was slowing down, and she yawned. *Maybe I have time for a nap,* she thought, as she felt more and more relaxed in the darkness of no space or time.

Brightness abruptly enveloped her, as if a light switch had been turned on, and she squeezed her eyes shut against the pain of it. *Am I dead?* she wondered, half hoping she'd see her dad soon. Then she was falling, fast, and Mairi landed hard with a thump in a patch of tall, dry grass. Sucking in a deep breath and letting it out, she was amazed she could breathe freely again. Stretching every limb, she expected to see they had been flattened like dough under a rolling pin, but they were completely normal. The necklace still dangled from her left hand.

She peered around, but a thick white fog was surrounding her, so she could barely see past her outstretched hands. Surprisingly, Jamie was lying next to her, holding his palm to his forehead. *Hadn't he stayed on the bus?* She saw a trickle of blood seep between his fingers. He gestured at a rock sticking through the grass where he'd apparently hit his head when they landed.

"What happened?" Mairi asked as she automatically started to check he was okay, caring for him the way she'd had to the past several weeks, but he waved her away.

"Listen!" he whispered.

In the distance, she could hear a lonely, haunting sound, like a thousand bees playing a melody in unison. It was somehow familiar, but she couldn't be sure why. All she knew was it made her feel both sad and excited, as if something amazing was about to happen. She couldn't imagine what.

As she grasped for Jamie's hand to reassure herself this was real, she heard the tune change tempo. The fog began to lift, golden sunlight started to filter through the white tendrils, but before she could see more than tall grass stretching far in every direction, she again felt herself being sucked up and away. The feeling wasn't as shocking as before, seeming familiar and safe, like when she was little and her preschool teacher would roll her up in a blanket and say she was a burrito. She found herself wondering, *Where am I going this time? Will Jamie be there, too?* Then it was over, and she was back on the bus, snug in her seat, Jamie next to her staring with wide-eyed wonder. As if they were of one mind, they looked to the front of the bus and across the aisle. Neither the bus driver nor the few passengers around them acted as if two children had disappeared and reappeared right in front of them. They wore the same bored expression as before.

"What happened?" breathed Jamie.

Mairi shook her head slowly. "I have no idea." If Jamie hadn't been with her, she would have thought it was only a dream.

DISRUPTION

Isle of Skye, Scotland
June 23rd, early 1700s

Ian MacDonald sat alone on the burial mound, the very one all clan members knew to be an underground entrance to the land of the dead, one of the doorways to Avalon. The lesser clan members were afraid to linger here, only coming when a family or village member was laid to rest, scurrying away like frightened kittens as soon as the blessings were invoked. That's why Ian had picked this place for thinking. He knew he wasn't likely to be disturbed.

The sun was shining bright overhead, but he barely noticed. The hood of his white druid's robes was pulled low over his eyes, shadowing his face to match the darkness of his thoughts, hiding his limp gray hair, his long gray-white beard flowing over his chest and ending in a point at his belt. It was the day after the Summer Solstice, and once again he'd been disappointed. *Surely something new will happen to give me a lead to where it is,* he found himself wondering, yet again.

For over four decades he had been searching for it,

the silver faerie chanter. Three times before he'd been close to snatching it back from either the MacCrimmons or the MacLeods, the clans who had taken it, and each time he'd just missed it. *How dare that girl defy the order of law and presume bagpipes were for her gender? Bagpipes have always been and always should be for men alone.* Not knowing what had possessed the girl to steal the chanter in the first place truly vexed him.

He balled up his claw-like hands into fists, the sharp nails he kept perfectly filed digging into his palms. Though the skin of his hands was brittle and dry like a shed snakeskin, and his fists shook like leaves in a breeze, they were still more powerful than any other druid's on Skye. *Except for my son, who is now more powerful than I.* His mind drifted to his son, Ewan. Ian did not like his son being so powerful because Ewan was next in line after Ian as head of their Grove of Druids, so the more powerful Ewan became, the less powerful Ian felt. This troubled Ian, night and day, keeping him awake, preparing for every full moon so he could attempt new rituals thought to grant eternal youth. None of the rituals had yet to work, so Ian held onto his one true hope, gaining the power thought to be contained in the silver faerie chanter.

"If I can't reclaim it soon," the old man sighed, very much feeling the aches and pains inflicted on him by his aging body, "Ewan will replace me before the solar year completes one more pass."

SNAP! A twig broke nearby and Ian looked up sharply. Striding toward him was his son, a man who stood as tall as the shoulders of a warhorse, with a broad chest to match. Ewan's long red hair and beard, not unlike the hair and beard Ian once wore with pride, flowed around his head and face, practically crackling with the power Ewan possessed.

"Da!" Ewan's deep voice, a voice to rival the war drums of the Romans, boomed. "I knew I'd find ye here. Moping about, planning yer funeral we're sure to soon have, are ye?" Ewan's long legs quickly brought him by his father's side. Squatting down beside the old man, Ewan laughed heartily at his own joke as he slapped his dad none too gently on the back.

Ian scowled and attempted to burrow further into his hood. *Oh, how I regret letting my son in on my secret thinking place.* Rubbing his hands together, he waded through his crammed mind working up a retort, but before he could clear the phlegm from his throat, he felt the hairs on his neck rise.

Stilling his body, slowing his breath, and clearing his mind, Ian pulled his powers from the very earth as he let himself be drawn into the feeling he was experiencing. Ewan also stilled his body, a trick Druids learned early on in their training in order to tune into the natural world. This allowed Ian to focus. After over two decades of no signs at all, the Macleod family that Ian had spent nearly a lifetime chasing had finally used their magic, and the silver faerie chanter, too. This turn of events rejuvenated Ian, who now felt the adrenaline coursing through his body as he became excited for another opportunity to take back what belonged to his clan, and ultimately to him. The MacLeod's must not be allowed to survive such use. Not this time.

THEORIES

Northern California
June 23rd, present year

"I'm sure it was a wormhole, like how they traveled in *A Wrinkle in Time*." The redwood groves zipped by the bus window as Mairi and Jamie argued about what exactly had happened to them. Jamie insisted he knew exactly what had spit them out in some random grassy field mere moments ago.

Mairi rolled her eyes. This had been Jamie's all-time favorite book when he was ten, and although he'd been sorely disappointed there wasn't more of a battle involved, he'd talked incessantly about it for weeks afterwards. Despite the lack of battles, he had gone on to read all of Madeleine L'Engle's books.

Mairi shook her head. "I'm not so sure it was a wormhole." She looked down at the necklace in her hand. It wasn't humming anymore and the electric charge was much fainter. "It has something to do with this necklace, I'm sure of it. Mom never wanted us to touch it, hiding it in the bag or shoving it under a pillow or whatever every time I caught her looking at it. Then, the first time I touch it, something weird happens."

"Really? Well, a wormhole can be as tiny as a necklace. My theory still works."

Mairi barely heard him she was so lost in her own thoughts. *What is mom hiding from us? What is it about this necklace? What made it hum and is the electric pulse important?* She held her breath to see if she felt or heard anything more coming from the necklace.

When Mairi didn't jump on board with his theory, Jamie immediately threw out another one. "Well, it could be that the necklace is an alien machine connected to an ancient civilization. Maybe they were passing overhead in their spaceship, and we triggered their tractor beam to grab us." As if to demonstrate, Jamie grabbed Mairi's shoulder.

The breath she held escaped in a rush. "Geez, Jamie! You watch too much *Ancient Aliens* on T.V. Leave it to you to choose some strange show when you aren't buried in a book."

"So what? You have any better ideas?"

Mairi shrugged. She really didn't have any idea whatsoever. "Your ideas are all about science."

"Theories." Jamie pointed out. "Not ideas. In science, we have theories."

"Fine!" Mairi could feel her frustration rising into anger. But she didn't want to be angry with Jamie. At least he had ideas. "Theories, then. What about magic? What if this necklace is magic somehow? Like in Harry Potter. Isn't there a magic necklace in that book?" She couldn't explain it, but magic felt right.

Jamie grinned. Mairi stared back at him, then sighed. *Of course he likes this idea. He's read all of the Harry Potter books, too.* She'd only read the first one, but she'd watched all of the movies.

"Wizards are cool!" Jamie was talking, again. "Okay, maybe Mom bought this necklace from a weird old witch lady who put a curse on it like in *The Half-Blood Prince,* and now Mom is worried because maybe it caused Dad's cancer."

Mairi flinched at this. She grimaced and went to yell at Jamie that his theory was lame, but saw that he wasn't grinning anymore. *He must not like this theory either.* "It's not likely. Mom told me that this necklace has been in our family for centuries. It didn't cause Dad's illness." She huffed, wishing it did have the power to bring him back to life, though. Glancing down at the necklace, she stared in wonder. *Could it bring him back? Would Jamie think it's possible?* She shook her head incredulously. *That's too easy. Life doesn't work that way.*

For the rest of the bus trip, they argued every possibility they could come up with, so that by the time they arrived at their destination, they realized they had absolutely no idea what had happened.

THE CASTLE
Northern California
June 23rd, present year

Mairi saw her Granda through the windows as they got off the bus. There was no mistaking him, his white hair hanging a bit past his shoulders, fluffy like a cloud with tiny curls at the ends like wisps of stratosphere. His meticulously trimmed beard let loose the secret that he cared a great deal about his appearance. His piercing eyes, the same exact shade of green as Mairi's, stared directly into her soul. Dressed in a green plaid shirt and blue jeans, even in the summer heat, he stood straight and proud.

Her mom had told her his name was William MacLeod, and that he was her Granda, but Mairi still wasn't sure what to call him. *We're supposed to spend an entire summer with a virtual stranger? There is no way I'm going to enjoy any of this!* Mairi thought with frustration. He stood at the base of the steps looking like he might awkwardly hug them, then with barely a hello, he turned and walked so they could retrieve their bags from the underbelly of the bus. Mairi and Jamie followed and unbelievably Granda did not even lift a finger to help. Mairi and Jamie struggled under the weight of their bags.

"This is not a great start," she muttered under her breath.

What possessed me to bring so much? Mairi wondered. *Oh yeah. Mom. She told us to be prepared for anything.* She'd told them about swimming in the neighbor's pond on hot dry summer days and, on cold foggy nights, huddled indoors with a good book. *Ha!* Mairi almost laughed aloud at this thought. Books weren't her thing. There had also been suggestions of treks through muddy marshes and hikes up rocky cliffs, which meant she'd had to pack rain boots and hiking gear. Mairi was certain all these things wouldn't make the summer any less boring, just her luggage that much heavier.

They lugged their bags across the main street and over to a dirty white 4-door Toyota Highlander. Their granda opened the back-hatch door, displaying an impeccably clean interior, while they grunted and heaved in their belongings. Then, she began her usual silent battle with Jamie to see who got the front seat, but her Granda glared over the roof of the Highlander. "Jamie, in back, now." His quiet, matter-of-fact demeanor squelched any of the customary rebuttals Jamie would have thrown at their mom. Granda left no room for argument. He was clearly an adult you obeyed. *At least his command was in my favor,* Mairi thought, stifling the shred of hope she felt at this small win, determined to *not* enjoy anything about the summer.

After leaving the bus station, they briefly passed through town, stopping only to order burritos as take-out dinner. Mairi looked incredulously at the Mexican food. She doubted it would be any good, this far from Baja, and had been proven right with every bite. The flavor was bland, and the beans tasted like they came from a can. Still, it was better than the granola bars Mom had given them to munch on the bus ride up.

After ordering burritos, they'd turned up a steep, paved road, heading East out of town. They quickly ascended the surrounding mountains via a switch back until Mairi could look out her window and see the tiny town below them, nestled in a valley next to a meandering blue-green river. The mountains surrounding the river valley were covered in a dense forest of pine trees, as if the Christmas tree lots in the city had gathered there for a convention.

For every mountain range, they crested after that first one, another one, both higher and farther away, replaced it. More and more trees covered the mountains in waves of velvet green. Fiddling hopelessly with her cell phone, Mairi felt any likelihood for a social life disappearing behind the car. *Granda really lives beyond civilization,* she thought.

They passed through the shade of a tunnel of trees into the bright sunlight of wide, open expanse. In stark contrast to the previous tree-lined road, the one they were on now was flanked by meadows of tall grass turning golden in the dry summer heat. The fields were spotted with fluffy white sheep and sleek black cows calling back and forth in plaintive tones. After what seemed to be an hour of zipping along, they left the paved mountain road and turned onto an all-dirt, ditch-ridden road leading deeper into nowhere.

The three of them bounced along in silence. Finally, hot from the windows being rolled up, Mairi asked if she could roll down the window.

"I don't like dust in my car," was Granda's gruff answer.

Mairi took a deep breath and braved asking, "Ummm...then can we turn on the AC?"

Granda frowned, "It's not good for the car engine on these mountain roads."

Mairi hunched her shoulders and let out a sigh, staring into the distance of the expanse of blue sky, not a cloud in sight.

Finally, they turned into a gated dirt driveway. Grass was sprouting up between tire tracks, so Mairi guessed Granda didn't get many visitors. *Maybe that's why he doesn't know how to talk to people,* she thought. Her imagination returned to her earlier images of prison. She squeezed the necklace through the velvet bag, remembering what had happened to her and Jamie, wondering if it would make life more interesting now, like in *Harry Potter* when Harry had been given his Hogwarts letter. *Though I'm not sure I want anything to happen again. That was kind of scary!* she admitted, if only to herself.

Granda set the emergency brake, letting the car idle as he got out and proceeded to manually unlock the shining steel gate. Mairi gazed at it through the dust-covered windshield. It was a designer gate with an intricate pattern twisted into it. Mairi gasped with recognition just as Jamie tugged on her sleeve.

"Isn't that the same design as on mom's old necklace?" Jamie whispered from behind her.

Mairi nodded her head. Carefully, she began to pull the bag out of her pocket, but quickly stuffed it back in as Granda returned to the car. She suddenly wondered if her mom could have told Granda about the necklace going missing. She sat stiff with anticipation until he pulled the car through, waiting restlessly as he got out again to close the gate.

Quick as she could manage, Mairi dumped the necklace onto the palm of her hand. She gasped as Jamie cried out, "It's an exact match!"

Both the pendant and the gate were designs made of metal twisted into intricate knots created by intersecting continuous lines. Mairi knew she had studied it in art class last year, definitely a type of Celtic Knot. This one had three stylized triangles with a circle intertwining them. She tried to recall what the symbol meant, but she couldn't. *For once, I wish I'd paid more attention in class!* Mairi sighed, *instead of daydreaming of the perfect wave.*

At the sound of Granda's returning footsteps, Mairi hastily replaced the necklace in the bag and shoved it into her pocket, half wishful she'd been pulled away again like on the bus.

That was close! Granda had come to her side instead of the driver's side of the car. He pulled open her door, telling her and Jamie to get out.

"This is the best view of my house and land. Take a look." As usual, he wasn't asking but commanding. Still, Mairi detected a hint of pride in his voice.

They quickly unbuckled and stepped out, standing near the edge of a steeply sloped grass covered mountainside. Mairi followed Jamie to the very edge of the road, looking down into the valley where she could see the back of a circling Red tailed hawk.

Jamie swayed a little. "I'm on top of the world! This place is amazing!" he shouted, voice echoing in the valley, arms stretched open wide. "This is like being in Middle Earth with the hobbits and wizards." As Jamie looked around with awe, Mairi rolled her eyes at her brother.

"I love it here already," Jamie said, grinning up at Granda. "This is better than a city any day."

Mairi glared at him. "Traitor!" she growled.

To the left, below where the driveway wound down

and around the mountainside, a large oak tree stood on a knoll, branches reaching out over the edge, towering above more groves below it. To the right, and far below, a large stone house was towering above the many smaller oak trees surrounding it. The house was massive, with a huge wooden door and rock walls surrounding the entrance. It looked more like a mini castle than a house, complete with a tower off to one side and what appeared to be a moat around the house and immediate yard. Beyond it, a vast valley stretched out and more pine-covered mountains rose above and beyond it. Mairi shrugged, observing that it was just endless mountains with trees and no ocean in sight.

Mairi got back into the car with a sigh, frowning at Granda as he kicked the dust from his shoes before getting in. *What's the point? This whole place is a dust bowl.* Then he slowly, carefully drove over the rutted driveway, down and around the lone oak tree. As they made their way through a shady grove of trees at the bottom of the driveway, Mairi leaned her head against the window, her mind drifting to waves crashing on sandy shores. She vaguely registered glimpses of red- and purple-topped thistles poking out amongst the moss-covered rocks peeking through the grass. Here and there a glint of light caught her attention, as it seemed to dance from thistle to thistle. Mairi frowned when the light took on the shape of a tiny humanoid figure with wings for half a second. *Weird!* she thought, shaking her head, wondering if she was hallucinating.

They pulled up and parked under a rock walled carport. Climbing out of the car, they once again struggled under the weight of their bags as Granda watched. Mairi felt as if he were sizing them up, seeing how strong they really were. *Well,* she thought, *I'll show him!* She decided right then and there, no matter what he made her do, she wouldn't complain.

Mairi wrestled with her bags as they followed a pebble path past the carport, across a ravine with a trickling stream via an arched stone bridge, which explained what had looked like a moat from high above. The pebbled path took them through what must have once been a vast garden, but now consisted of dead plants and dry leaves. Gardening reminded her of her mom; she was always bringing home new herbs to plant in their yard.

Who used to do all the gardening here? Could it have been my mom? Or maybe it was my mom's mom? For the first time since she was a little girl, Mairi realized that no one ever mentioned a grandmother. *Do I even have one, besides Granny Kate? But she's my dad's mom, so who is my mom's mom? And why the heck am I only meeting my granda now, when I'm already 15?* Questions kept tumbling into her mind, questions she'd stopped asking in elementary school when she was never given any answers.

At that moment, her eye fell on a fluffy white cat languidly lying on an old bench that had green paint peeling off the graying wood. The cat was taking in the last golden rays of the evening sun. As they came closer, the cat stretched and leaped off the bench. She slowly walked over to Granda, gracefully wrapping herself around his ankles. Mairi realized she still didn't know if her mom had ever found Peaches. *I'll text her tonight, except I doubt there's a connection,* she thought with a snarl.

"Hello Star!" Granda said with the first true smile Mairi had seen on his face. He reached down and gently stroked Star's forehead.

"Meeeow," Star answered, purring her approval.

Picking up the cat, which nestled comfortably in his arms, Granda walked up the expansive stone stairs that covered the whole front of the house, leading to a porch flanked by two lion statues. The massive wooden double doors proved to be more impressive up close than Mairi had expected. They were made of heavy, light brown wood. The same Celtic Knot design on the gate and on the necklace was carved into the doors, the seam of the two doors dividing the knot into two equal parts. Jamie elbowed her and pointed at the door, "Look!"

As if I can't see for myself! She pushed him and gestured for him to keep quiet. *Doesn't he realize Mom doesn't know I have the necklace?*

The doors opened onto a large rectangular room. The floor was covered with thick wool rugs in faded designs of more Celtic patterns. To the right, a wooden piano stood against the far wall, a painting of a beautiful red-haired woman with pale skin and piercing green eyes looked out over the room.

"Who's she?" Mairi asked, pointing at the portrait.

"Your Gran." Granda stared wistfully down at the white cat he'd scooped into his arms. Then he looked back at Mairi and said sharply, "You look just like she did at your age."

Mairi smiled in spite of herself. *Am I really as beautiful as my grandmother?* Before she could ask what had happened to her, Granda continued walking. Mairi barely had time to see that a faded green velvet couch sat against the wall near the piano and a dark wooden dining table and chairs occupied the area to the left of the entrance, looking over what had once been the garden. A thick layer of dust blanketed everything.

Then they were passing through a kitchen with a sink and stove to her left and a fridge and cupboards to the right. There was a door nestled in the wall between the cupboards and Granda indicated it to Jamie.

"You'll take your Uncle's old room."

Mairi raised her eyebrows. *An uncle?* She never knew her mom had a brother.

FAMILY PHOTOS

Harris, Northern California
June 23rd, present year

Mairi watched Jamie open the door to their uncle's room. Looking over his shoulder, she saw that the room was dimly lit as the fading sun shone through a window on the opposite wall. Under the window was a table completely covered with dusty figurines of soldiers clearly at battle with each other.

Jamie "whooped!" and dropped his bags onto the floor near the bed to the right. He'd always loved setting up battle scenes. By 10 he was a whiz at the game of Risk and now, at age 12, he was into reading about the history of battles, true and fictional ones, and re-enacting them.

Stepping into the room, Mairi could see that the rest of the walls in the room appeared to be completely lined with shelves packed full of books. There was an entire set of encyclopedias on one of the shelves. *Who keeps encyclopedias anymore?* She'd only ever seen them in libraries. Mairi realized she'd barely see Jamie with all those books to read. Normally this wouldn't bother her, but he was her only lifeline in this wilderness of no technology.

Leaving her brother to his games, Mairi followed her grandfather past the kitchen and into a living room with high vaulted ceilings. They paused as they entered, as if Granda wanted to show her the room, and Mairi dutifully looked around. One half of the far wall consisted of a giant rock fireplace; the massive chimney reaching up to the ceiling. "Does it really get so cold here you need such a huge fireplace?"

Granda shrugged, "It can, but I just like fires. They're good for telling stories around."

Mairi nodded as her mind briefly drifted to how her dad used to tell stories about past surf trips while they sat around the campfire. Shaking her head to push away the memory, she noticed that next to the fireplace there was a giant sliding glass door. The door opened onto a deck sweeping out into the tree-covered valley beyond the house, reminding Mairi of the canyon behind her own house. She and her brother used to love exploring the canyon, often not coming home until their mom yelled for them to return.

"That's your mom as a little girl," Granda's voice broke into her thoughts. He was pointing to a large, single-family portrait hanging above the mantel in a wooden frame carved with more Celtic Symbols. The portrait was of an auburn-haired man (*Granda?*), the red-haired woman from the previous painting, and two blonde-haired children, her mom and most likely the mysterious uncle.

"Oh!" was all Mairi managed in response. *It's so weird to finally see Mom's family.* Feeling the necklace in her pocket, Mairi decided she might as well spend the summer learning what she could about her mom's mysterious family. *I haven't got anything better to do, and this necklace definitely needs an explanation. I wonder if I should ask*

Granda, but he'll probably just think I'm crazy.

Glancing one more time around the room, she saw that a big leather couch, a faded wingback chair, and a tall wooden chair were the only furniture in the room. Next to the wingback chair was the case that Mairi had seen her grandfather put his bagpipes into at her dad's funeral. Mairi caught her breath and stuffed the memory away as quickly as it surfaced. Blinking back the tears threatening to break free from her eyelids, she tightened her grip on her bags.

Granda swept her through the room and up a set of wooden stairs, their footsteps cushioned by a lush old carpet. They zigzagged back, the faded carpet continuing along a hallway with a balcony overlooking the living room below on the right and two doors on the left. Her grandfather held onto Star in one arm and opened the first door with his other hand.

"Your room. It was your mother's. She said whatever you find in there can be yours now." He paused, looking directly at her, and Mairi felt certain he was making some point she didn't understand. "I'll see you in the morning." Granda left her then, moving on to the second door, which was probably his bedroom. Mairi ignored his blunt exit, happy to be alone for the first time all day.

Mairi settled herself into her mother's bedroom, putting her bags on the floor. Pushing open the faded curtains covering the two windows, she noticed that they were still a cheery cerulean blue in the creases. The setting sunlight reaching through the branches of the trees created a speckled leaf pattern on the desk below the window, drawing her attention.

A movement beyond the tree caught her eye. She looked outside and saw a deer with 3-pronged antlers munching on a plant growing in the garden below. As she stared at it, the deer lifted its head, long ears almost like a rabbit's sticking out to the sides, one of them notched as if it had been torn. It looked intently back at her. They remained locked in what seemed a staring contest for several long seconds, until a sound in the nearby woods caught the deer's attention. He glanced in that direction then leaped over the twisted chicken wire fencing enclosing the garden in a single bound. Mairi had never seen a deer in the wild before, and stood transfixed for a moment longer wondering why she felt as though the deer had been trying to tell her something. She shook off the feeling.

"What a ridiculous thought," she muttered to herself, turning back to do her unpacking.

Mairi found an old towel tucked into a desk drawer, and was able to wipe the layers of dust that covered all the surfaces. She felt a little better about unpacking after that. An antique dresser stood against the wall opposite the window and the desk. Mairi finished putting all of her clothes into the drawers, then tried to use her cell phone, but her mom had been right. No connection. She played music instead, a mix of modern punk and classic 80s Metal, hoping to quiet the questions tumbling around in her head like an off-kilter washing machine. *At least there's electricity to charge my phone,* Mairi thought, with some relief.

Opening a desk drawer, she found a collection of photographs tied with a plaid ribbon. She sat down on the queen-size bed against the third wall, which was under another window overlooking the front walkway, and switched on the lamp on the bedside table. The photos were of her mother at various ages with a group of friends. The younger pictures showed her laughing and occasionally a young boy pushing his way in. *Photo bombing*, Mairi thought, automatically. She guessed it was the mysterious uncle because he looked like the boy in the portrait above the fireplace mantel downstairs. Flipping the photo over, she found several names scribbled on the back. His name was James, like her brother.

In a few pictures, there was a dark red cat in her mother's arms. *I didn't know she even liked cats,* she thought, *all she did was complain about Peaches when we first brought her home.* Weirder still, the cat's name was Star. *Did they name all their cats Star?* There weren't any pictures of Gran, but there weren't any of Granda, either.

Maybe Gran left Granda, taking my uncle with her? Probably it was a big scandal and that's why Mom never talked about it, Mairi decided, trying to make sense of everything she'd just learned.

The pictures of her mom as an older teen were even weirder. She had dark circles under her eyes and hollow cheeks. She looked like one of those Goth kids, dressed all in black, but she didn't wear any of the tell-tell black eyeliner.

She looks depressed! Mairi realized, all too familiar with that look on her mother lately. *Why would she be depressed?* There were no more photo bombs by her uncle. *Maybe whatever happened to him happened in their teens and that really messed up my mom. Like how she is now, ever since Dad died,* Mairi thought, *a total mess.*

Mairi thought about all the dust she'd wiped up and the faded furniture, and her quiet, stern granda. *Everything seems so old in this house,* she thought, *and sad. I need to figure out what happened!*

Standing up and stretching, she decided it was time to get ready for bed and took out her favorite Mickey Mouse pajamas to change into. They looked more like yoga pants and a t-shirt, and were extremely comfortable, though even Mickey couldn't make her smile these days. She didn't want to remember the last time she'd been to Disneyland, right before winter break, and then her dad had surprised her with the pajamas for Christmas. Mickey was his favorite Disney character, too. "Old School," he'd told her when she was a little girl.

Mairi shook her head and buried her head in the pajamas. They smelled like home . . . like the lavender sachets her mother was always placing in drawers and under pillows. Out of curiosity, Mairi reached under the pillow on her bed. No sachet, but at least Granda had been decent enough to put fresh linens on the bed for her, evidenced by the lack of dust.

Getting ready to change, she reached into her pocket and felt the velvet bag containing the necklace. She could feel a buzzing of energy radiating from it, which felt reassuring. *Maybe that's why Mom always held it. There's something comforting about it.* A twang of guilt for taking the necklace from her mom passed through her chest. *Maybe I should give it back.*

No! I won't give it back, Mairi argued with herself. On top of being angry that her mom was a depressed mess who neglected her children, now she was also angry her mom had never told her anything about their family. *What is up with my family and this necklace?*

She mulled over everything that had happened since leaving home. Her mind could barely process the fact that she'd been whisked off the bus this afternoon then pulled back on by some inexplicable force. *Would Mom tell me what happened if I simply asked her? If I can't figure it out by tomorrow, I'll find a way to call her and ask,* Mairi resolved, finishing pulling on her pajamas.

Turning off her music, she grabbed her travel bag with her toothbrush and other toiletries. She was heading out of her room when she realized she had no idea where the bathroom was. Flipping the light switch on in the hallway, she cautiously moved along the balcony to her grandfather's door. She raised her hand to knock, but hesitated when she heard him talking to someone.

He must be on the phone, Mairi thought mindlessly, before remembering her mom had said there wasn't a phone in the house. *How does he call my mom?* Mairi wondered.

She waited for a pause in his talking then hesitantly knocked, unsure of how he'd react. Just before he opened the door, she thought she heard a woman's voice murmur something. She shook her head. *Must be a TV or something.*

Granda opened the door, with Star twining between his ankles. "Yes?" he asked, raising his eyebrows. Mairi glanced past him, catching a glimpse of a tartan-patterned bedspread before he pulled the door closed behind him.

"Uh…" Mairi stuttered, almost forgetting why she'd come. "Um…I don't know where the bathroom is…"

"Go downstairs. It's directly under the staircase." He stepped back into his room and closed his door with a click.

I will never get used to his directness. Not a very chatty guy, Mairi thought, *except he was definitely talking to someone, or a tv, or something. Weird!* She turned around and headed down the stairs. At the bottom, she walked around the big leather sofa and found a door on the other end of it, almost directly under her bedroom door. She twisted the knob and opened it, just to feel it shove closed on her again.

"Hey! Don't you know anything about privacy?" It was Jamie. Obviously, he'd found the bathroom first.

"Jamie," Mairi called through the door. "Do *you* know how Granda calls our mom? I mean does he have a cell phone? There's no reception here, so he wouldn't have one, would he? Does he have an old-fashioned phone or something?" She heard her brother turn the water on and splash a bit then shut off the water before he replied.

"You mean a land line," he patronized, "and Granda doesn't have one. Mom said he doesn't have a cell phone, either, so he rarely calls her. Only when he goes to town or a friend's house."

"Oh. Well, then, does he have a TV? I heard a woman's voice coming from his room."

Jamie poked his head out of the bathroom. "That's strange. Mom said he doesn't care for modern conveniences. Except for the car and lights, he doesn't have anything electronic here, not even a radio. He uses solar panels and batteries so he keeps it simple." Shrugging his shoulders, he retreated into the bathroom, leaving Mairi to brood over what she'd overheard coming from her granda's bedroom.

BAGPIPES

Harris, Northern California
June 24th, present year

The next morning Mairi was sitting on her brother's bed watching him arrange the miniature bagpiper figurines at the front of a team of ancient Highlander warriors. Jamie was giving a long-winded explanation about the purpose of the bagpipes in battle. He'd just read about them in some book he'd found on a bookshelf in their uncle's room. Apparently, their uncle had also been really into history and had collected a huge assortment of books.

"…. and the sound alone of 30 bagpipes playing was often frightening enough to scare the enemy before the battle even began," Jamie was explaining. "Except they were banned from Scotland, along with tartans…"

"Jamie, I'm hungry," Mairi said as she jumped off his bed. "Help me check the kitchen. I can't find Granda, but there's got to be something to eat in all those cupboards. Then we can explore the house. We've got to figure out what is going on around here."

Jamie frowned at her, probably for interrupting and

for showing so little interest in his latest battle facts. He let out a sigh and put down the miniature bagpiper he'd been holding.

"Fine. I'm hungry, too."

As they searched the cupboards, Mairi told him about the photos she'd found in her room and promised to show him later. Jamie held up a cylinder container he'd found with dry oatmeal in it saying, "I wonder what happened to our uncle. Seems so weird that he'd just stop being in our mom's life. And our Gran, too, what do you think happened to her?"

Mairi put a pot of water on the stove to boil, about to say she didn't have any idea about their Gran when they heard it: a haunting sound drifting into the house from far away. *It sounds like what we heard in that meadow...*

"Bagpipes!" Jamie declared, almost triumphantly.

Mairi looked at Jamie, confused. "Bagpipes?" Some little piece of a puzzle was about to fit together. The tune she and Jamie had heard when they magically ended up in the field of grass . . . bagpipes!

There was a crash in the living room, and a plaintive "mew."

Mairi dashed into the living room, but didn't see that Star had knocked anything over. She only saw the tip of a fluffy white tail retreating up the stairs.

Odd, she thought, and then she heard a distinctive humming. Looking around she saw Granda's empty bagpipe case was lying open beside his tall wooden chair with the velvet bag holding the necklace lying inside.

Not realizing Jamie had followed right behind her, she bumped into him in her haste as she turned around. "His bagpipes are gone and somehow the necklace got here. I'm sure I left it on my dresser upstairs." *Did the cat just put it here?* Mairi glanced back up the stairs.

"So...?" Jamie slowly asked. "Granda must be playing the bagpipes right now."

"Maybe . . . " Mairi was thinking. She picked up the velvet bag and plopped down on the couch in a poof of dust, carefully dropping the necklace out of the bag and into her hand to inspect it. She could feel the electric energy radiating from it, and the humming was getting louder. Looking around the room to see if she was transporting, she let out the breath she was holding as she saw nothing had changed.

"What does the necklace have to do with Granda playing his bagpipes?" Jamie asked, sitting next to her.

"I'm not sure, but I think it's connected. The symbols on the gate and the front doors match this necklace that Mom says has been in our family for centuries. I wonder if it belonged to Granda before she got it? The connections must mean something, and I'm certain this is the sound we heard when we suddenly left the bus and landed in a field, the sound of bagpipes playing. Let's see, the necklace was humming like it is now, and you had grabbed onto me and wished to be somewhere . . . Let me try something." As she said this, she put her hand on Jamie's knee and said, "I want to go to Granda."

She felt a rush as darkness once again enveloped her and the now familiar sensation of what could only be explained as being squeezed through a tube. She wasn't sure if her plan to take Jamie with her had worked, but she was most definitely transporting. These thoughts were short lived, though, as she quickly felt like she was melting into nothingness.

Then they were once again landing in a heap in the grassy meadow, Jamie luckily not hitting the rock next to them. This time it wasn't a foggy day. In fact, the sun was shining warmly on them. When they looked around, they saw that a giant oak tree towered over their heads nearby. But the most amazing thing was their grandfather, who stood under the oak tree, bagpipes resting on his shoulder, and an unfamiliar smile gracing his lips.

"I've been expecting you," he said.

REJECTED

Los Angeles, California
June 24th, present year

Danny lay on his twin bed, the crumpled sheets bunched up at his feet. He let out a big sigh. "How am I ever going to get to Northern California? My car will never make it and mom doesn't have any money!"

Closing his eyes against the dawn light starting to fill his room, he thought again about how he had ended up on what was hopefully not a wild goose chase. After he'd proved to himself that the silver chanter he'd seen on the old man's bagpipes at his uncle's funeral was indeed the same one that kept slipping through his ancestor's fingertips, the first chance he had gotten he'd called his Granny Kate to ask her what she knew about the bagpipe chanter and to see if she knew anything about the old man at the funeral. Granny Kate had been in a hurry, packing for her annual summer trip to Scotland. She'd found his Aunt Shaylee's phone number and given it to him, and that was all the time she had for him, other than to mention she'd heard his cousins would be staying up in a little town in Northern California for the summer with the old man, who turned out to be his Aunt Shaylee's dad.

Danny had immediately called her. "Hi Aunt Shaylee. This is Danny. . . . Yes, Adair's son. . . . School is good. I did enjoy my senior year, thank you for asking. … Well, I'm wondering if you can tell me how I can get in touch with your dad. I really enjoyed his bagpiping at Uncle Aiden's funeral and I wanted to talk to him about it…umm, for my major …" *(ahem)* Danny cleared his throat, "…at UCLA, when I go."

Danny had tried to stick to the truth as much as possible, hoping to get the information he needed without revealing his true intentions. Shaylee had told him her dad didn't have a phone, but she'd pass on his message when her dad called next which, she'd warned, was very rarely. Danny felt a little like he'd been brushed off.

Pulling himself out of his pool of self-pity, Danny crawled off his bed, adjusting the clothes he'd fallen asleep in, wondering if there would be anything in the fridge that might resemble breakfast. He rummaged through the contents, deciding it all required too much effort to cook, when he was struck with sudden insight. *I'll ask my dad for a business loan! He's told me in the past that he'd help me out if I ever had a real plan, which college apparently doesn't count as one, according to my dad. Well, now I do have a real plan.*

Feeling hopeful, Danny turned from the fridge, flipped open his archaic cellphone and dialed his dad's number with his thumb, drumming the fingers of his other hand on the dining table as he tried to find an outlet for his nervous energy.

The phone rang once before a woman's nasally

clipped voice answered. "Adair MacDonald's residence. He is in a meeting. Can I take a message?"

Danny let out a big sigh. *Of course! He has a secretary even for his private line? Sheesh!* "Yeah...uh...this is Danny."

"Danny *who*?" the terse voice asked.

"His son, that's who! Can I talk to my dad? Uh...please." he added, trying to remember he was calling to appeal to his dad for a loan to begin his new venture of finding ancient Celtic artifacts, not to air his grievances.

"Oh." She sounded genuinely caught off guard. "He didn't mention he had a son. I'll just check if he's available." The phone clicked over to country music, Danny's least favorite, and he found a chair to sink into. *Who knows how long this will take?*

Ten minutes, and a glass of milk with toast and jam later, his father's booming voice came on the phone. "What do you want? I was on the other line with a potential new client. This better be important!"

Not even a 'How do you do?' Nice, Dad! Taking a deep breath, Danny launched into his carefully rehearsed speech. "Okay, I'm hoping you'll help me become an antique dealer, you know, as a career. I want to specialize in Celtic artifacts." Danny paused as his dad took in a deep breath and huffed it out.

"Umm...well, anyway, Celtic artifacts sort of like the Fairy Flag in Dunvegan Castle on the Isle of Skye in Scotland. I bet museums would pay loads of money to me if I tracked down antiques like that and brought them in. And I'm sure there are tons of Celtic antiques here in North America because of all of the Scottish families that moved here in the 1700s after the Highland Clearances started."

"Just *what* are the Highland Clearances?" his dad

interrupted, sounding impatient, but maybe a little interested.

"I learned about it in history class. The Highland Clearances were when all the Clan chieftains told their poor relatives, the ones who farmed for them in exchange for a home and land to live on, to pack up and leave so that sheep could be raised on the land instead. The poor Scots were shipped off to Australia and North America without any notice."

"Look, I don't have time for this. Get to the point. Now!" Adair's voice dripped with impatience.

"So," Danny hurried to get to his request, "I bet there are plenty of Celtic artifacts I could find and sell back to Scotland. In fact, I am positive I found one at Uncle Aiden's funeral. It's a silver chanter that a piper had attached to his bagpipes. I'm so sure it's the silver faerie chanter once given to our MacDonald ancestor by a faerie, the one from the legend Granny Kate told me." Becoming more excited, Danny blurted out, "It's the real deal, Dad! You've got to help me get it. It belongs to *our* family!"

By his dad's sudden intake of air, too late Danny realized his mistake.

"I've *got* to help you get it? I don't *got* to do anything for anyone unless I decide to." Danny cringed. "Daniel Adair MacDonald, I didn't get rich chasing after fairy tales. I worked hard, through aching back and calloused hands, to get where I am. And do you realize where I am now?"

"Not really," Danny muttered.

"I am the top contractor for building oil pipelines on US soil. People look up to *me*, turn to *me* for solutions to *real* problems like bringing fuel to the enormous number of cars on the road. People rely on me, and what do you want me to say about my only son when they ask? That you want to prove that *fairy tales* are real? You sound like my mother. That old bat filled your head with too many crazy notions. You make my brother's lifelong obsession with surfing sound like a real job, and look where it got him...six feet under and nothing for people to remember him for. Call me when you have an actual career plan." The line had clicked off before Danny could even let out the breath he'd been holding, his father's tirade ringing in his ear.

Danny slammed his phone down on the table, knocking over the vase of flowers his mom had brought home from the Farmer's Market. "Aargh! Why!?" Danny shouted up at the ceiling, pumping his fists in frustration.

Fighting back the tears threatening to spill like one of his father's broken pipelines in the mid-west, he stomped into his room. "Uncle Aiden was ten times the father you ever were!" he shouted to no one, wishing he were brave enough to really say it to his dad. "Fine! I'll figure out how to get the faerie chanter myself!"

Looking around his messy bedroom, feeling his heart beat racing, an idea occurred to him. "I guess I can sell my car and take a bus to Northern California and take back that chanter on my own. I'll prove to my dad that I'm not chasing fairy tales."

He grabbed his empty trash can and began throwing old receipts and candy wrappers in it, searching for the number of a friend who had offered him $500 for his pile of scrap metal on wheels he called his car. Pulling away a slightly moldy towel, he saw the picture of his dad, mom, and him as a toddler. It was the only picture he owned of his family together, taken on the rim of the Grand Canyon, his mom's long blonde hair mingling with his dad's even longer red hair as it blew in the wind. Danny shook his head. His dad looked nothing like the Metal Head engineering student he'd been when Danny's parents had met at Cal-Poly in the late '80s. Flipping the picture over, he turned to his bedside table.

Rifling through the junk that had piled up there, too, he found the stray business card his friend had hastily scribbled a number on. Gripping the card until it crumpled, Danny grumbled aloud, "I don't need him! What a jerk!"

Returning to the room that served as both a living room and a dining room in five quick steps, he picked up his phone and dialed the number. *My dad's wrong! He hasn't seen the silver chanter like I have. He hasn't felt the power of it. I'll get that chanter and prove to him I'm right.*

DRUIDS

Harris, Northern California
June 24th, present year

"What do you mean you were expecting us?" Jamie asked, looking earnestly up into his granda's eyes.

Walking back from the meadow, Granda stood between Mairi and Jamie carrying his bagpipes under his right arm, the tall pipes resting on his shoulder.

"I knew you would come," he said.

"But . . . " Mairi hesitated. Mairi tucked the necklace back into the pouch in her pocket. She was waiting to see if she should show him or not. *Does he know about the necklace? What did he see?* "Did you see us arrive?"

"Yes."

Was that a twinkle in his eye? Mairi felt as if her grandfather was teasing them now. *Maybe two can play this game.*

"So, you saw us materialize as if from nowhere?" She could always pretend she was joking if he didn't know what the heck she was talking about.

"Yes."

They stepped off the grassy trail and onto the dirt driveway they had driven down the day before. They hadn't actually gone far at all.

Ugh! He isn't making this easy. She was carefully picking her way along the road, avoiding tripping over the deep ruts angling sharply across the driveway and down the mountainside. She tried again.

"You don't seem surprised that we appeared under that oak tree from out of nowhere. Why aren't you surprised?"

"Because, I'm a druid...and so are you and Jamie. At least, you will learn to be."

Jamie whooped! "Just like Harry Potter! So cool!"

Mairi stopped walking, "Wait! How is a druid like Harry Potter? What is a druid, anyway?"

Jamie looked at her with an exasperated expression. "A druid is . . . was," he shook his head, "anyway, a druid was a person who not only possessed magic, but also advised the chieftains of the Celtic Clans. Some druids were bards, singing epic songs and telling stories to keep the Celtic history alive, since they didn't believe in writing anything down. Other types of druids were healers and the highest in the Order of Druids were advisors. All were magical in their own way."

Granda looked down at his grandson, pride showing on his face.

"So, a druid is kind of like a wizard." Mairi stated, stepping over a deep rut in the road.

"Yes," Granda replied, "druids are essentially wizards."

"So, how does it work?" Mairi asked, fiddling with the necklace she'd pulled out of her pocket.

"Well, the necklace and my bagpipes have to be used

simultaneously to magically travel through space and time in order to work. But, it only happens with very specific songs and to people who already possess magic in some way." Granda shifted the bagpipes under his arm after responding.

A sunbeam glinted off the silver faerie chanter gripped in Granda's right hand and Mairi's eyes were drawn to it. She felt a strong tugging sensation coming from it, not unlike someone grabbing her shirt and pulling. "Does the magic have anything to do with this chanter?" she asked.

"Yes, only bagpipes with this chanter attached will work the magic," Granda answered.

"Okay . . . " Nearing the house, they crossed the little bridge spanning the stream in single file. "Umm . . . does mom know about this magic? Is that why she always forbids me to touch this necklace?"

"Yes. Your mother and uncle used the magic to time travel many times with your Gran and I, but the last time they did it they were teens and they were on their own," Granda paused in speaking, his voice catching a little. "Something went terribly wrong and your uncle never returned."

They entered the house quietly, each lost in their own thoughts. Mairi and Jamie sat down in the sunshine at the dining table, waiting for the breakfast their granda promised to make them after he put his bagpipes away.

Oh wow! Mairi was thinking. *This is so cool! And scary! And amazing!* Her mind whiplashed, thinking of the implications of what she had just learned. *Why did I never know any of this before now? Why did Mom never tell us?*

"What happened to our uncle?" Jamie asked. Getting information out of their grandfather was still so difficult.

Leaning casually against the counter, as if it were only the weather they were discussing, he told them, "Your mother and he traveled back in time to ancient Scotland to try to undo the faerie curse that turned your Gran into a cat and he never returned."

"Wait! Gran's a cat?" Mairi exclaimed. *This just keeps getting weirder and weirder,* she thought, shaking her head. "How is any of this even possible?"

STAR

Harris, Northern California
June 24th, present year

"Gran is a cat?" Jamie repeated Mairi's question.

Granda sighed, putting down the wooden spoon he was using to ladle oatmeal into bowls for them. "Yes. Specifically, Star is your Gran."

"Wait. What?" Jamie and Mairi jumped in shock.

Right on cue, Star, the white cat, jumped onto the table and sat there primly looking at all of them with her big green eyes, fluffy tail wrapped around her little feet.

"Hello." She calmly spoke to them. "I am your Gran, Caroline Star. Nice to finally properly meet you."

Mairi felt as if the whole world had been ripped out from under her feet. *This is weirder than magically traveling from one place to another, almost as weird as a world without Dad...no, not the same, but...druid curses? Talking cats?* All her teacher's lectures in science class were trailing away like a barely remembered dream.

Jamie, on the other hand, was laughing and hugging Star. "I'm not sure how this is possible, but this is so cool!"

Mairi stared suspiciously at her Granda, wondering if there was an electronic device making it seem as if Star could talk. But such an elaborate electronic prank did not fit the granda she was getting to know. It had to be yet another weird part of her family. Then, Mairi remembered the photos from her mom's room upstairs, "Wait…" she addressed her granda, "has she always been a white cat? Or was she once a dark red cat?"

The cat answered instead, "Yes, I was once a beautiful redhead like you, Mairi. But time has turned me white, like your granda."

Mairi frowned, "Okay…" Her mind whirled, trying to adjust to talking to a cat…her gran. *So, this explains the cat in the photographs. But…* "What happened to my uncle? Did he die?"

"No, my dear, your uncle is alive. At least, I hope he is. He just chose not to return," she said wistfully. Star was obviously the talker in this house. "Your mother said she tried to convince him to come back with her, that they would try again another time to undo the curse, but James said he had so many ideas he wanted to work on there that he wasn't ready to leave. Your mother tried to return to him many times, but couldn't. A druid's curse had destroyed her powers. Her only choice was to accept that her brother had chosen to stay, and someday she might get her powers back and be able to take up the battle again."

"She never even talked about magic, though. It's like she pretended it never existed," Jamie pointed out.

"No, she didn't talk about it because something unexpected happened. When she moved to San Diego, I guess to get away from all these bad memories, she fell in love with a descendant of the very druid who had cursed her family. The druid's name was Ian MacDonald, judging by

Shaylee's description of him and we believe he's your very distant relative."

Oh wow! My last name is MacDonald so could Ian MacDonald really be my ancestor? Mairi rested her head on her folded arms on the table...it was spinning with all the implications. *But Dad didn't seem like the type to even know about magic. Did he know about Ian MacDonald? Mom...now she definitely seems like the type to be into magic with her herbs and Ayurveda medicine stuff. To think she battled a druid once? And now her brother is stuck back in time...what if Jamie were stuck back in time? And Gran is trapped as a cat...forever? My family is a bigger mess than I ever imagined!* Mairi sighed, looking up from her inner struggle and into the gentle eyes of Star and Granda.

"Why did that druid curse my mom?" Mairi asked.

"He wanted revenge on our families, the MacLeods and the MacCrimmons, for taking the silver faerie chanter from his clan, the MacDonalds" Granda answered.

"Is there anything our family can do to fix this?" Jamie asked. "Is it too late? Couldn't we just return the chanter to him?"

"No!" Granda answered. "He will only use the chanter's powers for evil. He's the cruelest druid I know of, full of darkness and greed. Besides, we'll never know what happened to James if we can't time travel."

Mairi stared at her granda, showing so much passion when he was usually so calm. She was unsure of what to say or do.

"Did you tell them, William?" Star directed her question to Granda, incongruously sharpening her claws on one of the carpets where she'd jumped to the floor. "About them being druids, too?"

Granda nodded in answer.

Mairi sputtered, "But we know nothing about being druids!"

Star looked back at Mairi, "Nothing to worry about. We will teach you two. You can learn spells from me," Star answered, "and family lore."

"You can learn to play the bagpipes with me," Granda added, finally setting their cooling oatmeal down in front of them, "and learn Scotland's history."

"Then what?" Mairi asked, ignoring her oatmeal while Jamie wolfed his down.

"Then you two are certain to be the most powerful druids any clan has ever seen." Star reassured her, a subtle purr to her voice. "You're sure to be stronger than Shaylee and James ever were since you are descended from both MacLeods and MacDonalds. Most important, you'll be safe, able to protect yourselves from ever being harmed by the magic in our world. Plus, with the proper studies and your natural abilities, you could reverse the faerie curse on me, maybe even restoring your mom's and granda's magical abilities."

"You mean…but…how…?" Mairi tried to form her thoughts into coherent sentences. Star jumped onto her lap and curled into a comfortable ball.

"No pressure or anything," Mairi hissed under her breath. *So now there's an evil druid Granda is afraid of, Gran's a cat because of a faerie curse, mom and granda have no powers because of a druid's curse, and Jamie and I are expected to be able to fix everything because we're supposedly powerful druids . . . without any powers, except for a magical necklace and a silver faerie chanter? Great!*

THE CELTIC WHEEL

Harris, Northern California
June 24th, present year

"Ahem," Granda cleared his throat, sitting on the velvet couch in the sitting room, across from the dining table. "So, we were thinking that, if you two are ready by August 1st, then you, Jamie, and I will go back in time and try to find the faerie who gave my parents the necklace and ask her to reverse the curse." Granda looked at Mairi, full of hope, his green eyes shiny like wet leaves after a rain, his cheeks actually flushed.

Her breath caught and Mairi again stared at her granda, eyes wide. "I almost forgot about there being time travel, too. But...how does it work? How can we possibly travel from place to place and back in time? Could we really go back and meet up with my uncle's time? How would we control what year we land in? What if we are a hundred years too late, or too early?" Mairi absent-mindedly petted Star as she worked through her confusion, her strokes becoming more frantic, her voice threatening to rise to hysteria.

Star purred happily before answering, her body

vibrating under Mairi's hands, calming her a little. "You could meet up with James' time with ease, because you can only travel 300 years forward or backwards in time. I guess it is 300 years and not 200 or 400 because three is a magical number for faeries."

Jamie leaned forward eagerly. "I've noticed that in fairy tales, there's always three of something."

Gran purred louder before answering. "Yes, all fairy tales work in powers of three...three brothers, three sisters, and three chances. So, I know you could travel exactly 300 years back from today. At least, that's been our experience."

"Wait!" Mairi took a deep breath, shaking her head. "What does that mean for us, specifically?"

"This means that your Uncle James will have aged the same amount as your mom, so he will be a grown man now. Then, however long you stay back in time, a day or six weeks, it would be that much later when you return to the present." Star patiently explained. "There is a catch, though. There are eight magical days of the year often referred to as The Celtic Wheel. You can only travel through time on one of those eight magical days.

"Why?" Jamie asked, eyeing Mairi's oatmeal. "If we can time travel, why not every day of the year?"

"Picture a bicycle," Star clarified. "There are two wheels that travel at the same speed, rotating at the same rate. The front wheel is the present, while the back wheel is the past. Pick a point on the present wheel and it will rotate around until it is right below the frame, the only thing that connects the present to the past. When your point is near the frame, the coinciding point on the past wheel is also below the frame. You can jump through time at that moment. But it only happens eight days during the year."

"So, if we didn't return in the 24 hours of one day,

would we have to stay in the past until we reached the next magical day, however much time later?" Jamie spoke slowly, trying to make sense of all this information.

Star purred, "Yes, there are actually almost exactly six weeks between each magical day."

Something clicked in Mairi's thoughts. She fiddled with the necklace that she'd pulled out of its pouch. "I know this is a Celtic Knot." She shook her head, trying to clear it and get her questions straight. "It has three triangle parts and a circle. Does it have anything to do with the power of three?"

"It's called the Trinity Knot," Star answered. "It is also called the Triquetra. It represents the past, present, and future, and the circle means that all are unified. Over the centuries other meanings have been attributed to this knot, and they might be true. However, given that it helps us travel through time and space, this is the probably the truest meaning."

"So, August 1st is the next magical day?" Jamie asked.

"Yes," Granda answered.

"If you don't go then you will have to wait for September 22nd," Gran explained, "and that might be too long for some of us to wait."

Nodding, Mairi stared at her Gran trapped in a cat body. Then she looked up at her stern and, she now realized, probably lonely granda. Finally, her gaze rested on her younger brother she'd unwillingly been charged with watching out for while their mother took a swim off the deep end. Mairi felt very small for such enormous problems, frightened by the idea forming in her head. *Could I really help? I know I don't have any powers, regardless of what they say, but if I don't try to help them, who else can they turn to? Oh Dad, I wish you were still here to tell me what to do! What would you do if you were in my shoes? Would you dare to go back in time and attempt to save Gran from this curse and at least check on my trapped uncle? Or would you run for the nearest beach and hide in the waves? What should I do?* Mairi longed for the normalcy of her life before everything seemed to crumble, before her dad had died.

DARK POWERS

Isle of Harris, Scotland
June 24th, early 1700s

The flickering flame from the nearly extinguished candle held in Ian MacDonald's right hand caused the words to dance, making reading nearly impossible. The druid raised his grey shrouded head from reading over the manuscript. He'd fished it out of the old trunk at the back of the small dark room earlier that evening.

Where did it go? He asked himself again, just as he'd asked this question for over 40 years. *It can't have simply vanished off the face of the earth...could it?* Ian contemplated, not for the first time, the real possibility that the chanter had disappeared into the Faerie Realm from which it had first come. "No," he said, shaking his head, though no one else was in the room to hear him. "I'd have figured that out by now. So, where is it? I've got to find it!"

Setting the manuscript on his lap, he avoided crumpling up the precious parchment in his aggravation, running his left hand through his greasy hair instead, a guttural growl of frustration escaping his cold thin lips. It always came to this point, no matter how long he'd been searching. He couldn't let go of the anger he felt for the disappearance of his clan's precious chanter. He had searched for over two decades with no luck and then that young woman had shown up unexpectedly with it 20 years ago. He'd been leading his Grove of Druids through their Summer Solstice ritual when a young woman came running into the oak grove, oblivious to his circle of druids. She appeared to be running from someone, and indeed she had been, evidenced by the English soldier that burst into the grove directly following her disappearance.

Yes, right before his eyes she'd begun to play a song on her bagpipes, standing still long enough for him to realize she was playing on the silver faerie chanter. Without thinking, he'd put a curse on her, a curse strong enough to take away all her natural magical abilities. He couldn't be sure his spell had succeeded, as she had managed to escape, though he was pretty sure his curse had hit her before disappearing. The tracking spell he'd woven into the curse had worked. He knew this because he'd detected the magical use of the faerie chanter a few times over the years, the most recent being just two days ago as he'd been sitting on the burial mound thinking. Too bad the spell hadn't included telling him *where* the chanter actually was.

Ian sighed, completely exhausted. Immediately after having realized the faerie chanter had been used for magic again a couple of days ago, Ian had hired passage on a ship setting sail for the Isle of Harris. Upon arrival, he'd pushed his old tired bones as fast as they would carry him across the moor, to a hut built directly over the mouth of a cave, far from any villages. He'd had to unbury the manuscript from the many stacks of parchments he had gathered here over the years he had been trying to reclaim the chanter.

Ian let out another growl of pure frustration before returning to reading, turning the page to a drawing he'd never noticed before. A thin smile slowly formed, further creasing his already lined face. *At last!* Here was proof that the journey to the Isle of Harris had been worth it.

He set the manuscript on the intricately carved table beside him and reached for his solid oak staff, standing up to his full crooked height of 5'10." He had once been as tall as his ox of a son, but the Fates had wreaked their havoc on his previously beautiful body. Running a gnarled hand up the length of his staff, he admired the exquisite carvings of Celtic Knots on the handle. The knots were the same ones he remembered seeing etched onto the silver faerie chanter and he'd carefully replicated them when carving the handle of his staff. The knots aided his powers, and when carved by actual faeries as they were on the silver faerie chanter, the magic was immensely stronger.

He was never so upfront with his fellow druids about his love for the powers he believed the faerie etchings held. Oh, he'd tried once, long ago to bring others of the MacDonald druids to join him in his search for the silver faerie chanter and its magical powers, but they had not cared, being much more interested in the politics of the clans and the struggle with the English. Even his own son, Ewan, did not realize how much Ian dreamed of power and eternal youth.

Ian now realized he must turn to the faeries in order to finally discover the whereabouts of the lost faerie chanter, thanks to the drawing he had just discovered. Certainly, the Unseelie Court, the Dark Faeries who dwell in the darkest depth of the Faerie Realm, would have their ways of helping him reclaim it. When the chanter finally returned to the Isle of Skye, as he was certain it would, he'd be ready to grab it.

The faerie chanter would be returned to the MacDonald clan. More specifically it would be returned to him, and the power it possessed would finally be his.

FAERIE KIN

Harris, Northern California
June 25th, present year

Mairi woke to sunlight filtering through the window over her bed, angling in from the East. It hit the sloped wall of her bedroom, lighting up a picture hanging there she hadn't noticed before. Pushing back the covers, she crawled across her bed and sat up directly in front of it, her breath catching in her throat. It was of her mom, she was sure, as a little girl dressed in a light green plaid dress tied with a velvet ribbon. She was in a garden full of flowering rosemary and lavender bushes, the sunlight touching her hair, making her blonde curls look like a halo of light as she danced with several monarch butterflies, the sound of her laughter almost audible through her open-mouthed grin.

Behind and to the left of her, sitting on the ground with a pair of pruning shears in one hand, a bundle of herbs in her other hand was Gran as a young mother. Red hair pulled back in a low ponytail, dressed in overalls, she was smiling with such obvious delight at the antics of her daughter. Mairi realized that there was a time when her Gran had led a normal life, had held her children and cultivated her garden. *What must it be like to be stuck in the body of a cat? Was it fun, full of carefree days or was it terrible, not being able to hug her family anymore or simply keep a family garden?* Mairi shook her head. She had no idea what Gran's life was like for her, but she knew what it was to want to live a normal life when that choice was taken away.

This made her realize she truly needed to do something to help heal her family from this curse. *I can't bring my dad back, but maybe I can stop my mom's depression by helping Gran find happiness. I know Granda wants me to help her return to human form. I don't know if I can do that . . .* Mairi pictured the dried up garden in front of the house and snapped her fingers, *but I do know I can help her in the garden like I used to help my mom.*

Mairi dressed in a hurry and ran downstairs to grab her brother. She dragged him upstairs to show him the picture on her wall, and shared her idea that she thought they should help in the garden. "Okay, but first I want to finish the chapter I was reading before you interrupted," he grumbled and stomped back to his room.

Later that morning, Jamie, Mairi and Star were out in the old garden. As Star instructed Mairi on which weeds to pull from a particularly small garden bed, Jamie was digging and turning the soil in a bigger plot with a long-handled shovel. The rhythmic sound of his digging created a calming background noise. Mairi noticed that round green rocks, angular turquoise rocks, and numerous gray stones of all sizes defined the border of each space. For a moment, Mairi rested her hand on one of the green rocks as she leaned forward to dig out a clump of weeds. A vibration ran through her hand from the rock and Mairi pulled away.

"What's up with these rocks?" Mairi asked, not ready to reveal what she'd felt.

Star explained, "They all came from the various rivers and creeks around our county that I used to visit with your mom and uncle during their summer vacations."

Mairi smiled, rubbing her palm. "My mom used to bring home rocks from all of our trips to different places in Baja." *I miss those trips, before cancer and depression...* Mairi sighed, staring at her hand. *But they never vibrated like these.* She returned her attention to Star.

"I'm happy she carried on the tradition. I'd like to trade with her someday. Rocks, stones, crystals; all are powerful allies to druids, and each place they come from carries a different strength that represents the part of earth they belong to." Star purred for a little while after that, staring distantly into a ray of sunshine touching the ground in front of her. *She misses my mom...her daughter,* Mairi realized, the thought springing to mind. *I wonder if my mom misses me...* She made a decision.

"Is it weird that the rock vibrated just now when I touched it?" Mairi asked.

Star appeared to raise her eyebrows, a funny look for a cat. Mairi smiled. "Well, that's a good sign of your growing powers."

To which Mairi could only answer, "Oh."

"How come I don't feel the rocks vibrating?" Jamie asked.

"Because you are still a wee bit young, lad," Star said, rubbing against his ankle. "You'll come into your powers more as you grow. Be patient."

Mairi frowned. *Have I really started coming into my powers now? Does that explain anything besides the vibrating rocks? I remember feeling tingly when I would catch a wave when I surfed. I wonder if Dad felt that way. I just assumed everyone did, but now I wish I'd asked him.* Sighing, she thought through this while she continued pulling weeds.

As the sun moved overhead, Star seemed to be getting a great deal of satisfaction at being able to work on her garden again with her grandchildren's help and was proving to have a lot to say about it. Mairi sat back on her heels and looked at the dirt caking her fingers and embedded in her nails, wondering more about the vibrations she felt coming from the rocks, as Star rubbed up against a clump of grass. Star was telling them how they would need to plant a whole new herb garden so they could begin to mix necessary ingredients for the spells she wanted to teach them to cast.

"But Gran," Jamie interrupted, "how come our family are druids? What makes us a druid verses a regular person?"

"I suppose it's the faerie blood that runs in our veins," she answered.

FAIRY TALES

Isle of Skye
Long Ago, Once Upon a Time

Star came over and rubbed up against a stunned Mairi's leg. Jamie stopped shoveling and stared at the little fluffy cat.

"Faerie blood? How...?" Mairi had never been a big believer in fairy tales. Sure, as a kid she'd believed in the Tooth Fairy, but was she actually real? As Mairi thought about it, she couldn't be certain her parents had ever actually said the Tooth Fairy wasn't real. They had just sort of nodded when Mairi had declared herself too old for such silliness. Mairi shook her head in disbelief. *Maybe that isn't the kind of fairies Gran is talking about?*

"Let's go in for a drink of cold lemonade and I'll share a tale with you."

Settled on the green velvet couch in the sitting room, Mairi and Jamie had scrubbed their hands clean and were sipping on lavender lemonade. Star was curled up on a pillow between them, facing the picture window looking out over the garden they'd worked in all morning.

Star shared her tale. "It all began centuries before even your granda was born."

There was a young MacLeod, in line to be chief of the MacLeod clan, who awoke one night to the loveliest singing drifting through his window, which overlooked the moor behind the family home of Castle Dunvegan. He couldn't resist such an enchanting melody though try as hard as he might, so he got to his feet, wrapping his tartan around his shoulders to protect him from the cold. He ran through the castle, quiet as he could, so as not to awaken anyone else, in a hurry to hear the melody a bit more.

As soon as he was out on the moor, he once again heard the lilting tune. He felt drawn to find the source, as though his very heart depended on it. He followed the trail on the moonlit night, as though floating on a dream, not stumbling as one might expect in the moon-shadows dappling the trail. As he approached the stone bridge spanning a little stream trickling into the sea, he saw the most beautiful maiden glowing in the silver moonlight, singing. He stopped before she should see him, for he dared not frighten her away.

He knew not how long he stood watching her, but when she had stopped singing, and he shook himself as if from an enchanted sleep, he saw the moon had moved so far across the sky it kissed the edge of the ocean. Lest he lose the maiden to the darkness soon to follow the setting moon, he dashed across the moor. As he reached the bridge, though, the maiden had vanished and it was too dark to properly search for her.

Returning in the sunlight of the following day, the young MacLeod searched all around the bridge hoping to find any sign of the maiden. There was nothing, not even a footprint in the soft grass of the moor. It was as though she had never existed.

For the next month, the young laird could not stop thinking of the singing maiden, waiting up every night hoping to hear her enchanting song again. Throughout the entire cycle of the moon, she did not return. Then, on the third day of the full moon, he finally heard her again. This time he was ready. He had started letting his dog sleep next to his bed for just this moment. He called him to his side and they raced toward the bridge.

His dog was a well-trained hound, taught to stay by his master's side until commanded to follow a scent. However, as they came closer to the bridge, and the vision of the beautiful singing maiden became clear, his dog took off from his side, ending up next to the maiden. She turned and looked directly at the young laird, before turning and disappearing with his dog.

Devastated that he had not only learned nothing new about the maiden, he'd lost his faithful pup in the same moment. He returned to the Castle Dunvegan, feeling defeated. He could not eat or sleep, wasting away from longing for the next full moon when he would surely get another glimpse of the young woman.

A third time the full moon arrived, and the laird took to lying out on the moor at night, right next to the bridge, waiting. On the third night of the full moon, the unthinkable happened. The young laird heard the enchanting melody just before he fell into a deep sleep. He was wakened by the wet tongue of his dog and opened his eyes to see the beautiful maiden's large green eyes staring into his own blue ones.

She offered her hand, and like the fool love had turned him into, he took it and willingly followed her under the hill into the realm of the faeries. There he was given food to eat that instantly returned him to his original healthy self. He and his pup followed the maiden all over the land of faeries, dancing through flowering meadows and splashing in crystal pools of water. He soon forgot his name and stayed he knew not how long.

What he did not realize was that his faerie maiden loved the land of humans, for the moon did not shine as bright in her realm. She longed to return to the moor by Castle Dunvegan and sing to the heavens above. She brought her faithful dog and human friend with her as she passed back out of the faerie kingdom.

The moment the young laird smelled the salty sea air, his mind cleared. He looked about himself and realized what he'd allowed to happen to him. He had willingly come under the spell of a faerie, a faerie he'd come to love very much. He looked to the maiden on the bridge, took her hand, bowed over it, and kissed it softly.

"My lady," he began, but she silenced him with a kiss. She had come to love her human companion just as he loved her. He returned to his family in Dunvegan Castle, and she returned to her father under the hill, each to ask for permission to marry the other. They were both denied.

On the following full moon, bathed in the silvery light, they permanently sealed their love for each other. Hoping this would change their fathers' minds, they once again returned to their respective homes and begged for marriage. Seeing that there wasn't really much choice in the matter, the fathers reluctantly gave their blessings, and their restrictions. The faerie maiden could live for one year with the humans, until the baby was born, then she must return to her faerie family, or risk severe illness.

The baby was born, a healthy son, with the MacLeod blonde hair and the green eyes of the faerie folk. As promised the faerie maiden left her son in the care of his father and a nursemaid, returning to her faerie folk under the hill. The boy was named Alberich, meaning "faerie king," and while the baby thrived, his father did not. He missed his true love, and began to perish from lack of food and drink.

In a desperate attempt to revive his son and heir, the laird's father held a grand gathering of clansmen. The babe was left with his nursemaid who wrapped him in plaid blankets, and leaving him in his cradle, went out of the room to better watch the revelry. The babe began to cry, and as his cries went unanswered, he went on to kick and thrash so that his blankets no longer warmed him. Becoming cold in the Scottish sea air, his cries became more desperate.

His mother heard her son's pleas through the thin veil between the faerie world and the human one, and unable to ignore them, she hastened to his side. Wrapping him in a blanket of faerie material, she held him and sang to him the very same melody that had drawn the baby's father to her the previous year. The babe quickly calmed down, and fell into a contented sleep.

Below, even surrounded by the noise of the festivities, the young laird's keen ear heard the faerie's song and immediately rushed to his son's room hoping for a glimpse of his love. Alas, when he'd arrived, she was no longer there, but the blanket she'd wrapped their son in remained. He longingly touched the faerie fabric.

The baby Alberich grew to be an unusually handsome man, as well as a most accomplished clan druid. Alberich's grandfather, who was also clan chief, was unwilling to recognize Alberich as heir, tainted as he was by the faerie world. So, it was that the title of clan chief was passed to Alberich's younger half-brother, born to his father and a second marriage enforced by the clansmen, and purely

Scottish. Alberich did not mind for he preferred the world of magic to the world of battles. Still, he went on to marry his own true love, and fathered his own children, many of which carried on the tradition of magic due to their faerie blood. His baby blanket of faerie fabric hangs in the castle halls to this day as the Faerie Flag of Castle Dunvegan on the Isle of Skye.

"Thus, all those descended from Alberich MacLeod have a touch of faerie magic in their blood, and the strongest become druids, some more powerful than others," Star concluded, looking pointedly up at Mairi.

ON THE ROAD
Northern California
June 26ᵗʰ, present year

Danny tried to sleep on the bus, awkwardly lying across two seats. He used his backpack for a pillow, intending to keep it safe from thieves. He'd jumped on the next available bus ride heading North, pulling everything he had from his savings, which really wasn't much, and selling his car. So here he was, hours into his bus trip, going to look for the proverbial needle in a haystack. He was heading to a little town without an address and only the last name of MacLeod. Shifting slightly as the bus hit a bump, he tried to get a few minutes of sleep in the dimly lit cabin. *Maybe Indiana Jones' life wasn't so amazing, after all,* he thought before drifting off.

Danny awoke later, to the bus winding through the redwood groves along highway 101. Unable to get comfortable, Danny sat up and looked out the huge window that took up half the wall of the bus beside his seat. He jumped a little, letting out a gasp as the bus passed shockingly close to the gargantuan trees flanking the narrow two-lane highway, only to have the grove open up to a 50-foot cliff dropping into a green-blue river below. *Oh crud! I hope this driver knows what he's doing.* Committing to the drive, entrusting his life to the bus driver, Danny shifted his gaze away from the precarious landscape, pulling from his backpack the picture of the silver faerie chanter he'd retrieved from his granny's attic.

Using a small magnifying glass to inspect the drawing, he looked closely at the etchings engraved in the silver chanter. He could see that the etchings were various Celtic knots. The only one he recognized was the Trinity Knot, the meaning of which he knew to be varied. *Why were these particular knots carved on it? Does the Trinity Knot refer to Father, Son, and the Holy Ghost? Or does it refer to Maiden, Mother, Crone?* Danny racked his brain, trying to think of all possible threes he'd read about. *Maybe it means Sky, Water, Earth? But what does any of it have to do with music? Would anyone want it for anything besides its historical significance, and proof of the validity of fairy tales?*

Scrutinizing the picture, he accepted that he couldn't see enough of the other knots in the photo to be certain which knots they could be. Looking forlornly at his antique cell phone, he again wished he had one that allowed him to search the Internet. His favorite self-pity mantra came to mind *being poor sucks!* His thoughts drifted into an adventure in which he was adeptly stealing artifacts and miraculously dodging spears thrown at him by generic native people painted with blue mud. *If only life were really so exciting,* he thought as he was jolted out of his reverie when the bus wobbled on a sharp turn.

He again picked up the paper, and began running his

fingers along the picture, imagining he could feel the etchings beneath his fingertips, wishing he held the real thing. Danny let his thoughts roam beyond fairy tales and folklore, beyond proving the stories to be simply a hint of history. He tiptoed into the possibility of magic. *What was the power I could feel coming from it? Could the chanter truly be from the faeries?* Danny almost laughed at himself. *Then that would mean faeries exist, and that isn't what I'm trying to prove... is it?*

JOURNEYS

Harris, California
July 1ˢᵗ, present year

"It will be August 1ˢᵗ soon. This is the Festival of Lughnasadh, and one of the eight most powerful days of the year." Star was explaining to Mairi and Jamie.

Mairi gulped her drink. "So soon? That's only…" Mairi counted in her head, "4 weeks away." They had arrived right after getting out of school in June, and had been there a week already.

"Is it one of the eight days that are the only days when we can time travel?" Jamie asked. Ever since learning their granda was planning on traveling back in time with them to try to reverse the curse on their gran, Jamie had taken it upon himself to quiz their grandparents for as much information as possible.

They were seated around the table, drinking lavender lemonade after another morning of gardening. They spent every morning of the past week gardening, and then had been left to explore the nearby deer trails and oak groves while Granda went off to his work tending sheep and mending fences on other ranches in the neighborhood.

Star nodded her furry head, answering Jamie's question, "Yes, and the next magical day after that is September 22nd, the Autumnal Equinox." Looking over at Mairi, Star scrutinized her. "Do not be concerned with how soon Lughnasadh is. You will be ready, I am certain."

Mairi took a gulp of her purple-hued lemonade and said, as calmly as she could muster, "Our garden won't be grown yet so how will you show us the spell recipes you said we need to learn?"

And we haven't learned very much about being druids! Mairi was searching her mind for some reason to put off the journey, to wait for Autumn Equinox instead, but she knew that wouldn't be possible. They were supposed to be back in school by then. Still, as she learned more about her family history, she became more afraid of the plan they were concocting. Excited, a little, but fear was definitely starting to take over. She really didn't like the idea of running into Ian MacDonald.

"I know, my dear, that is why Granda is going to take you into town in a few days to visit the local herb shop. I'll give you a list of what ingredients to pick up. You'll also buy some fresh herbs and flowers for us to plant in our garden. We don't want to put all that weeding and toiling to waste, now do we?" Star was looking smug, in that way cats do so well.

She planned this all along, thought Mairi. *She knew the garden wouldn't be grown before summer ends, but she had us do all that work anyway. Gran was probably just bummed she couldn't garden anymore and was happy to finally have two children to do it for her. I bet this was why Mom became so good at gardening, doing all the digging and planting once the curse had changed Star into a cat.*

Mairi shrugged, *Oh well.* Gardening had actually proven to be kind of fun. Better than sitting around doing nothing, since she couldn't text her friends whenever she wanted, or go on the Internet. Getting her hands dirty in the warm soil had been strangely satisfying, and certainly helped ease her growing anxiety. *At least, I was able to help Gran in a non-magical, non-druidic way.*

Granda came into the house just then and stood leaning against the wall. As Mairi glanced up at him, she remembered a vital piece of time traveling. "Are you going to teach me how to play the bagpipes? I'm awful at playing instruments; Jamie is way better, but I'd like to learn, if I can."

Her granda's eyes twinkled merrily, and the corners of his mouth turned up slightly. "No need to worry about whether you can play or not, the faeries took care of that." He glanced down conspiratorially at Star.

"What do you mean?" Jamie asked.

"You'll see," Granda answered with his usual mystery. "Come with me." They followed him out of the house as he led them along the path to the driveway, carrying the case with the bagpipes.

"Never a direct answer around here," grumbled Mairi.

Standing in the meadow above the house, under the oak tree, the shadows growing longer with the sun's constant travel across the blue sky, Mairi felt mystified. She had successfully managed to play a tune on her Granda's bagpipes. Granted it wasn't quite the right tempo, but it still sounded good. This was bizarre because Mairi really didn't play an instrument of any kind. It was her brother who had always played the clarinet. She would rather surf or talk to friends on her cell phone. But Granda had insisted she'd be able to play *these* bagpipes.

Now Jamie was playing the bagpipes as if he'd been playing them his whole life. Even Granda looked pleased, leaning against the trunk of the oak tree, arms crossed over his chest, a faraway dreamy look in his eyes. When he stopped, Granda told them Jamie was playing an ancient tune passed down from one MacLeod to another.

"How come you always come out to this oak tree to play the bagpipes?" Mairi asked, as they made their way back to the house. "Why don't we play nearer to the house?"

Her granda looked down at her and smiled. Just a little smile, Mairi noted, but a smile none-the-less.

"Good question. Your training is truly beginning. An oak tree is powerful druid magic. Oak trees are the doorways between now and then and what is to become, between that which lies above us and that which dwells below. When playing the bagpipes, it is always best to find a beloved tree with which to share your music."

Mairi thought about this cryptic answer for a few minutes, trying to understand what he meant. Finally, she shrugged and decided he just really liked oak trees. Then she remembered she had a much more pressing question.

"How come Jamie could play the pipes so well? For that matter, I don't understand how I was able to play at all. Is it because of this silver faerie chanter you told us about before?"

"Ah, that is a fine tale," Granda said, not quite answering, "and not an altogether happy one. It is a tale of magic, and thieving, and ultimately, one of true love."

At Jamie's pantomimed gagging regarding yet another tale of love, Granda harrumphed. "Ah Jamie, you remind me of your uncle at your age. He too had little regard for tales of love, yet he soon came to realize that all the best stories, whether they are historical or fantastical, are based on love in some form or other. Love for another person, or love of one's clan; it is still love. This one is about both."

Jamie jumped back and forth across the ruts along the weather-worn road, and Mairi stumbled to avoid twisting her ankle as she attempted to step around a loose rock. She waited for Granda to begin his tale. He remained silent, though, walking along, deep in thought. She was a bit afraid to ask him if he was ever going to start, and soon realized he had no intention of telling the story at all as they arrived at the house and went through the front doors.

"Uh...Granda, what about the story you were going to tell us?" Jamie spoke up.

Whew! Mairi thought, *I'm glad he asked.*

"Hmmm? Oh, yes, well.... I will wait for Star to tell it. I am not the storyteller." With a wave of his hand, they were dismissed to go wash up for dinner.

The dishes from dinner having been cleared away, Granda was sitting up straight in his wing back chair in the living room, Star curled in his lap. They had feasted on lamb chops from sheep Granda had raised in a co-op on a neighbor's land, and they were all enjoying a rare summer fire in the huge rock fireplace in the living room. Outside, they were enveloped in a thick fog that had rolled in while dinner was being prepared, drenching the house in a wet cold. Mairi automatically thought of *June Gloom*, a term used in San Diego this time of year. Granda had actually smiled at the fog, saying that stories are best told around a fire.

Star intoned...

A FAERIE'S GIFT

Isle of Skye
Long Ago, Once Upon a Time

*I*t began long ago, in the highlands of our home country of Scotland. A MacDonald crofter was out tending his sheep, fiddling around rather awfully at playing a tune on his bagpipes, when one thing led to another and he managed to do a favor for a faerie.

In exchange for the favor, the faerie rewarded him with a gift, a silver chanter to place on his bagpipes. Upon doing so, the crofter found that he could play the bagpipes almost as well as anyone trained in the art. So excited was he that he rushed home, driving the sheep as fast as they could safely go, to share his lovely new treasure with his family.

Unfortunately for him, as he made his way, he passed his clan leader, the Chief MacDonald, who asked why he was rushing madly through the hills. The crofter answered honestly, as he'd been taught to do by his da, that he'd just that very day been given a gift from a faerie.

In his pride, he blew up his pipe bag, and played a tune. It wasn't the best playing the Chief had ever heard, but he knew that farmers aren't trained in the art of the Highland Bagpipes, so there was obviously something special about these pipes. His eyes were immediately drawn to the silver chanter on the end of the bagpipes, and he knew that to be the faerie's gift. He bade the crofter good night, and the chieftain set off for the MacDonald castle, making plans for how he would get his hands on that chanter.

Before a week had passed, a tax collector set out into the villages of the MacDonald clan, demanding an additional tax for it was sure to be a terrible winter in which the chief would need to be prepared to care for the needy. When the tax collector came to the crofter's home, he fished around their hut until he saw the one thing of value their family had: the silver faerie chanter. He made it clear that the crofter must make payment with the silver chanter, and nothing else, for his chief demanded it of him.

The chief was delighted in his new chanter, and happily gave it to his son to compete in the upcoming Clans Competition, in which each clan would vie for the title of Head Piper. Alas, MacLeod bandits overtook him on the way to the competition, and the silver chanter made its way into the hands of the MacCrimmons, head pipers to the MacLeod's. Needless to say, the MacCrimmons won the title of Head Piper on all of Skye, and since they were aligned with the MacLeod clan, sworn enemy of the MacDonalds, this really put a burr in the division between their clans.

The story does not end there, though. The daughters of the clans were not encouraged to play the pipes, even though they had equal talent to their brothers. Bagpipes were for heading into war, and girls were not encouraged to go to war. Now, this didn't actually stop the lasses. Scottish lasses are just as feisty as their brothers, and so they would secret themselves into underground caves to practice the art of *playing the bagpipes.*

It just so happened that years later, on the night of the annual Clans Competition, Mairi MacCrimmon, the daughter of the MacCrimmons' chief piper, overheard the story of how the MacCrimmons came by the famed silver faerie chanter. She had a strong sense of justice, so she stole the chanter from her brother while he slept off his drink, intending to return it to the old farmer's family. As she ran across the moors and marshes, she became hopelessly lost in a thick fog that rolled in suddenly, something that shouldn't have happened to her, being as she'd been traipsing all over the highlands her entire life, so she knew it was the work of faerie magic, or something akin.

As she took refuge in a grove of oak trees, a young druid approached her, materializing out of the fog. She saw it was her love, young Liam MacLeod, a druid and descendent of the faerie line of MacLeod's. She told him what she was doing, and he applauded her endeavors, but explained she was in grave danger as her brother had awakened to find what she had done. Now, led by their druids in finding her, the MacCrimmons and the MacLeods, united with the MacDonalds, were competing to see who would get to her first and claim the chanter. He had only just managed to conjure up the fog in time to hide her.

The young MacLeod druid took her hand and led her to the safety of a nearby Faerie Door, hoping that they would be able to lie there unseen, to make their escape the next morning. They knew not where they would go, for returning to their homes was out of the question, just as going to the crofter would surely endanger him and his family. Mairi wept bitterly at the turn of events, when all she had wanted to do was put everything to rights.

As they lay against the Faerie Door, clinging to each

other for warmth, a beautiful maiden seemingly shimmered into being right before their eyes.

"Mairi, I am the faerie who bestowed the silver chanter upon the crofter, and have been most displeased with all three clans. You alone tried to do right by my gift, and so I have come to help you and my kinsman."

She pulled from her sleeve a silver necklace, a pendant of intertwining triangles wrapped in a circle dangled from the chain. Mairi recognized it as one of the four knots etched into the chanter itself.

"With this necklace, combined with the powers of the silver chanter and your faerie kinship, you will be able to go wherever you wish, whenever you wish, thus escaping the men who would kill you. However, you must return to me each year without fail or your family will suffer. This will hold true for all of your descendants for all time, whosoever claims ownership at the time of the tithe. Abide by this one rule and all time will belong to you." *And so it was the faerie left their side.*

Star became still, closing her green eyes in a deep slumber on Granda's lap. Granda gently petted her, a look of deepest sadness on his face. The fire had burned down low. No one had turned on any other lights, so the room was bathed in an eerie orange glow. Mairi had many questions, but didn't dare disturb anyone as the energy in the room had become somber, like when a test has ended and no one wants to jinx their scores by speaking about the experience. She and Jamie exchanged a silent nod and quietly tiptoed from the room, heading for their own beds.

PRACTICE

California
July 2nd, present year

Mairi's covers were a mess. She lay in bed, tossing and turning, unable to shut down her mind and go to sleep. She was struggling with how to make sense of everything she'd learned over the past week and a half. *Faeries are real? Time travel is real? This is crazy!* Except she knew it wasn't crazy, because her grandparents were telling her it was real and she'd experienced something with the necklace. *But what did I experience? Traveling from the bus to the Oak Knoll above Granda's driveway, and then traveling from the living room to the Oak Knoll. Always with Granda playing the bagpipes. What if we go back in time and he gets sick or cursed or…*Mairi's stomach dropped with a reality dose…*or killed?* She realized that she would be entirely at the mercy of fate if she didn't at least learn how to use the bagpipes without Granda's help. *Except I don't really know the first thing beyond blowing in the pipe and fiddling with notes. I don't even know what songs to play.* She really needed to practice! She resolved to talk to her brother first thing in the morning. She could get him to help her practice. With this new plan, Mairi lay in her crumpled bed, focusing on her breathing as the light of the full moon highlighted the picture on the wall of Gran and her mom in the garden. *Next time the moon is full, I'll be heading back in time,* she thought, finally drifting off to sleep.

She awoke at the crack of dawn, a beam of light shining through the window above her bed, puffs of dust dancing through the sunbeam. She could hear her granda moving around downstairs, preparing to go out to check on his sheep on his neighbor's land or maybe inspect the fence, or do whatever he did for his work. She considered rolling over in bed and going back to sleep since she'd barely slept at all, but she had a plan that she intended to execute. As soon as she heard her granda close the heavy front door, Mairi quietly got dressed and gingerly crept down the stairs to her brother's room, hoping not to rouse Star.

"Jamie," she whispered as loud as she dared. She didn't know where Star was, but she didn't want to alert her Gran to what she was hoping to do this morning. "Jamie!" She spoke a little louder and shook her brother's shoulder.

"What?" He attempted to pull his covers over his head. Mairi grabbed them and yanked them down.

"Jamie! Get up. I want us to try to visit our house in San Diego this morning. Come on. I need your help to play the bagpipes! You know the songs better than I do." Mairi whispered hoarsely, wanting to be heard, but stay quiet at the same time.

This caught Jamie's attention and he grunted that he would meet her outside in five minutes with the bagpipes.

Pacing back and forth on soft feet, Mairi tried to

control her patience. Before she got angry, her brother came through the front doors, carrying Granda's pipe case. Together, they made their way up the hill to the Oak Knoll, hoping they could travel home and back before anyone figured out what they were up to and stop them. Glancing over her shoulder, Mairi thought she glimpsed a white cat sitting in an upstairs window wearing a feline grin. *Why do I get the impression I'm not fooling my Gran one bit?* Mairi wondered.

Trudging through the tall grass still wet from the fog the night before, Mairi's feet were soaked through. She should have realized wearing her high-top sneakers was not the best idea. *Oh well,* she thought, *we'll be there and back in no time.* "Hurry Jamie! We're almost to the oak tree."

Jamie scowled at his sister from several feet behind and below her. "I'm carrying these bagpipes, and they're heavy! I now have more respect for the pipers who carried them to battle."

Once they reached the Oak Knoll, Mairi laid out a blanket she'd hastily pulled from the back of the couch, and helped Jamie put the suitcase with the pipes on the blanket. She watched as her brother fumbled through putting the pipes together, attaching the chanter and reed to the bag, less sure than he on what went where. When it was finally put together properly, she listened to Jamie huff and puff into the bag, inflating it until it was taut under his arm.

"Do you think it matters which song I play? I don't know that many." Jamie asked her.

"How should I know? You're the one who is supposed to know music!" She struggled to keep the alarm out of her voice. All the same, it sounded shrill, and Mairi knew she was beginning to panic.

"Mairi, I do know which song. I was just testing you, because we both need to know the songs that take us where we want to go. If something happens to me, you have to play, even if you don't play well."

Mairi sighed. "You're right, Jamie. That's one of the reasons I wanted us to do this today. Do you think you can teach me? I don't even know how to read music."

"I'll teach you," Jamie said with much more confidence than Mairi felt. "For now, listen to the song for a few minutes before wishing us at home. Then we'll practice the traveling song when we return from Mom's."

Jamie played the song that allowed them to travel. After he played it through a few times, Mairi held onto the necklace in one hand and placed her other hand on Jamie's shoulder.

"I wish we could be at home in our living room," she said. At the same time, she visualized the living room in her cozy little house in San Diego. She imagined the brightly dyed blankets patterned with mandala symbols covering the furniture, the moss green throw rugs scattered on the barely varnished wood floors, the leaf-patterned shadows that adorned the walls as the morning sunlight flooded the windows this time of year, filtering through the jungle-like yard her mother over planted but rarely pruned, and finally the smell of lavender and sandalwood that almost constantly permeated the whole house.

She experienced the usual feeling of being squeezed, surrounded by instant darkness, and suddenly felt herself sit softly on the plump couch her Granny Kate had charitably given them years before.

"I think we are getting better at this," she whispered to her brother, who was grinning at her, pipes resting on his lap. He nodded his agreement, looking around him, wide-eyed.

It's so nice to be home! Dang! I should have brought my phone. Mairi realized she would have actually been able to use it for the first time in over a week. Shrugging her shoulders, she looked around the room.

The house was quiet, except for the drip-drip of a leaky faucet they thought their mom had fixed before school let out. Mairi could see it from her seat on the couch; the kitchen sink was barely visible to the right past her brother through the arched opening from the living room into the kitchen. The edge of the dining room table could be seen to the left of the opening. Now that her attention was focused in that direction, she realized she could hear another sound. Someone was crying. She could see that her brother also heard it, so she put her fingers to her lips and tiptoed to the kitchen.

Peaking around the corner, she saw her mother seated at the table, head bowed over her folded arms, pictures of Dad spread out. It looked like her mother had been sorting photos to put into a photo album, which lay askew amongst the piles of photos. Mairi barely stopped a sob from escaping her chest at seeing her mother missing the same person Mairi also longed to see. She found herself wishing for the thousandth time that the magic her family possessed would bring her dad back.

Obviously, her mom thought she was alone, and not wanting to explain how she got there, Mairi snuck back to her brother and waved at him to follow her out the back door. Once outside, she told him what she had seen. Worried they would give themselves away with the bagpipes, they snuck through the back gate of their house and down into the canyon below. Carefully picking their way through cactus and sagebrush, they found relative safety in a gorge and they quickly slipped back to their granda's property.

Sitting up in the grass, Mairi didn't know whether to laugh or to cry. Seeing their mother weeping had been difficult, but the elation at having deliberately and successfully made a journey on their own was exhilarating.

NEW BEGINNINGS

Harris
Then, and Now

Back at Granda's house, as they sat at the dining table eating their lunch of potato stew, Mairi brought up the tale they had heard the night before.

"How does that story end, the one about Liam and Mairi? I mean, where did they go? Who are they?"

Granda went on chewing his stew, while Star perked up, happy to tell more stories.

"They would be your great-grandparents, of course. Mairi is your namesake and your granda is their child. For, you see, once the faerie gave them the necklace, Mairi immediately played the tune the faerie instructed her to play and they wished to be far away on the Isle of Harris. Of course, Harris is part of the holdings of the MacLeod clan so they had to be careful not to be found. They built a little house in the side of the hill in an isolated area. Their house backed up to a cave and they only played the bagpipes in the cave where they were sure not to be overheard, using the combined magic of the necklace and the chanter to whisk them onto nearby farms where they could acquire supplies. They were cautious to only take from the wealthier clansmen, never the poorer farmers, and only a scraggly sheep here or a scrawny sheep there. Soon they had built up a simple little home for themselves and were blessed with a wee bairn of their own, your Granda William, on the Summer Solstice."

Mairi glanced at her granda, quietly sipping the broth of his stew, and she realized, *He really is from the dark ages...born hundreds of years ago! And Mairi is my great-grandmother...I wonder if she spelled it the same way I spell my name?*

Mairi returned her attention to her Gran, who went on with her tale. "Your granda was schooled in both the arts of the MacCrimmons' pipes and the druidic skills of his MacLeod ancestors. He was a bright little lad and learned quickly. Of course, the faerie magic that surrounded him was helpful. Still, being an only child, he became bored and started wandering away from his home, looking longingly towards the other clansmen's children, wishing to make friends. It wasn't long before the other children discovered him, and he especially caught the eye of a shepherd's sister."

Granda looked up lovingly at Star, then quickly scowled and grunted something about having to tend his own sheep. He was out the front door before anyone could say a word.

Star sighed. "He doesn't like the rest of this tale."

"Why? Because you're a cat now?" Jamie asked.

"No, because his curiosity and new friends got his parents found out. On his 18th birthday, as I sat in his home alongside his parents, celebrating with their meager rations, the MacLeod Chieftain came with his brothers to take back what they believed to be theirs, the silver faerie chanter. Under your great-grandparents' insistence, your granda played the traveling tune, the one that takes you where you wish to be. I held tight to his shoulder, unable to imagine my life without him, and he wore the necklace under his tartan. His parents were just about to grab hold of us so they could travel, too, when the MacLeod Chieftain himself broke down the door and grabbed them both. We landed in a foreign land, and a foreign time, without his parents. We never found them again, though we've searched all the castles of Scotland, from castle dungeons to castle keeps, for a trace of them. We have finally come to accept they must have been captured and most likely did not survive."

Mairi shivered at the thought of her granda holding so much heartache inside him. *I've lost my dad, but he's lost both his parents, and he doesn't even know what happened to them. And, in a way, he's lost his wife and his children.* Jamie's next question broke into her thoughts.

"You landed in the future? In this time now?" Jamie asked, piecing together the information they were being given.

"Well, about 45 years ago, but yes. The future, from the time when William and I were born, in the 1600s."

Mairi's mind was whirling. "Okay, so did you know you had traveled into the future?"

Star shook her furry white head. "No, nor that we were no longer in Scotland. At first, we thought we had landed in another part of the Highlands. We searched all day for any familiar landmarks, but none were to be seen. The grassy meadows, the rock outcroppings, even the oak knolls all looked like they belonged on the Isle of Harris, but they were all wrong somehow. We were sitting in the middle of the field wondering where we were, looking at the sheep grazing there, sheep that were certainly sheep, but unlike the wooly sheep we usually saw in the Harris of Scotland, when a man came riding up on his horse. We jumped with fright, certain he was an English soldier, though his uniform was different. Now we know he was a cowboy, out checking on his ranch, but at the time, when he spoke to us, we thought one of our worst fears had been realized, for he spoke some form of English."

"How did you figure out where you were?" Mairi asked.

"And *when* you were?" Jamie added.

"The cowboy was intrigued by your granda's pipes, and our clothing, asking if we were part of a theater group. He explained that his ancestors were originally from Scotland and had come over to the Americas on a ship in the 17th century. That was our first clue we were no longer in Scotland, and that it was no longer the 17th century. It took several more days to find out it was 1970, and that we were in a mountain community called Harris that's part of California, USA. Luckily for us, the rancher was a kind man who wasn't as angry with all the hippy kids who were moving into rural communities to homestead. He assumed we were one of them, and in trade for teaching him about our Scottish customs, a few stories and bagpipe songs, as well as working for him with his sheep, he eventually granted us this piece of property."

"But how did it happen?" Jamie pressed for more information. "Why did you time travel this time, when you'd always just stayed in your own time before?"

"We soon realized that because we had been traveling on one of the magical days of the year, the Summer Solstice, we had been able to time travel as well as travel from place to place. We tested out our theories, secretly revisiting Scotland over the years, both ancient and modern, but quickly became leery that we might get caught. We soon had our own bairns, your mother and uncle, and so we settled into our new life. All would have been good until the day we die, except one day I woke up as a cat. We realized it must be due to the faerie curse, but we aren't sure how to reverse it." Star gave a big sharp-toothed yawn, circled on the chair cushion once, and fell asleep in the sun, just like any ordinary cat would.

Except she's not an ordinary cat, Mairi thought, *she's my gran and I need to fix this. Before she dies, she deserves to be human once more.*

"She's dying."

Mairi turned at her granda's voice. She hadn't heard him come back in. "Dying?"

"But she looks so healthy," Jamie added.

"She isn't…healthy, I mean." Granda came over and sat on the arm of the couch, shoulders drooping under the weight of his sorrow. "She has to sleep most of the day and night to be able to have enough energy to be with you two."

"Why is she dying?" Mairi could feel her heart breaking. *Not her, too!*

Granda shook his head, looking down at his shoes. "I don't know. I've tried everything. I can't take her to the vet, for fear they'll notice she's not a typical cat. I've asked my neighbor, Helena, for her help as she's a midwife and knows quite a bit about animals, too. She brings ointments and unguents to sooth your gran, but…"

"It isn't working?" Jamie asked.

"Nothing is working. Star…Caroline…" Granda sighed. "Your gran tells me she can feel her life slipping away. So I decided to defy your mother's wishes to keep you children away from magic, and ask for your help. When your father died," Mairi cringed at the reminder, "I saw an opportunity to help your mom and also, maybe, help your

120

gran." Granda scooped up Star and carried her upstairs where Mairi imagined he was tucking her into the blankets on his bed.

Mairi thought of the hole in her heart from losing her dad mere months before, and her resolve to help lift the curse from Gran solidified. *I will go to ancient Scotland where I'm sure the answer to curing Gran must be. I can't let her die, too! Not if Granda thinks I can help.*

INTO THE DUNGEONS

Isle of Skye
July 2nd, early 1700s

Ian MacDonald leaned against the moss-covered wall, the cold damp seeping through his druid's robes. Clasping a hand to his chest, he concentrated on taking deep breaths of the stale air, trying to slow his heartbeat after traveling the stairs leading to the dungeons. The stairs were a labyrinth of twists and turns, ups and down, spiraling around deep into the bowels of the earth under the ruins of Dun Sgathaich, the former MacDonald castle on Skye. Very few people realized there were dungeons under the ruins, and Ian liked it that way. He liked his secrets. Here he kept his favorite prisoners, Mairi and Liam MacLeod. He'd had to bargain for their lives with rare manuscripts when the MacLeod clan chief had captured them, but now it was going to finally pay off.

Holding tight to the skirts of his robes as he attempted to keep them from dragging in the pools of stagnant water, Ian limped the last leg of his trip. He'd pushed himself harder in the last few weeks than he had in the past 10 years, but he knew this might be the only remaining chance he'd get for reclaiming the silver faerie chanter. He just had to push a little bit more. When he finally held the chanter, he was certain the faerie magic in it would feed his own power, curing his ailments and maybe reversing his aging. All his studies of the Fair Folk had pointed to this possibility, that their gifts to humans held a greater magic than most people ever imagined. But he was not like most people. He was a druid, and a powerful druid who, unlike his fellow druids, had specialized in the study of the faeries. He knew the effect their magic could potentially have, and he'd spent his life in search of anything made by them.

Coming to a dead end, Ian reached out his twisted hands, wincing with the pain of stiff joints in the chilly underground, and held tight to the dungeon bars hewn from the very stone. Squinting in the gloom barely illuminated by the elaborate cracks in the walls leading up to the surface, Ian called out in a hissing voice, "Mairi, Liam. You've got company."

Slipping out of the blackest crevices of the prison cell, a thin wisp of a man stepped forward, rags of what might have once been brightly dyed tartan fabric barely clinging to his sagging skin. Patches of white hair sprouted from around his head, hanging down to his shoulders. Blinking his sunken eyes, Liam spoke, his voice coming out sounding like rocks scraping against each other. "What do you want, you old lizard?"

"Don't look at me like that, Liam, we've been through so much together." Ian laughed to himself. "Where's Mairi? Where's your dear wife?"

"She passed on a long time ago. You'd know that if you visited more often."

Ian sucked in his breath at this news, folding over like

he'd been punched in the gut, his hands on the bars the only reason he didn't fall over. Mairi had been the one he'd wanted to talk to, the one who had drawn the picture of the faerie handing her a necklace while Liam stood behind her playing a tune on his bagpipes, the ones with the silver faerie chanter attached. He'd have to hope Liam would know what the necklace signified. Gifts from faeries always meant magic for humans. After several gulps of air, Ian regained an upright stance.

"Ah, well, my friend, I still have you, don't I?" Ian said decidedly. "What can you tell me about the necklace the faeries gave your wife?"

Liam gasped and stepped back from the bars. Straightening up and breathing deep, he answered, hatred oozing from his every word, "I have no idea what you are talking about, old *friend.*"

Ian stared at Liam with his vibrant blue eyes, scrupulously sizing him up. "You lie!" Ian pulled power into his hands from the very darkness surrounding them, unleashing a shock of electricity into Liam's old bones, momentarily lighting up the dungeon. Liam's eyes rounded in surprise before he fell down on the stone floor, unmoving, the stench of burnt flesh permeating the cold, dark room.

Ian stared for a moment at Liam's crumpled and singed body. He hadn't meant to kill the old man, forgetting how fragile they had all become over time. He shrugged his bony shoulders and turned away, his mind already thinking on how he would find the answers he needed elsewhere. Liam's reaction had told him enough. The necklace was important.

Ian made his way out of the dungeon without a backward glance. If he had paused, even for a moment, and looked behind him, he would have seen Liam's body being borne away on a cushion of light.

NEIGHBORS

Harris, California
July 4ᵗʰ, present year

Mairi awoke the morning of July 4ᵗʰ, excited because they were going to a neighborhood party. If she was honest, she was enjoying her time with her grandparents, but she really missed seeing people her own age, people that weren't her little brother. Granda had told them the night before that they would be going to a pond a neighbor had built next to the creek and there would be food and fireworks and "all the kids will be there," as he put it. They were planning to arrive at 2:00, after the scorching noon day sun began to settle behind the trees, shading the area where the food would be set up, but still plenty hot enough to swim.

She spent all morning under Star's direction, making potato salad, mixing in dill and mayonnaise, which was apparently her mom's favorite recipe when she lived at home. Scooping it out of the mixing bowl and into a beautiful blown glass bowl the color of the sea, Mairi remembered the glasses of the same color and style in her cupboard at home. A thought occurred to her.

"Hey Gran. We have glasses that match this bowl exactly. Did you give them to us?"

Star purred. "They're from a local artist. I had your granda buy some dishes to match our bowl, then mail them to your mom as a reminder of her childhood." Gran licked some potato salad mix off her soft white paw.

Mairi nodded, *I think my grandparents never stopped caring for us, even if Mom tried to keep us separated.*

Now the potato salad and a six-pack of ginger ale sodas sat in a small ice-chest waiting downstairs to be taken to the party, while Mairi searched through her suitcase, trying to find her one-piece swimsuit. *Or should I wear my bikini?* She wasn't sure what the local teens would be wearing and she didn't want to stick out like a sore thumb. Finally, she decided on her black two-piece and a Hawaiian print sarong beach cover up she'd picked up in Baja on her last trip with her dad.

As she slathered on her coconut-scented sunscreen, a longing for the ocean and surf trips with her Dad welled up inside of her. She had never in her entire life spent more than a week away from the steady crash of the waves and feel of sand between her toes. It wouldn't be the same in the least, swimming in a freshwater pond. Yet, Mairi couldn't wait to feel her body enveloped in water again. Shaking off her melancholy, she took the stairs two at a time to join her granda and brother downstairs.

Mairi walked behind her granda in his Bermuda hat, red t-shirt and blue plaid shorts, snow-white legs practically blinding her from their lack of exposure to the sun. Still, it was good to see that her granda didn't always wear plaid shirts and blue jeans. That he tried to be a part of the modern world, no matter how silly he might look, was a good thing.

They made their way around the edge of the round pond, which was a giant sloping hole in the ground covered in cement and filled with blue-green water flowing from the creek and through a pipe to one side. The sound of the constant trickle of water entering the pond could be heard in the background of the party. They set their cooler down under a table at the far end, past a giant rock that stuck out into the air above the middle of the pond. Taking her potato salad out of the cooler and setting it on the red-white-and-blue-checkered tablecloth, Mairi jumped in surprise as she heard her brother shout "Geronimo!" followed by a loud SPLASH! He had wasted no time in jumping off the giant rock into the pond. She turned to see him swimming toward a tall tower of inner tubes, where a crowd of boys ranging from 12 to 17 were playing King of the Hill, ruthlessly pushing each other off the tower and back into the water. She noticed some of the older boys were even kind of cute.

"Hi!" A woman's cheery voice interrupted her thoughts. "You must be Mairi, William's granddaughter."

Mairi turned to look into the turquoise-blue eyes of an older woman, who was possibly one of the most ornately dressed older women she'd ever seen. Her long gray hair hung in a sheet down her back, accented by a streak of purple dye. Ruby red crystals hung from her ears and her fingers were adorned with ruby and silver rings. Her dress was cobalt blue cotton reaching from neck to ankle, edged with designs embroidered in silver thread, and a Celtic cross hung around her neck along with the same ruby red stones. The woman was sitting comfortably on a beach chair in the cool shade of a large leafed maple tree. Mairi nodded her head and smiled politely.

"I'm Helena Doane, one of your neighbors. Your granda co-ops his sheep on my land and he's told me all about you and Jamie visiting him for the summer. He seems happier than I've seen him in a long time." Her genuine joy practically radiated from her.

Mairi nodded again, unable to hide a look of surprise that Granda had been talking about her.

Intuiting Mairi's look, Helena went on to say, "Oh, he didn't talk too much, he never does. I've just known him long enough to see the change in him without him saying anything. He must get so lonely in that big house with no one but his cat for company."

"Yeah, I think he must." Mairi's mind drifted to Gran. Looking at all the older women and men happily chatting in groups here and there around the pond, Mairi realized how sad it was that Gran couldn't be here. Maybe if she had been cursed into being a dog instead she could have joined them, but a cat that travels to parties would be more conspicuous. Mairi's resolve to help her Gran overcome the curse, especially because she was dying, was strengthened with this latest realization.

Turning from Helena, Mairi saw a couple of girls walking towards them. "These are my granddaughters, May and Rose. Girls, this is Mairi. Her grandfather is William. Why don't you three go swimming now?" They each wore simple bikinis, one in bright red and the other in white. Mairi was relieved to find her bathing suit choice fit right in.

"What a beautiful sarong! Is it from Hawaii?" One of the girls asked Mairi.

"Um…no. I got it in Baja."

Smiling their approval, Helena's very friendly granddaughters led Mairi away to tell her all about the neighborhood gossip and hear about her surfing trips. Their giggles were infectious and Mairi couldn't help but join in with them. After a while, they jumped into the pond to swim in the cool water for the next few hours, even taking on the boys for who was King of the Hill.

When Mairi finally got out of the water to dry off, she had to leave the other girls for a moment to retrieve her towel on the opposite side of the pond. She took it out of her bag and had just begun rubbing the droplets off her arms when dancing lights in the trees beyond caught her eye. She looked up the hill rising away from the party, her heart skipping a beat as she looked directly into the soulful eyes of a deer. It reminded her of the deer she'd seen outside the window at Granda's the morning after she had first arrived. She noticed this one had a notch missing from an ear and the same splay of antlers. *Could it be the same deer? Is that possible? How far do deer roam?* She wondered.

Once again, Mairi felt as if the deer were trying to tell her something as their eyes locked. A crackle in the woods, as though someone had stepped on a branch, startled the deer and it ran off farther up the hill. Mairi continued staring, lost in thought, until she felt someone's hand set gently on her shoulder. She turned to see Helena staring in the direction the deer had gone.

"She's a messenger. She's trying to tell you something," Helena told her in a soft tone of voice.

"What…she…? I thought deer with antlers were male." Mairi took a deep breath to regain her thoughts.

"Usually only male deer have antlers, but this deer is special," Helena told Mairi, in a matter-of-fact tone.

"Okay…" Mairi hesitated. "But why is she trying to tell *me* something? *What* is she trying to tell me?"

"When the time is right, the message will become clear. There is something very special about you. I can see it in your aura." Helena smiled gently at Mairi, piercing her with her gaze. "Now, let's go eat before the food is all gone."

"My aura?" Mairi asked as they walked back to the food.

"Yes, all living creatures have an aura, an energy field of various colors surrounding them. Auras have several layers and the different colors mean different things about how someone is feeling, or what they're thinking."

Trying to picture what Helena was describing, Mairi put her towel back on her pile of stuff. "Is an aura similar to chakras?" She had just had a lesson in the seven different chakras she, and all people, apparently had running through her body, each one a color of the rainbow. With a slightly sinking feeling, she remembered she had a book she was supposed to study before tomorrow's lesson with Star. *Ugh! Studying to be a druid is vastly better than regular school, but homework is homework.*

"Yes, a little bit. It's a lot to understand in one conversation," Helena went on, "but you and your granda have unique auras, especially yours. Most people have faint auras, where as your aura is like a neon sign to the trained eye. Like I said, there is something special about you."

Mairi nodded her head, trying to wrap her mind around this latest information. Shaking the last drops of water from her hair, she pulled it up into a loose bun and wrapped her sarong around her damp bikini, tying it at her waist. She made her way back to her new friends after getting a plate of potato salad and someone's blackberry pie. She didn't have much of an appetite after all. She didn't know if she liked being "special" when normal had always been so much easier. She was actually relieved when Granda said they needed to be home before dark. Deep in thought on the long bumpy ride home, she tuned out Jamie's muttered complaints about missing the fireworks as she tried to puzzle out the significance of a deer stalking her.

TOWN

Northern California
July 7ᵗʰ, present year

"Good news, children!" Star called out as they made their way through the kitchen a few days later. Star was perched on one end of the kitchen table in a pool of sunlight. She had been staring out the window at the freshly turned garden bathed in the golden light of the morning sun, but now she was looking intently at them with her green eyes.

"You are heading into town this morning with your granda, as soon as he returns from checking on his sheep. And guess who will be waiting for you at the bus station?"

"Mom?" Jaime asked. "She told me she might be able to come up after a couple of weeks."

Mairi's stomach turned. *Does Mom know I took her necklace? What is she going to say to me about it?*

Mairi frowned, then remembered she had her own questions for her mom. *What's Mom going to say when I ask her about being related to faeries and these faerie gifts, and what about never telling me about time traveling?* She wasn't sure how to feel about her mom, but all of the fantastical family lore they had learned really gave her a headache. Not to mention how heart wrenching it had been, seeing her mother sobbing over the pictures of her dad.

Then she realized what all of this really meant. *I'm going to town! Maybe there's Wi-Fi and I can finally call my friends!* She had tried to text her best friend every night since coming, not to talk about magic because who would believe her, or even to discuss family drama, but just to gossip about normal high school stuff. Like, who was dating who this summer, and where everyone was hanging out, what parties she was missing. Maybe she'd even tell her friend about the neighborhood pond party she'd gone to. Predictably, there had been no connection, ever. She'd heard there was more consistent cell reception in town and she was really hoping she could sneak away from everyone for a little bit. Getting to see Mom was a complication she didn't feel like thinking about anymore, but like a burr in her sock after hiking around the mountain meadows, the thought stuck with her.

"Geez Mairi!" Jamie broke through her thoughts, setting a bowl and spoon down in front of her on the table. "You look like you're arguing with yourself. Aren't you happy to see Mom?" Mairi just scowled up at him.

They quickly ate their breakfast of hardy cinnamon oatmeal, which was pretty much the only thing they could find in the cupboards. *Poor Granda, he really doesn't know what kids like these days, and Gran sure isn't able to help much. Maybe Granda will let us do some grocery shopping. Better yet, maybe Mom will do the shopping while I call my friend.* Mairi carried her bowl and spoon to the sink, ignoring Jamie's questioning looks.

"Do you think this means Mom is doing better since Dad...you know...?" she asked Gran, remembering her mom's depression.

"I really don't know," came Star's soft reply. "We'll have to hope for the best."

Mairi looked away from Star, continuing to wash her dishes as she raced through all of the questions she'd been building up ever since discovering she had magic in her family, questions she still needed to ask. *Is the faerie curse really the reason Gran is Star the Cat? If so, why haven't Granda and Gran returned to a faerie door each year? Had something prevented them before Mom was cursed and my uncle left behind? Were the MacDonalds and MacLeods and MacCrimmons, all of whom were obviously her ancestors, still angry at each other? Dad must not have been angry, or he wouldn't have married Mom, but did that mean none of her MacDonald relatives knew about the faerie chanter?*

She tried to remember her dad's funeral, but it was all a blur of sadness. She quickly shoved that memory out of her mind. It made her want to curl up into a ball and cry. She wished so badly that her dad was only a phone call away. *What would Dad say about these family stories? Too bad I can only time travel 300 years back. I'd go see my dad if I could go back just a few months.* Mairi frowned as she dried her hands, fumbling with her phone to try to find music that would get her dad off her mind.

Heading upstairs to get ready for going to town, she sent her mind further back to holiday gatherings and summer vacations with her dad's family. *Did anyone seem to dislike Mom? Maybe Granny Kate was a little judgmental of Mom, but she was judgmental of everyone. No one ever dressed good enough for her, or used the right manners, or brought the right food. No one except Dad, her first-born son; he was perfect in his mother's eyes.*

What about Dad's brother, Adair? Mairi shook her head. She barely knew her other uncle. He'd only come to a family gathering one time, when she was ten, and she just remembered him scowling at everyone, even his son. *Poor Danny! What a bummer his dad is such a jerk!*

She remembered the last she'd seen of her uncle he'd been arguing with her dad in the kitchen about him being a fool for not investing in Adair's oil company. "You're missing a real opportunity! Don't forget I tried to do something nice for you by inviting you to be part of my company." *Or something like that.* Mairi couldn't exactly remember. Adair had stomped away, shouting at the whole room of people gathered there, slamming the door on his way out. Mairi had been pulled into an embrace by her dad who'd whispered something about "some people only care about money and power."

Other than Uncle Adair, I think my MacDonald family can't possibly be evil, let alone magical druids. But Granda is certain I'm related to the MacDonalds from his past. Mairi considered asking Star all these questions, but ever since learning she was sick, Mairi didn't want to bother her anymore.

With these thoughts whirling in her head like a hive of angry bees, Mairi managed to be ready in time and not make everyone wait too long for her. Before she knew it, they were bouncing over the mountain road, heading down the switch back curves into the valley where the little town was nestled. It felt weird to be wearing make-up again, but Mairi didn't want to look too much like a country bumpkin. She might even run into May and Rose in town, since they had explained they lived with their parents closer to town than where their grandparents lived. Either way, she hoped she would fit in with any other teens she might run into, and couldn't wait to call her friends in San Diego.

SEARCHING

Northern California
July 7ᵗʰ, present year

Danny was dirty, tired, and hungry. He'd been wandering around town for nearly two weeks, hoping he'd find out where Mairi and Jamie were staying with their granda for the summer. His fists clenched just thinking about their granda. For the hundredth time, Danny went over everything he knew. Starting with William MacLeod, who'd had the gall to show up at Uncle Aiden's funeral with the faerie chanter, the very chanter that had been stolen from his family, the MacDonalds.

Danny had read in an old manuscript from the library that the chanter was thought to still be in the MacLeod clan, but it had disappeared from all references in about the 1670s. He'd frantically searched every piece of writing he could get his hands on, but had found nothing new to fuel his research, except a faded charcoal drawing he'd discovered in his Granny Kate's attic. It was of a faerie and a woman talking while a bagpiper played in the background, which wasn't very helpful. Luckily, he happened to be in the right place at the right time when he was at his uncle's funeral, or he never would have known the chanter still existed.

Thinking about the conversation he'd had with his Granny Kate after the funeral, he remembered how shocked he felt when he'd found out Uncle Aiden's wife was a MacLeod. *How had I never known before? I was always visiting my aunt and uncle, playing with my cousins Mairi and Jamie, but not once did I hear anything about their mother being a MacLeod. Of course, why would I?*

No one else in his family seemed the least bit interested in their ancestry. He alone had picked through family diaries, read every bit of history he could Google on the Internet about the MacDonalds, their lifelong feud with the MacLeods, and by default the MacCrimmons. He alone seemed to know about their ties to a magical heritage, one taken from them by the MacLeods and MacCrimmons, by Mairi and Jamie's ancestors.

When Danny had arrived in this little town, he'd paced up and down the one main street, hoping to catch a glimpse of Mairi or her brother or their grandfather, but no such luck. Their grandfather only had a post office box for an address, so there had been no way to track down his physical address, no way to find them.

He'd asked around, but everyone looked at him suspiciously and shook their head. It was like everyone knew the answer, but no one trusted him enough to tell him. *So strange! What do they think I'm going to do?* He almost laughed out loud. *Probably exactly what I am planning to do. Steal something.*

Danny was worried he didn't have enough money with him for paying for a place to stay, so he'd gotten in with a crowd of young people who hung out on the wall in front of the local grocery store. They spent their evenings down by the river, sleeping in amongst the trees, staying warm by building bonfires and snuggling up with each other like a litter of abandoned puppies. They barely smelled better than stray dogs, either. Aside from swimming in the river, there wasn't any way to bathe. Danny didn't really enjoy this lifestyle, but he didn't want to give up, as this was the best, the only, lead that he'd had in his search. *This is probably the kind of thing Indiana Jones would go through, anyway.*

But what would my dad think of me now? Danny thought, sourly. *Never mind, I know what he'd think, and I doubt I want to hear him say it.*

He kicked a rock on the ground in front of him as he walked along Redwood Drive, the town's main street. *What am I supposed to do now?* Absentmindedly, he watched the rock sail through the air and plunk against a white Toyota Highlander. He couldn't see a mark on the dust covered car, so he walked away without concern, pulling his baseball cap further down his forehead.

WATCHED

Northern California
July 7ᵗʰ, present year

Mairi strolled out of the coffee shop in time to see a young man kick a rock, and to hear it hit Granda's car. The guy shrugged and walked away.

Weird, Mairi thought, *he kind of looks like someone I know,* but she couldn't really see his face under his ball cap. Hurrying out of the shade of the awning protecting the front of the coffee shop, she crossed the street to her granda's car. She looked carefully, but didn't see any damage so she crossed the street again to meet her brother at the library. She'd promised she would catch up with him, as soon as she'd had a few minutes to chat with her friends and drink a chai tea, treating herself to a little taste of the So Cal life she still missed, in spite of the exciting discoveries about magic.

Danny glanced back over his shoulder at the car he'd hit, feeling slightly guilty that he hadn't double checked to be sure there wasn't a scratch, when his eyes lit on a girl crossing the street. He almost tripped over his feet in his shock that it was his Cousin Mairi. He couldn't believe his luck! Pulling his baseball cap further down over his eyes, he quickly scooted behind a parked truck so she wouldn't see him.

How will I explain my being here? Danny thought, suspecting it was a bit late to solve that piece of the puzzle.

Mairi inspected the car Danny had just hit, then turned and re-crossed the street. Danny waited until she'd gone around the corner of the building housing the coffee shop and several other small shops before he darted between cars on the street in order to follow her. Staying in shadows and waiting for her to pass corners, Danny was able to follow her to the town library. He'd already checked it out in his frantic search for his cousins' whereabouts, so he knew that there wasn't a whole lot to learn from the short supply of books within.

He paced back and forth while he waited for her to come out. *What is she doing in there?* Luckily, he remembered to be wary of people driving into the parking lot and people exiting the glass doors, because he barely had time to duck behind a bush when Mairi and Jamie came walking out.

"What were you looking for in there, anyway?" Mairi was asking her brother.

"I don't know," Jamie shrugged. "I like to check out the history of different places. Did you know that there's an Indian curse on the beach town a bit West of here? Apparently, the pioneers killed a whole tribe of local Indians so they could take their land."

"Ugh! That's terrible, Jamie! How can you enjoy reading stuff like that?"

"I don't enjoy it. History is really important, don't

you think? We shouldn't forget it."

Danny followed as close as he dared, trying to hear their conversation, but they were too far ahead now. *What am I going to do? I should have really thought this through. Do I just go up to them and tell them I happen to be in this town visiting a friend, and oh, happy coincidence, I ran into them? Actually, that might work,* he decided.

He continued to follow his cousins back onto the main street of town, and was in time to see the Greyhound bus pull up. His cousins' grandfather came out of a sporting goods store and joined the few people waiting for friends to come off the bus. Danny stayed hidden in the shadows across the street, mulling over what to do next.

Mairi looked around anxiously as she waited near the bus for her mom. She had the strangest sensation that she was being followed.

"Jamie, do you think someone is watching us?" She stared towards the shadows across the street, squinting to see better. "I have this creepy feeling that somebody is."

Jamie dismissed her feelings, "It's probably Mom looking out the bus windows at us."

Mairi wasn't sure it was so simple as that, but she had no proof. Shaking off the feeling, she walked forward to meet her mom as she stepped off the bus steps. She was dressed all in black, her clothes looking like they'd been slept in for a week, and there were dark circles under her eyes. *Great! She isn't better.* Before Shaylee even had a chance to say hi, Granda was hugging her.

"Welcome, Shaylee."

"Hi Da," Shaylee said, kissing him gently on the cheek. Then Shaylee turned her green eyes to gaze upon her children. She hugged Jamie tight, reminding him that he looked exactly like his father, her voice catching a little and causing Jamie to stiffen and pull away.

Geez Mom, way to bring us all down! Mairi thought it, but wouldn't say it. Her mom looked really beat up, and Mairi didn't want to start an argument in the first five minutes.

Mairi gave her mom a one-armed hug, and received a bone-crushing squeeze in return. "I've missed you two so much!" Shaylee looked both of her children up and down, causing them more embarrassment than she probably realized.

Oh god! She might cry. Mairi stepped aside to avoid any more of a scene, and was grateful when Granda led the way back to his car, carrying their mom's bag for her. Mairi could see her mom needed the help. She seemed to droop as she walked.

"Before we head up the hill to Harris, we need to stop at Oak & Moon Herb Shoppe, then the grocery store," Granda said to her mom.

After putting her bag in the Highlander, they walked down the street to the little herb shop, sandwiched between the 1950s style theater and the western bar.

What a funny little eclectic town this is, Mairi thought. *It can't make up its mind what era it's part of: hippy, country, or retro Fifties.*

Shaylee took a deep breath and sighed, "I remember this place."

Mairi took a deep breath, too, and was hit with the scent of hundreds of different herbs: rosemary, lavender, comfrey, dill weed, chamomile, and so much more. It smelled a bit like their home in San Diego. The woman running the store saw them and scurried out to give Shaylee a big hug, saying in a loud whisper, "I'm sorry about your husband."

Shaylee just nodded in return before finally remembering her family standing behind her. "These are my children, Mairi and Jamie." Shaylee introduced them to the older grey-haired woman, whom their family used to sell herbs to years ago. Mairi smiled and Jamie said, "Hi."

The older woman was she a talker...she went on and on about how sweet and pretty Shaylee had been as a teenager, and how she remembered their grandmother, who Mairi was "the spitting image of."

Mairi wished she'd waited in the car.

"You know, it's weird, you showing up today, Shaylee. A boy, young man really, one of those street urchin kids who hang out by the store wall all day by the looks of his filthy clothes, he was asking about you kids. He was asking where you were staying, and about your grandfather mostly. I wouldn't tell him anything. Probably here to rip you off or something! I kept my mouth shut. But I'm telling you now because here you are, and it seems like a really weird coincidence."

Granda looked quizzically at the woman, then questionably at Mairi. "Any idea who she's talking about?"

Mairi shook her head no, but couldn't help wondering if it was the kid who had kicked a rock at their car. He had looked familiar, but she wasn't sure since he had a baseball cap shadowing most of his face. Still, this proved her feelings of being followed might be true. She elbowed Jamie. "See?" she whispered in his ear.

"What?" he asked, too loud, causing the adults to turn and stare at them. Mairi smiled sweetly and steered her brother down an aisle full of chunks of crystals and other colorful rocks.

"Someone *is* following us. Why would somebody be asking about us up here? We don't know anyone!"

"Mairi, it's probably just some kids from the pond we went to on the 4th of July."

"But, I think those kids know where we're staying." Mairi wasn't convinced, but decided to let it drop. *Someone is looking for us, but who?*

After purchasing several herbs for tea, a few for spells, and some packets of seeds for planting, they left them in the car and walked up the street towards the Town Square.

"Hey! Aren't we going to the grocery store?" Jamie called out.

"We're going to the health food store around the corner," their mom replied. "We've always shopped there. It's owned locally, and the food is chemical free. Exactly like the co-op we shop at in San Diego."

Jamie groaned, but Mairi told him he should have expected it. Mom was a health nut, after all, even when depressed. It had been their dad who would take them shopping and conveniently forget that most of the ingredients were considered poison by their mom, buying them sugary, dyed cereal and soda.

"Besides, the Farmer's Market is setting up in the Town Square and we can buy fresh fruits and vegetables from the local farmers," Granda added.

The Farmer's Market actually proved to be fun, with music playing and a few people her age working in the booths. Everywhere they turned, people recognized her mom and exclaimed over her "beautiful children." They all wanted to know why she hadn't been back in ages, and how she was dealing with her husband passing away.

Mairi and Jamie escaped the first chance they got and sat down at a little bistro style table, painted in bright green with mismatching blue and red chairs. The sunlight beaming on Mairi's face felt good and she marveled at the way she could almost see every golden molecule as it danced in front of her. She shook her head to clear it. *What am I thinking?*

Instead, she turned her attention to the band that was playing in the center of the square. The music was a low-key reggae band, with a guy playing real African drums and a female singer with dreadlocks down to her knees. Jamie got up and wandered over for a closer look.

Mairi looked past him to where her mom stood over by the wild flower stand, trying to laugh with her old friends as if she were a young girl at a festival, not the widowed older woman she obviously was. Mairi could tell her mom was still barely holding it together by how thin she was now compared to the beginning of summer. Mairi sighed, her shoulders tensing up with frustration.

Why is Mom even here? Mairi wondered yet again. *She shipped Jamie and me away for the summer, supposedly because she had to work all day to pay bills and couldn't be with us, yet here she is.* Mairi couldn't figure it out. *We lost our dad in May, but we also lost our mom. She's not how she used to be.*

Mairi remembered her mom just this past spring, before the first doctor's diagnosis, laughing with her dad in the backyard garden. She felt the resentment she'd been carrying ever since her dad had died growing strong again, in spite of having mellowed out with the distraction of magical faerie necklaces and evil druids. *Mom should be stronger than this. She should be holding our family together, not sending us off to an odd little town far from our home.*

A shadow fell across Mairi's face. "Can we sit with you?" someone asked.

Mairi looked up, startled. May and Rose, the girls

from the 4th of July party, stood next to the table looking down at her.

"Oh hey! Yeah...okay...sure..." she said, pointing at the empty chairs next to hers. *I forgot they might be around.*

"We usually come to town on Fridays so we can hang out at the Farmer's Market. We haven't seen you here before." May smiled at her, friendly and warm, lips rimmed in berry colored lip balm.

"Oh, we don't come to town much. We had to pick up my mom so I guess that's why we came today," Mairi replied, starting to feel comfortable with the girls again.

"Yeah, our grandma does a lot of shopping for your granda...for you guys." Rose picked at her brightly painted watermelon-colored nails.

If I weren't caught up in a magical marathon to disenchant Gran, I'd much rather hang out all day and listen to music with May and Rose. Mairi sighed. *I miss being with friends and just being normal.* Before she realized it, the time had passed and her mom was waving at her to head back to the car.

On the other side of the square, in the shadow of a large maple tree, Danny spoke to a man in a beat up 1960s VW bus. Handing him $40, Danny climbed into the ripped-up passenger seat, instructing the man to where the Highlander was parked.

I sure hope this works! Danny thought, not at all certain it would. "Follow that car."

FAERIE DOORS

Northern California
July 7th, present year

Mairi and Jamie were eating dinner at the dining table. It was roast beef with cooked carrots and potatoes, and a slice of homemade bread on the side. Jamie was inhaling his dinner, asking for seconds before Mairi had barely eaten two bites. She wasn't very hungry. Her nerves seemed to have chased away her appetite. She stabbed her fork into a potato and swiped it around her plate several times before she finally put it in her mouth. When she finished chewing and swallowing she asked the question on her mind.

"I'm wondering about the faerie that gave your mom and dad the necklace, Granda. Is she still alive?" Mairi glanced at her mom, who seemed deep in concentration over her own plate of food. *She didn't even flinch that I brought up faeries.*

Granda simply answered, "Yes" so Star clarified. "Faeries live for hundreds of years. She should be very much alive in the 18th century, maybe even now in our current time. Why?"

"I'm just wondering, how are we supposed to find her? I mean, when we go back in time..." It all seemed so daunting.

"Where is the Faerie Door our great-grandparents, Liam and Mairi, first met the faerie?" Jamie added.

"It's in Scotland, on the Isle of Skye. Truly, all faerie entrances lead to the same Faerie Realm so you don't need the exact one. You see, it's another dimension, so the rules of space and time run a little differently than our rules in this dimension." Star explained it all in a calm voice.

"I know you have explained faerie lore to me before, but it's so confusing. Can someone really go into a faerie door at one end of the Isle of Skye and be at the same place in the Faerie Realm as they would if they walked through a faerie door miles away?"

"I think the doorways into the Faerie Realm are magic, and they're given the same enchantment, so that when you walk through one door or a different door, the magic acts upon you and you step into the throne room of the Faerie Queen," Star explained. "She wants to see all visitors rather than have strangers, especially humans, running amok in her Realm. Still, humans must remember not to actually go into the Faerie Realm. Time runs differently there and they might end up thinking they are staying a day while a whole year or ten years pass in the human dimension."

"Then how do people ever talk to the faeries? Do I stand at the knoll and call out 'yoo-hoo?' and wait for someone to answer the door?" Mairi asked.

"Yes, sort of," purred Star in response to Mairi's agitation. "Stand at the faerie door, whichever one, and then make an offering of dried herbs and crystals, like I taught you about the other day. Play them a tune on the bagpipes, if they're handy. Faeries love human music as much as we love their own faerie music, and they are happiest when they feel worshipped. They are known for being slightly narcissistic. Doing this little ritual is certain to get someone's attention."

Mairi nodded her head, daring to hope it would be so easy, and that she would get the attention of the right 'someone.'

"Are there faerie doors in different places, other than on the Isle of Skye?" Jamie asked.

Granda shrugged as Shaylee glanced up from her barely eaten dinner. Star answered again, "There were plenty of faerie doors all over the British Isles when we lived there. Scotland, Ireland, England, and Wales are all countries known for their connection to faeries, even to this day. But this time, this land is different. I think it must be the modern technology and how everyone who lives here and in this present time seem disconnected from the earth, from nature. Faeries and Nature live in a symbiotic relationship. When an area of the earth is mistreated, it becomes ill; then the faeries in that area are weakened.

"When I was a little girl, my gran and my ma would take my sisters and I out to the spring near our house and we would leave offerings. Every family did this, so our respect for the earth was very clear, and our respect for faeries was also obvious to the Fair Folk. When they feel appreciated, and the earth is healthy, the faeries show themselves, interact with humans more. But people nowadays take the earth for granted, so the faeries are hidden, or disconnected; their doors can't be located here."

Mairi was lost in thought. *I think I saw a faery the first day we drove down granda's driveway. I didn't know it was real, but now I think it must have been. But they're so sure no faeries would be here that it must have been a trick of the light.*

Jamie took up Mairi's questioning. "You seem like you take care of the earth. Wouldn't the faeries show themselves here, at least? Shouldn't there be a door here, and we could just call for the faerie who gave our family the necklace, without going back to ancient Scotland?"

"By the time we settled here," Granda answered for Star, who lay with her eyes closed, "this land had been logged to the point of being almost barren. Over where the pond is, that used to be called The Black Forest because it was so dense with huge fir trees and ancient oaks and madrone. However, it is mostly giant stumps now. Some folks did replant, so there are baby trees sprouting up again, but it has never been enough."

"We tried to reverse the curse when it first happened," Shaylee finally spoke up, "but our little altars were too weak, the damage to nature too intense here. The faeries must have abandoned this part of the world."

"What about the Native Americans of this area? They took care of the earth before the white settlers came. Maybe they could help now," Jamie added.

"We asked," Shaylee looked sadly at her children. "They call faeries Nature Spirits or Little People, and I hoped they might help, but they say the damage done requires a stronger magic than anyone today possesses. It would take a combined effort of the whole community, and not everyone believes in faeries or nature spirits anymore."

"So, our best shot at getting help for Gran is to go back in time to one of the faerie doors you are familiar with," Mairi stated, resigned to the inevitable.

Everyone nodded in agreement.

ANSWERS

Northern California
July 7th, present year

With dinner cleared, brewed tea steaming in their cups, Mairi and Shaylee sat on the end of her bed. Her mom was staring at her intently, obviously wanting to ask Mairi questions, per usual, but showing unusual reserve. *Fine!* Mairi thought, *I have a few questions of my own, but first, I better to get this part over with.* Mairi groaned internally.

"You know I took the necklace."

"Yes. I told your granda it was missing that morning when he called from Helena's house. Your granda called me back a few days after you arrived, telling me you had accidentally used it."

Mairi frowned at her mom. "And you aren't mad at me?"

"Relieved is more like it." Shaylee let out a long breath. "Relieved that you have only used it to travel around in California, and nowhere else."

Mairi suspected her mom knew she and Jamie had visited her at their house in San Diego. "Why didn't you tell me about the necklace? I would have loved knowing our family was magic while I was growing up."

"Magic isn't all fun and games, you know. People get hurt. I got hurt." Shaylee wrapped her navy-blue tartan shawl tighter around her shoulders, warding off a chill Mairi didn't feel.

"What happened when you were a kid and your brother got left behind in ancient Scotland?"

"Oh, I don't want to talk about it…not yet." Shaylee looked down at her weather worn hands. "But, I guess you do deserve to know, a little bit."

"Deserve to know?" Mairi exploded, jumping up and forgetting to keep her voice down. "Why have I known nothing of this all my life? Why didn't you tell me about my ancestors, and my grandparents, for that matter? Why all the secrecy?" Mairi didn't mean to sound so angry, but she realized she was actually extremely mad about being kept in the dark all her life.

"I guess I always meant to tell you. I kept thinking 'when she's older', but when each new birthday came I couldn't bring myself to tell you. We had the perfect life. We didn't have magic getting in the way and ruining our lives." Her mom sighed, walked over to the dresser and put down her cup of tea, wringing her hands together. Mairi had a sudden flash of her mom looking so happy as a teen, even if her own mother had already been cursed into being a cat, and then her mom looking so sad once her brother had disappeared. Mairi walked over and gave her a one-armed hug.

"I'm sorry magic made your life so miserable, Mom. At least there's a chance your brother will return and your mom will become human again. My dad is dead. The cancer killed him and he'll always be gone." Shaylee flinched and

Mairi dropped her arm. She hadn't meant to say anything about her dad, but she couldn't help it. She missed him so much, and she wished more than anything that the magic they had discovered had been the type that brought people back to life.

She heard a scuffle outside her room and glimpsed blonde hair through a crack in the door. "Jamie, come in. You don't have to hide."

Jamie walked in wearing the cut-off sweat pants he usually wore to bed. "Sorry, I just want to hear what Mom is telling you. I'm curious, too." Mairi and her mom sat down again. Their mom patted the bed next to her and Jamie flopped down beside them.

"Well, I was about to explain that your uncle didn't return with me from ancient Scotland for a number of reasons. The primary reason was that he actually loved it back then. He'd always read all of those history books, and played Risk and other battle games, and he loved that rugged life. Remember, if the faerie chanter hadn't come into our family, my brother and I would have been born back in the 1700s. That time is as much our own as this time is."

"With that logic, Mairi and I could have just as easily been born in the 1700s, too." Jamie chimed in, grinning and clearly taken with the idea.

"Maybe," Shaylee answered, "but your dad's time was now. His family lineage has no time travel in it. So, following this same logic, you two are in the time you are supposed to be in."

Mairi shook her head to clear the confusing timeline she'd tried to imagine in order to follow their *logic*, a timeline that looked more like the curving mountain road leading to granda's property rather than the straight lines she'd learned in math class. "This is a weird conversation.

You said, 'one reason' our uncle didn't return. What was the other?"

"The other reason he didn't return might be more relevant. The English soldiers were closing in on us, and my brother thought that if he led them away from me, I could safely get home, but return soon after to get him. Meanwhile, he might be able to learn about how to turn our mom back to her human form. The trouble is, as I played the pipes and wished myself home, I ran into a Grove of Druids with Ian MacDonald heading it. He sent a curse at me and wiped me of my magic skills. I knew, in that moment, that I was lucky to have gotten home, and that I might never see my brother again. I've hoped every day, ever since, that he is happy in the life he chose. It's a much rougher life than we live these days, and I believe in my heart he has survived it."

I wonder if I would miss Jamie if he got stuck back in time without me. Mairi knew she didn't really mean this. She knew she would miss him, but the thought slipped through all the same.

"Why doesn't granda just go back and get him?" Jamie asked.

Before Shaylee could answer, Star walked in on silent cat paws. "He's tried to time travel once since Ian cursed your mom. He played the tune, held the necklace, and made the wish, but nothing happened. I guess the faerie curse that turned me into a cat diminished his powers, too. He can still play the pipes beautifully, so the silver chanter is still magical, but the only reason he could help you kids travel from place to place was because you two are extremely powerful." Star curled up on Mairi's lap.

"I don't get why you keep saying we're so powerful. I don't feel powerful. I can't do anything magical unless I have the help of the faerie gifts," she held up the pouch containing the necklace as she said this.

"My dear granddaughter," Star said in a soothing tone, "you are becoming more powerful by the day. Have you not noticed how the creatures in the forest catch your attention more than ever before? Do you not have an awareness of the elements; the earth, the air, the sun, the water, as never before?"

"How..." Mairi stared at her gran. "How do you know this about me? Other than the rocks vibrating, I haven't told anyone that this is happening."

"I know because I am a cat right now, and in this form I can feel the energy currents running through every living being. Besides, I experienced it myself when I was young, just as every member of the druid order grows closer to the elements in nature as their powers begin to appear. You are older than most in our family," and Star stared pointedly at Shaylee for a moment, "but that is only because you were kept apart from magic for so long. Still, I've heard about your surfing and I think you had a stronger connection with waves than most surfers because of your magic."

At this, Star stood up, yawned, her feline teeth showing, and stretched right to the tip of her tail. Silently, she jumped to the floor and rubbed up against everyone's ankles before she walked out of the room.

"That's enough for one night. She's exhausted and so am I. Off to bed with both of you." With that, her mom shooed Jamie out of the room and gestured to Mairi to get into bed, crawling in herself. They would share a bed since there were no more spare rooms and sleeping on the couch seemed like it might be dusty. Mairi had tried to tackle the dust in the house, but it seemed engrained in the very fibers of the walls and furniture. Maybe her mom would have better luck.

Before turning off the light on her bedside table, Mairi completed her new nightly ritual. She looked at the calendar she'd picked up in town, counting the days until she would time travel. Her breath caught, *17 days before I go. Less than 3 weeks!* But thinking about her Gran, she hoped 17 days wouldn't be too late.

As they drifted off to sleep, Mairi asked her mom why she rode the bus and didn't ask Mairi and Jamie to bring her with the necklace. Her mom patted her hand, saying, "Some things in life are very frightening, and almost impossible to overcome." Mairi could see why her mom was afraid to use magic and that it didn't matter if she did not have magic anymore because even if she did, she probably wouldn't use it. Mairi shivered as an image of crazy druids cursing her mom went through her mind. *Could he really be that terrible?*

UNDERGROUND

Isle of Skye
July 7th, early 1700s

Using the last of his dwindling energy to push aside the boulder, Ian ducked his head and shimmied his way through the narrow entrance leading into the burial mound. Days of endless travel had left him with very little strength for what he hoped would be the final leg of the plan he had come up with.

He'd almost lost hope when he discovered Mairi MacCrimmon was dead, and had accidentally sent Liam MacLeod to join her. Then he realized the answer was in the drawing all along. *The faeries!* A faerie had given the chanter, a faerie had given a necklace, and so surely a faerie would have the answer for how Ian could gain both of those items for his very own. He didn't know what the necklace could do, nor did he care, for any gift from a faerie was sure to be powerful and worth owning. He'd defeat the MacLeod druids and grab both faerie objects in doing so, sure that the objects would make him the most powerful druid to ever live.

Trudging down the long entryway that widened as he

passed a catacomb of buried Highlanders, Ian shivered when a cold breeze blew past him. A sound up ahead caught his attention. He stopped and squinted in the darkness beyond, wondering if he should use what energy he could muster up to create a light to see by. Before he could even begin to call upon his powers, he saw an unearthly glow deeper in the mound.

A tall woman, illuminated by an energy source Ian had yet to figure out, made her way towards him. The ethereal light surrounding her entire being rose like wings above her shoulders. Perhaps they were wings; he'd never had an opportunity to find out, but certainly this was why faeries were so often drawn to resemble angels. As she drew nearer, her imposing regal stance caused Ian to shrink even more than his old age ever had. Stooped as he already was, his likeness to a bulky gravity bound animal became more pronounced next to her unearthly beauty. Ian gasped, awestruck by her inhuman splendor. Kneeling before her, he intoned, "Cali."

"You called, Druid of the Dark? What is it you wish to know this time?" Her voice, though airy and light, was stern and direct. "I thought I'd taught you all I could the last time we met. I still have not heard of where the silver chanter might be, if that is what you've come to ask. You must know by now that I care not for such human trifles, though they do alleviate one's boredom."

"I...I...ahem" Ian coughed, more to calm his nerves than to clear his throat. There were few in the world that caused him to feel timid as a mouse, and this Dark Faerie was certainly one who could. "I am here to seek knowledge about a necklace one of your sisters gave to a woman many years ago." He held up the charcoal drawing he'd brought with him, hastily yet gently unwrapping it from the wool scarf he'd carried it in.

Requiring no light beyond her own bodily illumination, or perhaps her eyes could simply see more than a human's, the faerie barely glanced over the drawing.

"Hmmm...my *sisters*," she said this word with such disdain that Ian wondered if this faerie could possibly ever love another, "do so enjoy meddling in human affairs. Such light-headed fools. It would be better if they left the human race to fend for itself, and perhaps get wiped out so that my race could tread where we will without any sort of secrecy."

She looked down on Ian as if she had only just remembered he was human. "Well, there are always such as you who give me hope." Handing the parchment back to Ian, she smiled slightly. Ian shrank deeper into his robes so frightening was her smile.

"Forgive my ignorance, but it seems like your kind could wipe out humans whenever you want, if you wished to, your power is so great." *If only I had such powers for my own.*

Looking down from her full height, like a bird of prey on a rabbit, she answered "Were it so simple? Alas, it is not."

"My lady, the necklace...?" Ian asked.

She shrugged, "It is a necklace with the power to travel both from place to place, and from time to time. I remember it a little. One of my faerie Sisters of Light made it for her own amusement, to see what mischief it would cause, assuming it would bring no harm. Perhaps it didn't, I don't know. She ended up taking pity on a young Highland couple being pursued by several clans at once. I don't recall when this was, but the necklace helped them to escape and that is the last I paid attention." Waving her long graceful fingers as if to shoo a fly, she turned to walk away.

"Oh, I do remember one more thing," she called over

her shoulder, and then pivoted gracefully on her bejeweled bare feet to face him. "That whoever was gifted the necklace must return to the faerie shrine annually or risk being cursed. I doubt the curse would be too terrible. Sisters of Light rarely deliberately harm anyone." She shook her head. "They are such frivolous faeries...such a disappointment. If only they would join me in my cause, we'd be so much more powerful."

"What cause is that?" Ian couldn't resist asking, though he feared her answer would be beyond his imaginings.

"Hmmm...it might be fun letting you know." She smiled slightly, eyes twinkling wickedly. "I am in a debate with the Summer Queen about whether we should take the Earth back from humans. Your kind does not take care of the world, not now in this time and definitely not in the future. Sadly, she does not agree with me, having a soft spot for those who are weaker. We'll see."

She disappeared then, leaving Ian to stand in the darkness and wonder at what he'd learned. *So Faeries are arguing over the worth of humans? That can't be good. All the more reason for me to find a way to gain more power of my own.*

Returning to his mission, a faint spark of hope kindled in his heart. *Place to place? Time to time? That explains how the MacLeod's keep disappearing without leaving a trace. And why they keep showing up at the Faerie Grove,* he thought, remembering what Cali had said regarding the curse.

Ian knew what he needed to do next.

AN UNEXPECTED GUEST

Harris, California
July 8th, present year

The waning moon made midnight darker than previous nights, as Danny lay hidden in the tall grass above the house he'd seen his cousins and aunt go into earlier. He rested his head on his backpack, staring at the night sky. *The stars up here are breathtaking,* Danny thought, enjoying the warm evening with no sign of fog. *Brighter than the stars in Southern California.* The night sky looked like a million fairy lights draped across a black velvet ceiling. Danny was entertaining himself by using his pointer finger to trace all the constellations he could recognize. Staying hidden and spying on his cousins might prove to be a good idea after all.

Earlier that afternoon, he'd questioned that decision as he'd used his last $40 to pay one of his river rat friends to drive a beat up VW bus and follow his cousins up the hill to their mountain home. The ride had been hot and dusty, with all the windows rolled down, not to mention terrifying as the driver took the corners as if he were the only car on the road, pushing the bus almost to breaking point. They had managed to keep the white car just in sight, and Danny had eagerly jumped out at the top of the driveway, muttering a "thank you" to the driver.

Now he dropped off to sleep, huddled under his jacket for warmth, the last bit of beef jerky in his belly, and stars for a night-light.

Mairi woke up with a start. *What are we going to wear?* They couldn't very well go popping into 17th century Scotland wearing blue jeans and sneakers. She pulled out her cell phone, hoping to use it to check out what kids wore way back in the 1700s, figuring even if her phone was old by modern terms, it would suffice to get her some information on the topic. However, after several attempts to get online, she threw it onto her bed in frustration. Typically, there was no reception today so she'd have to figure it out the old-fashioned way, with books.

Tip-toeing across the wood floor of her room, she slipped into a robe and pulled on socks to ward off the lingering chill brought on by the midnight fog that had rolled in. She quietly made her way downstairs without waking her mom, who had braved sleeping on the couch, so she could read whenever she woke up. Sneaking into her brother's room, she shook his shoulder until he awakened.

"Stop doing that!" Jamie grunted. "I don't like it when you wake me up early." He rubbed his sleep-deprived eyes and blinked in the gray gloom of the morning.

"This is important! What are we going to wear when we go back in time? I don't have internet access and I don't know what books are on these shelves, but we need to figure out what we need to wear to blend in, then we have to find those clothes and there aren't even any stores around here, let alone costume stores, and…."

"Stop! Geez, Mairi! Take a breath. I'm sure we can search the closets in this house once we know what to look for. They've all been back in time before," Jamie waved a hand indicating the rest of the house and its occupants. "And I do know there's a book on these shelves that will help us. Just give me a minute." Jamie slid out of bed with a thump, and picked his way through the piles of his dirty clothes all over the floor. Pulling a book off the shelf, he tossed it to Mairi, at the same time not bothering to stifle his yawn. A cloud of dust enveloped her, sending her into a sneezing fit.

"Thanks," she muttered to her brother, who was climbing back into bed without a backward glance.

Taking the book with her, she headed into the kitchen and turned the heat on under the hot water Granda had left on the stove. *He must have just left, off to work on the fence or something,* Mairi thought to herself as she prepared her cup of tea. She made an Awakening Tea, pouring the boiling water over a blend of dried peppermint leaves they had bought in town and adding raw honey from Helena's bees. Gingerly holding the hot mug, she snuggled up on the little couch in the sitting room.

Opening the book, she realized it was actually someone's drawing pad. Careful to turn the pages slowly for fear of ripping the fragile paper, she saw that on each page were sketches of men and boys dressed in kilts, and women and girls in long dresses with poufy sleeves, their own plaid shawls draped over one shoulder. Some girls were depicted dancing with little black ballet slippers and long socks, while boys danced beside them in similar shoes and socks. Feeling somewhat relieved that the outfits weren't too far-fetched, Mairi settled into sipping her tea and looking through the drawings.

She felt a hand gently rest on her shoulder, and she looked up into her mom's blood shot green eyes. *She was crying,* Mairi could see it in her eyes, but she'd also heard her mom's muffled sobs all night.

"Good morning, dear. I see you found my old sketch book."

"Oh! I didn't know you drew these pictures. I was just trying to figure out how people dressed in Scotland, long ago." *I didn't know Mom could draw. How come I know so little about her?* A twinge of guilt passed over her as she realized she used to spend most of her time with her dad.

Shaylee shrugged her shoulders. "Well, in that case, my brother and I had Scottish outfits from that era made for us each year, right up until the year we went back in time and lost James. I'm sure they will fit you, and they should be stored somewhere in this house."

Mairi felt some relief, but still she had a bubble of anxiety growing in her stomach, as she always did when the conversation turned to traveling through time. The peppermint was helping calm her nerves a little, but she wished she had added chamomile to the tea, or lavender. She needed all the help she could get. Star walked in purring and she rubbed her body against Mairi's calf. "Don't worry Mairi, everything will work out just fine."

Mairi stared at Star, wondering how she always seemed to know what Mairi was thinking.

"Scootch over, Mairi." As Mairi moved over her mom sat down next to her and took the book. Star curled up on Mairi's lap. "I don't think I've ever showed anyone this book. I was so distraught after returning from the past without James that I was sent to see an art therapist. To work through my feelings, I drew pictures of what I'd seen. The therapist probably thought I was obsessed with Scottish history, because it wasn't like I could even begin to tell her the truth."

As she talked, she turned the pages in her sketchbook, careful not to rip the old pages. She stopped at a picture with a broad-shouldered man in a grayish-white tunic and fiery red bearded face. He held some sort of staff and the anger radiating from his eyes was palpable.

"Who is this?" Mairi gasped, a guess already forming in her mind.

She felt her mom's body stiffen beside her. "That is Ian MacDonald, the druid who cursed me. I think he would have killed me if he'd had the chance. I suppose I should feel lucky I only lost my magic. I have to believe that James escaped his clutches and we'll see him again. The alternative is unthinkable. There is even a chance Ian never found out about my brother, since James was leading the English soldier away before I stumbled into Ian's Grove of Druids."

Mairi shivered all over. She sincerely hoped she wouldn't run into Ian. "He'll be an old man by now, like Da," her mom was saying to Star, who nodded in agreement.

So there's a good chance that when I arrive back then, hopefully he won't be up for battling anyone.

"He might even be dead already," Star was saying.

I really hope so! Mairi thought, feeling almost desperate.

As they continued looking through the sketchbook, Mairi saw images of a boy with reddish-blonde hair running through the jagged rocks of the Highlands, an English soldier on horseback closing in on him.

"My brother and I ran from the English soldiers, hiding in the crags between the sharp rocks on the Isle of Skye, and in the deep ravines. The English Soldiers and the Scottish Highlanders were fighting over who would be king,

Bonnie Prince Charles or King Edward of England. We accidentally ended up amid a skirmish. They'd noticed our bagpipes and assumed we were part of the battle. I think bagpipes were outlawed at that time."

Jamie came in and sat on the arm of the couch next to his mom, rubbing his eyes and yawning. "No, you would have been okay as far as the laws were concerned. Bagpipes weren't outlawed in Scotland until 1746. Still, if a soldier did hear you playing, you're lucky you weren't killed because pipe music was used to encourage the Highlanders in battle. The English feared the sound."

Shaylee looked at her son with pride. "I never stopped to check the history of bagpipes. It helps me to know that my brother might have found another set of pipes to play and would not have been an outlaw, though I'm sure he became a Highland warrior."

"Yeah, well, if he chose to fight alongside the Jacobites, he was an outlaw anyway. What's for breakfast? I'm hungry." Jamie stood and headed into the kitchen.

Just then there was a scuffling sound coming from the front porch and the heavy door swung open revealing Granda's tall, imposing figure holding a young man by the scruff of his neck.

"Look what the cat dragged in," he said and Star growled under her breath, to which Granda muttered, "Sorry, slipped out." She leaped over to land next to the distraught young man.

Mairi jumped off the couch, nearly spilling her tea, saying "Danny? What are you doing here?" Shaylee and Jamie stared, wide-eyed.

RELATIVE PEACE

Harris, California
July 8th, present year

They sat crowded around the kitchen table, with heaping bowls of steaming porridge topped with raisins, walnuts, and maple syrup sprinkled with cinnamon on the table in front of them. Shaylee had insisted that everyone needed a full belly before any more talk could take place. Granda had gone upstairs to change out of his work shirt and now sat straight and tall, washed up and digging into his breakfast.

Mairi stared at her cousin, not certain if she could trust him. She already knew that it had to be him sneaking around town asking people about their whereabouts. Her instincts were warning her against any possible logical explanation for his being there. Still, they had always been friends as children and he was related to her dad, which was making her emotions threaten to bubble up inside. *Is there a chance he knows about the necklace and the chanter? For that matter, could he know anything about their ancestor's feud?* She couldn't be sure.

Granda seemed to share her distrust, glancing over his bowl of porridge at Danny, barely keeping his questions bottled up. Her mom hummed a Gaelic lullaby tune, and Jamie gobbled up his porridge as fast as he could, taking huge gulps of ice cold milk to counter the heat of the cooked oats. Star stayed curled up on the couch in the sitting room across the way, pretending to be an uninterested house cat, but Mairi knew she was alert because one green eye periodically peeked at everyone sitting at the table, and her tail twitched impatiently.

Danny silently cursed himself for getting caught, even though the porridge was feeling pretty good on his empty stomach. One minute he'd been curled up in the grass, fast asleep under the starry sky, and the next this old man was yanking him to his feet demanding to know who he was and what he was doing on his property. Danny had quickly realized that keeping as close to the truth as possible was his safest course. He'd sputtered, "I'm Danny MacDonald, Mairi and Jamie's cousin. Aiden MacDonald is…was… my uncle."

"Get your stuff." The old man had gestured to Danny's backpack and jacket lying in the field of grass. "You can tell me *why* you are here and *how* you got here when we get home to breakfast."

The old man had yanked Danny along, following a faint trail down the mountainside, winding to the house below. Danny had stared in wonder at how it looked like a small castle nestled against the mountainside.

Mairi's mom finally broke the silence. "So, Danny, I thought I told you I'd have my dad call you. What brings you to our neck of the woods without an invitation?"

Danny took a deep breath. Ever since getting caught, he'd been trying to come up with some explanation. Again, he'd decided to stick to the truth, without actually revealing his true purpose. He was sure that if he could stay in the house with them, he would eventually get his hands on the silver faerie chanter. Maybe they didn't even realize the chanter was magic.

He started his explanation. "Everyone at school talks about how great it is to visit Northern California in the summer, that there are tons of jobs available. When I heard from my Granny Kate that my cousins had been sent up here to stay for the summer, I figured it was a perfect opportunity. But she didn't know where you were staying and you wouldn't tell me, so I just decided to get on the bus and start looking. You know, an adventure. I figured it was a tiny town, but when I got here, it wasn't as easy as I'd hoped it would be. No one knew where your granda lived, or they wouldn't tell me, and I couldn't get a job, after all. Finally, I guess I asked the right person, someone from that alternative college down the road, who thought they knew where you lived. Luckily, there aren't that many people who play the bagpipes around here."

Danny stopped and took a long drink from his milk. *Whew! That went pretty well, I think.* He braved glancing into the eyes of everyone surrounding him, and was relieved to see less suspicion than before. Except the cat, who was standing on a chair, front paws on the table, staring intensely at him. *What a strange cat,* Danny couldn't help thinking.

Everything went smoothly the rest of the day. Danny was taken up on his request for work and after a quick shower and fresh clothes, a mix of Granda's and Jamie's, he set back up the mountain to help Granda finish mending the fence. While they were out, Mairi and Jamie used this time to practice their bagpiping, to study the geography and history of the Isle of Skye, as well as their herb lore lessons with Gran and now their mom, too. When they finished, under strict orders from their granda, they locked away the bagpipes and the necklace, pretending that all they had been doing was learning to prepare traditional family recipes. This last part was a little true, as they had helped to cook dinner, which consisted of mashed potatoes and lamb, seasoned with herbs.

Danny proved to be genuinely helpful with Granda's work in the sheep pasture. He found he actually enjoyed the manual labor of digging new holes for fence posts and hammering the barbed wire to the posts. It was hot work, especially as the sun rose higher and higher in the sky, but at its pinnacle, William told him sternly that it was time for a break. They sat in the shade of an oak tree and ate the sandwiches that Aunt Shaylee had made for them. When the food was gone and water consumed, they went back to work.

"Does this fence run the whole length around your property?" Danny braved asking the stern older man.

"Yes."

"Looks like it gets a little difficult at the bottom." Danny was shading his eyes from the sun, looking down the mountainside where it seemed to turn into a steep cliff. Throwing a rock into the canyon to point out where he was looking, he hit the buckeye seed dangling from a buckeye tree branch, just as he had meant to. William raised his eyes at Danny's obvious skill.

"The sheep rarely get down that way, preferring the grass covered hillside," William answered. "I only have to walk the fence line after a storm. Plenty to keep me busy up here, most days. Once I get the fence mended I'll bring my sheep back from my neighbor's."

With that, the conversation ended, though Danny could feel William's eyes on him. He did not doubt he wasn't trusted. Danny tried to think of how to steer the conversation towards Scottish history and lore, but he was afraid to alert the man to his true intentions. He decided to just enjoy today, with good food and a real shower for the first time in weeks.

He'd figure out how to get the chanter soon enough.

SUMMER RHYTHM

Harris, California
July 15th, present year

The next several days passed quickly, with Mairi using the little calendar she'd picked up in town to keep track each night of how long until Lughnasadh. Before she knew it, there were only two weeks to go. In the meantime, they were enveloped in a typical California summer heat wave.

Mairi and Jamie hadn't expected the heat to be as bad in Northern California as it could be in Southern, but it most definitely was. They asked daily to go to the neighborhood pond to cool off. So their days fell into a steady rhythm with Danny and Granda working out on the fence each morning before the summer heat steadily crept up to the high '90s, while Mairi, Jamie, and Gran worked on bagpiping, faerie lore, and spells at home, with the help of their mother. Star spent more and more time sleeping and less time interacting.

As the air around the house became dryer each day, it was a luxury to escape to the cool water of the pond for the afternoon. The adults didn't care for joining them; so most afternoons the three cousins were on their own to walk through the woods, over the mountain, and down to the creek-fed pond a few miles away. Occasionally, other neighborhood kids would be there, too.

It was on these walks that Mairi, Jamie, and Danny became friends again. Or so Mairi and Jamie believed. For his part, Danny was torn up inside. On the one hand, he was angry because his cousins had access to a magical faerie instrument, even though he couldn't be sure they knew anything about it beyond its use for bagpipe music. On the other hand, Danny truly enjoyed his cousins. Jamie was smart as a whip and loved talking about history with Danny. His younger cousin seemed fascinated with battles and anything magical, while Danny could recount the history of various art forms such as storytelling and music. It wasn't long before they got onto the subject of druids. Young Jamie didn't realize that in that conversation alone, he told a lot more to his cousin than he probably had meant to, about how much he and his sister knew regarding magic.

For her part, Mairi was easy to be around, not talking too much, but not being unkind either. She seemed lost in thought, especially the one time Danny had accidentally mentioned her dad. He hadn't meant to, but the subject of surfing had come up and that always led back to Uncle Aiden, and before he knew it Mairi left their side. She took off to walk alone, eventually trailing behind the boys on the road.

Mairi had heard Danny's comment about her dad and hadn't meant to tune Danny out, but she had started thinking about her last surf trip with her dad, the one before he was diagnosed with cancer. He'd slipped so quickly into being bed-ridden because he was stage 4 before they even knew he had it. Mairi took a deep breath and tried to shake off the pain like she usually could, noticing it got harder every time, not easier as she'd been led to believe by her friends good-natured comments at the funeral.

Lost in thought, something caught her attention just off the road in the dusty woods. A flicker of big ears and once again her eyes locked into the deep brown eyes of a deer. This time the deer slowly turned away from her and walked a few yards, pausing and looking over its shoulder at her. Mairi felt compelled to follow, wondering what the deer wanted to show her. Accepting that the deer really was a doe despite the antlers, like the quirky neighbor, Helena, had told her at the 4th of July party, not a buck like she had thought all along, she puzzled out her personal knowledge of deer, which was minimal. She'd always thought only male deer had antlers.

After several minutes of following the doe, she realized it had disappeared. One moment she'd been directly in front of Mairi, then she'd stepped into a stream of sunlight filtering through the trees, and shimmered out of sight. Mairi looked around her, frightened that she'd gotten herself lost, but was relieved to see she was merely walking a parallel path to her brother and cousin, who were still traveling the hot dry road.

Looking closer at the path under her feet, she saw it was only a faint path, covered over in dry summer grass patted down by delicate cloven hooves. Feeling her own feet sweating in her sneakers, Mairi sat down and removed them. Stretching her toes and enjoying the soft air on them, she stood and took a gingerly step. *It's so good to feel the earth against my skin! It's not like the sandy beach I'm used to, but so freeing all the same.* Mairi marveled that it took her so long to try going barefoot. *I guess I have been distracted,* she admitted.

Peering around her in wonder, she noticed that she felt more at peace on the path and was no longer feeling the crushing weight of sorrow pushing her down into darkness. It was something in the way the sunlight filtered through the tree branches and the earth vibrated beneath her bare feet. It was energizing. Smiling to herself, Mairi quickened her pace in order to catch up with the boys, once again looking forward to jumping into the cool pond water.

This became the new way to travel to the pond, and the boys gladly joined her in walking barefoot on the soft grass rather than traversing the hard packed, dust covered road. It was cooler along the deer trail, where the fir trees were closer together letting in less sunlight. While they used to dread the hot walk to the pond along the sunbaked road, they began to look forward to exploring the path. They even became exceedingly good at noticing which critters had walked there the night before, noting the light scent left over from a skunk, the tiny pellet droppings of a cotton-tailed bunny, or the lost feather from an owl. When Mairi and Jamie relayed their discoveries to their granda, he was pleased and told them so, for becoming observant of Nature was part of their druid training. This was never said in front of Danny, but always in secret, yet Granda commented more than once on how enthusiastically Danny joined in with telling of their adventures.

Perhaps he really isn't a bad person, Mairi decided, happy to let go of being suspicious of her cousin.

TRAPPED

Harris, California
July 24th, present year

Mairi couldn't sleep again. There were only seven days until Lughnasad, and she wished more than ever since coming to stay at her granda's that she had Wi-Fi connection to keep herself busy. *What can I do?* She needed a distraction from her growing anxiety. Back home she would stay up late into the night and chat with her friends or watch videos online, but here there was nothing to do at night except read a book or listen to the crickets sing. All fine for Jamie who had always loved books as much, or perhaps more, than electronic media.

Sometimes Mairi worried that Jamie was a social outcast, always sitting around their house with his nose in a book. But she knew this worry was unfounded. Jamie was as equally outgoing as he was introverted, and had numerous friends to prove it. He seemed just as happy to put down his book, carefully bookmarked for where he'd left off, as he was to catch a ride to the beach and surf with friends or play an Xbox game with a school friend. Mairi would never admit it to his face, or to anyone at all, but she was sometimes jealous of her little brother's easy-going personality. She especially wondered if he was even affected by the death of their father because his smile never seemed to falter...*exactly like Dad, an optimist through and through.*

Mairi, on the other hand, was a worrier, and right now she couldn't sleep because she was freaked out she was on a suicide mission with all this time travel and rescue stuff. Pushing back the covers on her bed, she decided to go make a cup of hot chocolate and maybe find a magazine to flip through. Realizing her mother wasn't in bed either, she wondered if she would find her downstairs on the couch reading, or in the kitchen making tea. They'd often run into each other in the kitchen at home, late at night, both unable to sleep because something was upsetting them.

Pulling open the door of her room, grateful the door hinges were well oiled and silent, Mairi heard murmuring voices coming from downstairs. Stepping quietly across the padded carpet, she leaned over the balcony just enough to see her mom and Granda sitting on the two chairs, Star curled up in Shaylee's lap. Mairi quickly ducked down, kneeling on the floor and leaning against the railing.

"I really don't think we should send them back in time. I know that's what you're planning, and I can't sit by and do nothing. They're sure to run into Ian MacDonald or some other crazy druid. I'm their mother. I'm supposed to protect them! Not let them go on deadly journeys through time." Her mother was whispering, but Mairi could definitely detect a note of hysteria.

"I have been thinking about this, too," Granda spoke calmly. "I have been working on a Protection Spell that my parents taught me for when we used to pilfer sheep from the neighbors back on the Isle of Harris. I haven't done the spell in years, and my magic is weakened, but I think I can make it work."

"You know a Protection Spell? Why didn't you use that on James and me?" Shaylee looked like she wanted to shout at her dad, her fists clinched over Star's swishing tail. Mairi was sure she could hear Star's purring growing louder in an effort to calm Shaylee.

Granda smirked, "You do recall that you and James left without telling us, don't you?"

Shaylee was visibly deflated, her hands falling to her knees, her head drooping. "Yes...I'd almost forgotten. James was so sure we could sneak into ancient Scotland unnoticed. We planned to get the attention of the faeries and find a cure for our mother, then return home all before you came back from tending your sheep. We never expected to land in the midst of English soldiers and Highlanders battling. That completely threw off our plan. Then, when we thought we were safe, we ran into the grove of MacDonald druids. If only their spell hadn't cursed me! I can no longer return to bring my brother home, or help my mom...I feel useless."

Granda gently patted Shaylee's knee, saying, "Just as you were weakened by the druid's curse, I was weakened by the same faerie curse that turned your mother into a cat. It's as if a door was slammed shut on my powers, and it is only with great effort and nearly two decades of trying that I have opened the door a crack. I have powers again, but only minimally. I hope that by tapping into Mairi and Jamie's latent powers, I can put a spell on them that will protect them from harm. The catch is we won't really know if it's working, but I'll be with them and will physically protect them as best I can."

Mairi's legs were beginning to cramp from crouching so long at the bannister. Thinking that her mom or grandparents might glance up at any minute and catch her eavesdropping, she painfully crawled back to her room, feeling as though pins and needles were poking her legs all over. Making her way into bed, she massaged her legs gently until they felt normal again. Only then did she let her mind mull over the things she had heard.

It wasn't very reassuring to learn they were also worried about the plan, especially her mother. Mairi certainly was not nearly as confident in her powers as Granda seemed to be. Mairi was only a little more reassured by the possibility of the Protection Spell that may or may not work. She had actually understood what he meant about closed doors and latent powers, though. She did feel as if there were powers in her that wanted to come out and all she had to do was this one thing, but she didn't know what that one thing was. Like not knowing how to open a door, but knowing that if she did open it she would step through to the outside world.

Mairi lay her head on her pillow and stared at a cobweb she'd missed in one corner of her room, silken threads lit up by the nearly full moon. She felt a little like a fly caught in a spider's trap. Only she knew she wasn't really trapped. Her mother would support her if she decided not to travel back in time to attempt saving Gran. No, it was her empathy for her gran that decided it for her. She didn't want Gran to be cursed anymore. Gran was the one who was like a fly trapped by a spider.

But who's the bigger spider, the faerie who cursed Gran and Granda, or the MacDonald druid who cursed Mom?

DESPERATE MEASURES

Harris, California
July 25th, present year

Danny lay on a cot in Jamie's room. He had been at William's house and hanging out with his cousins for nearly three weeks and still he hadn't seen the silver faerie chanter. He couldn't even find the bagpipes William had been playing at Uncle Aiden's funeral, and Danny was certain that he occasionally heard far off bagpiping while he and William were out mending fences. He'd asked William about the sound of bagpipe music he thought he heard one day, and William had dismissed it as a trick of the wind. Danny knew he was being brushed off.

I have to figure out where they're hiding the bagpipes, and I'm sure I'll find the silver faerie chanter attached. But how can I even get into the house alone to look? I'm always off working with William, or I'm hanging out with my cousins. No one ever leaves me alone, or the house empty. It's like they don't trust me. Danny almost laughed at himself because he had actually felt insulted for a moment. *They have every right not to trust me. I'd steal the chanter in a heartbeat, if I ever get the chance.*

When Danny got up, William announced that the only step left in repairing his fencing was to walk the property line looking for any places they might have missed. He was certain there weren't any holes left, but he wanted Danny to make the trek just to be sure, mentioning something about his body not being what it used to be. He handed Danny a water bottle right after breakfast and instructed him to return before lunch with any news of necessary mending.

Danny followed the fence line down into the valley below the house as the sun cast long morning shadows through the trees. As he carefully placed one foot in front of the other, holding himself steady in the loose soil, he took a deep breath. *Ah! I'd forgotten what it feels like to be alone with my thoughts. It's so hard to be around other people all of the time.* Danny took a few more steps down the hillside, shocked out of his reverie when his hand brushed the barbed wire, pricking his middle finger.

"Ouch!" he exclaimed, looking from the wound to the rusty barbed wire. He glanced back up the hillside, past gnarly oak trees and manzanita brush sticking out at precarious angles, wondering if he should go back up and clean the wound in case of tetanus poisoning. He could almost make out the corner of William's deck where it stretched into the valley and was struck with an idea.

I could easily slip back up to the house and see what they do there when everyone thinks I'm out of the way. His feet acted without his full awareness, turning and hiking back up the hillside. *I'll sit under the kitchen window and listen in, then I'll return to this job. The fence can wait. And if they catch me, I'll tell them the truth, that I cut myself and needed to clean it.*

Danny knelt in the dirt under the kitchen window, his back against the stone tower rising above the house. He could hear his cousins inside with their granda and mom, their footsteps echoing under the house, but when he tried to listen to what was being said he couldn't understand a word over the whining of the solar batteries in the tower. Unfortunately, the window was too far above him to be of any help. *Okay, if not the kitchen window, then where?* Then he heard the front door open to his right, around the corner from where he sat.

"Let's walk the space near the oak tree, Granda," Mairi said. "I want to know exactly what we're going to do when it's time to go."

Almost too late, Danny realized they might be able to see him the minute they reached the bridge crossing the ravine beside the house. Quick as he could go without standing up, Danny scuttled around to the other side of the stone tower. Peaking around it, he saw Mairi leading William, Shaylee and Jamie across the bridge and along the driveway. Danny froze. If any of them looked back toward the house, they might catch a glimpse of him through the trees between the house and the driveway.

Should I follow them? See what they mean by "when it's time to go" or should I go in the house while all of them are gone and look for the silver faerie chanter, since none of them were carrying bagpipes? Deciding he didn't care if they were going anywhere, but he did care very much about where the bagpipes were being kept hidden, Danny chose the house.

As soon as he saw the parade of people head up the driveway and off into the meadow, he ascended the staircase leading to the deck. Pulling open the sliding glass door, he stepped into the living room. Electing to take a moment to clean the cut on his finger, he went into the bathroom and bandaged his wound first. Throwing the band-aid package into the trash, he stepped out of the bathroom door and right into the path of the cat staring at him with a perceptively suspicious look on her face.

Danny jumped in surprise. "What are you looking at?"

That is one weird cat! It's like she knows I'm here to snoop around. Shaking off the ridiculous feeling that a cat might know what he was up to, Danny made his way upstairs to first Mairi's room, then into William's, opening drawers and closets, looking under beds and on top of shelves. The cat continued to follow him the whole time. *If I'm not careful, I think she'll trip me.*

Certain that the bagpipes weren't anywhere upstairs, Danny continued his search downstairs, the cat hissing at him along the way. After as thorough a search as he dared, Danny growled his frustration and headed back out the way he had come in. *I don't understand! If they don't have the bagpipes with them now, where can they be? They have to be here somewhere. I hear them practicing almost every day.* Reluctant to give up, yet feeling there were no other options, he went back to checking the fence line.

DETAILS

Harris, California
Eve of Lughnasadh, present year

In the cool evening air, Mairi and Jamie were getting ready to try on the clothes their mom had dragged out of her closet. They had been neatly folded and kept in an old wooden chest that was hand carved with the same symbol as the necklace, on the gate and the front door.

"Who carved the Trinity Knot symbol into everything?" Mairi asked, as her mom gently closed the chest after removing the pile of clothes.

"Your granda. When I was very young, he would spend his evenings carving. Usually just small toys or spoons and knives to sell at the local Arts Festival, but sometimes he'd get to work on a big project." Shaylee set a neat stack of clothes on the bed next to Mairi. They smelled faintly like lavender, and Mairi wasn't surprised when she found dried sprigs of the herb laid precisely throughout the piles of tartan fabric.

Shaylee continued, "He stopped carving when James didn't return. It was one more blow in a long and hard life. I guess he didn't find joy in it, anymore."

Her mother went on to explain about the Scottish clothes; that every year, before becoming a cat, their gran had hand stitched her and her brother each a traditional outfit from tartan ordered through a store in town. It helped them feel connected to their old life, and Gran had wanted her children to know their Scottish heritage.

"Your childhood sounds like it was kind of mellow, mom sewing and dad carving. Were you happy?" Mairi found herself truly curious to know about her mom's childhood.

"Yes, I was happy. Maybe a little bored, even though James and I were raised fully aware of our family magic. Still, to everyone else, I think we appeared normal. Life was really good until the Faerie Curse took hold. A part of me wonders why my parents weren't more careful," Shaylee answered. "Maybe I was a little angry at them, all these years, so I turned my back on them and on magic."

Mairi nodded, pulling on one of the dresses. It felt strange to her. She wasn't used to wearing dresses that went past her thighs. Her dresses were usually short, with no sleeves. The only part in common was that both the modern dress style and the ancient dress style fitted her perfectly in the waist, although the Scottish dress had laces and cinched up much tighter. Having a dress that reached to her ankles and that was made of heavy cotton and wool felt suffocating. Not to mention the cumbersome tartan scarf her mom draped over her shoulder.

To finish off the uncomfortable ensemble, she squeezed her feet into a pair of stiff brown leather lace up boots. They weren't nearly as comfy as her sneakers. *How am I supposed to travel around the Isle of Skye in a long skirt and stiff boots?* At least her mom let her wear modern socks that were made of soft cotton, and her undergarments were her own.

Jamie came up from getting dressed in his room, and he didn't look much happier. He was wearing a skirt for the first time ever. His skirt, aka kilt, was short, coming to just above his knees. *At least he'll be able to move easily in it.* Still, he was trying to convince their mom to let him wear more than his boxers under the kilt, but his board shorts were so long that they showed below the hem. Finally, their mom went and got a pair of scissors and cut about three inches off the board shorts. Jamie noticeably felt more comfortable. He didn't seem to mind the shirt and tartan scarf, but he too complained about the stiffness of the boots.

It was the eve of Lughnasadh and Granda had gone to check on Danny, who had been brought to the neighbor Helena's house a few days ago under the pretense of not having any more work for him here. "The neighbors probably need help with their fences, too," Granda had told him, and it was true. However, Danny had really been sent away because Star had told them how Danny had come into the house to snoop while they were away. Everyone had been relieved he hadn't found the secret cupboard under the sink. It backed into the stone tower in which the hot water heater and solar power batteries were housed, and the bagpipes with the silver faerie chanter had been kept hidden. Now, Granda returned to the house just in time to hear Jamie protesting the aches the stiff shoes were causing his feet.

"Stop protesting, lad. You are showing your MacDonald side, whining and carrying on. You are a MacLeod and a MacCrimmon, too. Show your strength."

This shut Jamie up immediately, although Mairi suspected he had a whole lot to say to defend the MacDonald name. Not complaining anymore was probably the safest route to not angering Granda, though.

"You two look amazing! Exactly like the children of the clans ought to. We need to get your hair right, though, Mairi." Her mother's deft fingers quickly plaited her hair into one long braid that she pinned into a tight bun. This too was a foreign look for Mairi, who almost always wore her hair loose and wild about her shoulders, occasionally pulling it up into a messy bun.

Jamie's hair, which he'd always worn just long enough to look tussled, but not long enough to require a ponytail, was declared "perfect."

As if the two of them were off to the San Diego Highland Games or a school dance, their mother pulled out her phone and began snapping pictures of them. "You two look all set for the Lughnasadh celebration tonight." Jamie grinned, but Mairi stamped her foot.

"Enough pictures! I'm really tired. Let me close my eyes for a minute, and then we can make some tea and go over our plans again, okay?" Mairi caught her mother's worried glance in Granda's direction. *She's worried about this trip as much as I am! Are we actually doing this?* A part of Mairi still couldn't believe that magic and time travel could be real.

"Of course, we'll make tea," soothed Star, leading them all downstairs to the kitchen, tail twitching in the air like a flag on a pole. Mairi could hear her brother's shoes creak as he walked along the wood floors below. She wiggled her cramped toes, confirming that they were the least comfortable shoes ever invented.

Lying on her bed, she heard Jamie come back up and closed her door behind him. "What's up, sis? You seem really uptight."

Mairi sighed. "Aren't you even a little afraid of what

we're about to do?" she asked Jamie.

"Of course! But it's so awesome, and Granda will be with us, and we have magic. I'm too excited to be afraid!" Jamie's enthusiasm helped Mairi just enough to get her headed downstairs to join their family.

Danny was sure that he had been removed from William's house for a reason. He had noticed that his cousins would sometimes whisper together when they thought he wouldn't notice. There was something more going on than simply learning how to cook traditional Scottish food, although the meals had been delicious. Once, when he was talking to Jamie about historic battles, Jamie had excitedly declared that he couldn't wait until August 1st when he might get to see a real Highlander Jacobite. When Danny had looked at him curiously, Jamie had turned red and mumbled something about "wouldn't that be cool if I really could?" Danny knew his cousins would be doing something that day that they didn't want him to be a part of.

But that had been before he'd snuck back into the house while his cousins were out with their mom and granda. He didn't know how they had figured out what he'd done, but ever since then they had done more than whisper behind his back. They had actually avoided doing anything with him. Then he'd been sent away to the neighbor's and Danny had decided his only option was to return by August 1st to see what his cousins were up to.

Danny lay on the guest bed at the neighbor's house trying to figure out how he was going to get back to William's house, several miles away. It wasn't quite night yet, since it didn't get dark in the summer until almost 9 PM, but could Danny pick his way over the country roads before the night settled like a blanket all around him? He decided that he had to try because he was certain whatever was going to happen would happen soon. He had a feeling this might be the last chance he'd get to swipe the chanter.

WAITING

Isle of Skye
Eve of Lughnasadh, early 1700s

Pacing under the stars, the darkness of the moonless night a mirror of the darkness of his thoughts, Ian debated with himself. "The MacLeod's escaped my grasp 20 years ago at the Faerie Grove, where the oak tree canopy lends a home to our druidic meetings. Will they show up there tomorrow morning?" Ian was positive that his chance to regain the silver faerie chanter would be on the coming Lughnasadh, Harvest Day, it being one of the eight most powerful days of the year. He just could not decide which place to stand guard.

He began another pass around the base of the burial mound. "Or, will they arrive at the Faerie Door where Mairi MacCrimmon stole the chanter and whisked it away with the aid of Liam MacLeod? If the curse has come upon their son, William, as surely it must have or why else send children to do his work, then they will strive to beg the faerie's forgiveness at the very door they were first gifted the necklace."

Ian was so intently muttering to himself about where to best intercept the necklace and chanter, for he was sure they would be together based on what the faerie Cali had told him, he did not hear his son arrive.

"Ahem! Da, surely ye will wear a hole in yer sandals pacing so."

Ewan stood in Ian's path so that he bumped right into his son's imposing form. "Aah! Why must ye be so rude? Stand aside and alert me of yer presence like a proper man."

"Ho ho, Da, ye ought to notice my arrival like a proper druid. What has ye so entranced that ye did not hear my bulk traipsing through the woods to yer little hiding place?"

Ian cocked an eyebrow at his son. Of course, he should have heard his son coming, but he also knew Ewan's bulk had never caused him to make a noise unless he wished it so. Druids rarely alerted others to their presence unless they wanted to. Waving his gnarled hand at his son as if to send him away like a nasty smell, Ian answered as Ewan stepped aside, "I am wondering where best to catch the horrid MacLeods who stole our family's chanter. Will they come at the dawning of the morrow to the Faerie Grove or to the Faerie Door? I won't know until it actually happens, so I can't decide where best to wait."

"This still? Ye insist on chasing after ghosts." Seeing his father was once again resuming his pacing, Ewan took pity on the old man. "Vera well, I will assist you."

Ewan thought for a moment, looking first in the North-East direction and then in the South-West. "Da, it seems to me that this mound is fairly close to being equally in the middle tween the two spots. Wait here, and when the Earth Forces tell ye where they have arrived, go there. Perhaps I can borrow a horse to keep with ye, better to deliver ye quickly to intercept yer *mortal enemy*."

The last words Ewan uttered with such mirth, and laughed so heartily at his own joke, that Ian wasn't sure if his son was serious about helping. Ewan left right then, promising to return with a horse and Ian was too exhausted to not believe him.

He lay down on the mound, filling his body with all the Energy of Darkness he could draw upon, feeling the hum of the stars above and the earth below. He was drained from his travels, but he was also filled with more hope than he'd felt in decades. *Tomorrow... Surely tomorrow I will avenge my clan and will attain the necklace as a bonus. With two items enchanted with Faerie Magic, I will become more powerful, and then my boasting son will remember to be more respectful of his father.* Content for the moment, he drifted off to sleep.

Ian sat up, startled awake by the sound of horse's hooves galloping his way. "Da, here is the horse I promised you," his son called out from astride a tall black stallion, leading a smaller brown mare behind him. Ewan handed the reins of the smaller horse to his father. "I'll look for you at noon at the festival. Perhaps ye will be playing on faerie-enchanted bagpipes." Ewan's laughter echoed off the mound as he galloped away on his stallion.

Ian smiled, tying the reins of the mare to a small tree nearby. Sitting back down on the grassy mound, he waited.

THE STARS ALIGN

Harris, California
Lughnasadh 12 AM

Night finally came. The full moon shone down from above, lending enough light for them to easily pick their way over the deeply rutted driveway and up the grassy mountainside to the Oak Knoll. Their boots weren't too terrible for hiking in… so far. Mairi was glad she had thought to pack band-aids though, just in case she developed blisters from the stiff boots.

"This is, in fact, a Blue Moon," Star explained as they made their way, "because this is technically the second full moon in the month of July, making this particular transition a very powerful one. We are blessed!"

Mairi nodded, hoping Gran was right and that they would be blessed in their attempt to achieve all they planned on doing.

Once on the knoll, with the branches of the ancient oak tree reaching high overhead, they began the ritual of Lughnasadh. The light of the Full Moon shone eerily through the oak tree's branches, creating shapes in shadows all around their feet and over their faces.

Granda was dressed in his traditional Scottish kilt, and her mom had wrapped a colorful tartan around her shoulders. Even Star had asked Shaylee to put a tartan ribbon around her neck. Dressing up did make it sort of feel like a festival, Mairi had to admit.

Everyone stood in the four directions, and then carefully moved *widdershins* or counterclockwise, the opposite direction of the sun's path to indicate moving backwards in time in order to draw the Circle of Power. Star stopped to the North, Granda to the South, Mom to the East to indicate home and safe returns, while Jamie and Mairi ended to the West, the direction of new adventures.

In the center of the Circle was a stump, placed there earlier by Granda, on which were set symbols of the four Elements of Nature. There was a clay bowl for earth, which was filled with water, made silvery by the light of moon. A blue feather floated on the surface of the water and a candle rose out of the middle of the water upon which a flame suddenly ignited, honoring air and fire.

Granda started chanting in another language, which Mairi assumed to be Gaelic and she could hear Star take up the chant, followed by her mother. There was a shift in the air around her and she felt her brother shiver so she knew he must feel it, too. She sincerely hoped this was the Protection Spell working.

Danny lay in the tall grass surrounding the Oak Knoll where he could see William, his cousins, his aunt, and the cat whose white coat shown luminescent in the moonlight. Danny was grateful it had been such a bright night because hiking over the mountain roads from Helena's house would have been much worse if not for the moon. As it was, he had set out nearly two hours ago and was seriously worn out now.

He stared intently at the group gathered below him. *Why were they all dressed in Scottish clothes?* Mairi's clothes were especially questionable. Something unusual was definitely about to happen.

The droning of the bagpipes warming up pulled him out of his musing. He squinted through the grass, afraid to sit up too high and be spotted, and saw that it was Jamie who was handling the pipes. The silver faerie chanter glinted in the moonlight and Danny itched to grab it. There it was, so close to him, yet still not in his grasp.

As Jamie began to play a haunting tune, one that conjured up a feeling of homesickness, Danny noticed that everyone else seemed to be saying something in unison. He couldn't hear what they were saying, but he could see that they all had their eyes closed, even the cat seemed to be joining in. Danny started to feel a desperation welling up inside him. He needed to grab the chanter!

Mairi carefully pictured the Isle of Skye in Scotland in her mind, seeing it like a bird might see as it flew over the Isle. She began to intone "Isle of Skye in Scotland, 1715" over and over along with the music to help them stay focused on the proper place and time. Carefully narrowing the image down to the Faerie Grove her Granda had described to her that very morning, seeing it as one who stood there might see it. She waited to feel Granda's touch on her shoulder as she reached for the necklace around her neck where it rested safely in the folds of her tartan scarf. Her brother was busy concentrating on the song they had been practicing for the past several weeks, so it was up to her to reach her other hand out and grasp his shoulder. Just as she held the necklace, she felt the expected rush of traveling, but she also heard an uncharacteristic thumping like the running of feet. She felt someone dive on her and unexpectedly she was falling sideways.

Shock! Dismay! Worry! Fear!

So many unaccustomed feelings struck her all at once that Mairi's mind couldn't compute what was happening. Suddenly she was hitting the ground, the wind knocked out of her, and the music had stopped. She could feel Jamie under her, pushing her to get off him. She tried to roll away, but something…no someone…was on top of her, too. In a tangle of arms and legs, skirts and bagpipes, they tussled and tumbled around on the grassy ground, trying to separate themselves from each other.

Then she found herself alone, her hair loosed from the braided bun, sweeping down her back. She could hear the wrestling continuing to her left. The night had become weirdly dark, as if the moon had simply disappeared, and Mairi struggled to see what was happening around her. She heard her brother shout, "Get off me!" and "Hey! Don't break the pipes!" Then she heard her cousin Danny's voice laughing and could make out a dim shadow, a slightly lighter shade of dark, jumping up and down, clutching a silver glinting object in his hand. Before she could say anything, he had bolted away into the night.

Crawling across the rocky and grass-carpeted ground, as best she could in the tangles of her dress, she made her way to her brother.

"Danny took the chanter, Mairi. Doesn't he understand? We'll all be stuck here forever if he takes the chanter away from us!"

BETRAYED

Isle of Skye, Scotland
Lughnasadh 1 AM

"I don't know what Danny's thinking, Jamie. Does he even realize we're not on Granda's land anymore? At least, I'm pretty sure we're not. The moon isn't full like it was moments ago, so time has definitely changed, and this ground isn't the same. We were standing in long grass before...

"It must have worked, Jamie! We really time traveled!" In spite of the rough landing, she couldn't help but feel total amazement at what they had done.

Jamie clutched at her dress, and Mairi tried to focus on his face. "Mairi! We have to go after him. We have to find him! He has our faerie chanter, and without it we are all stuck here!"

That's when it occurred to Mairi she hadn't heard or seen her granda. "Granda? Jamie, where's Granda?" She grabbed her brother's shoulder, sharing his panic.

"He isn't here, Mairi! I think Danny must have knocked him away as we time traveled. We're here on our own," Jamie shouted at her.

Like a dye tablet at Easter slowly spreading through the vinegar solution, understanding of just what horrors Jamie was trying to get through to her started to sink in.

We're stuck in the 1700s.

Without Granda.

Mairi struggled to grasp the full extent of what it could mean . . .

For the rest of our life?

Ian jolted awake. *They've arrived. They're at the Faerie Grove, I can feel it.* He pulled his aged body up onto the mare with the help of a boulder, feeling grateful she was a smaller horse, and kicked his heels against her sides. He trotted along, wishing for a bit more light so the mare could go faster.

Danny ran madly through the brambles, stumbling over the uneven earth beneath his feet. *Where did all these dips in the ground and bushes come from?* He didn't remember the land around the oak tree knoll being anything but tall grass. *And where did the moon go?* He chanced a glance up at the starry sky. The stars were so bright, there was no way that the sky was covered in clouds, hiding the moon. One minute the moon was full and the next minute it was new and dark, as if a light switch had been turned off. He shook his head as he ran, trying to make sense of the world around him. *If only I can get to the main road, I can make my way back to town.*

He listened as he ran, and heard his cousins chasing after him. They were scrambling as fast as he was, intent on getting back what he had stolen.

Taken, he corrected himself, *and rightfully so. The*

chanter belongs to my family, my clan. Even if they are MacDonalds, too, they are also MacLeods and MacCrimmons, and so they are not deserving of the chanter, he reasoned.

Mairi had never run so fast and so hard in her life, certainly not under such conditions as being nearly blind from the night and across unfamiliar, uneven ground. She ran as though her very life depended on it, and most definitely her life did. Jamie was right behind her, proving he was no longer her "little" brother because now he was obviously as strong as she was, running just as fast.

She skidded to a stop, realizing she could no longer hear footsteps in front of her. Danny wasn't running anymore. Jamie slammed into her, unable to stop in time and unable to see much more than her dark shape. Again, they found themselves on the ground in a tangle of legs and skirts and bagpipes.

"What did you stop for?" Jamie whispered harshly in her ear as they rolled away from each other.

"Shhhh...I'm listening for Danny."

Sitting up, she tried to get her bearings. *Which way were we running?* In the dark it was almost useless. The adrenaline rush from time traveling and racing after Danny was starting to wear off and she was exhausted. *It must be almost one in the morning,* she thought.

"I can't hear him, he must be hiding. I guess we'll have to rest here and hope we can find him and the silver chanter before he gets away in the daylight," she whispered between panting breaths.

She could hear Jamie stifling a yawn off to her right. "You take the first nap, Jamie, I'll stay awake and listen for Danny."

She heard Jamie's muffled "no, I can't sleep at a time like this" and saw his greyish form lay down right where he was on the grass. *He's asleep,* she thought, and put her hand on his shoulder to reassure herself that she wasn't all alone in a foreign time, in a foreign land. To keep her mind awake, and her ears alert, Mairi stayed sitting up, leaning back on her other hand so she could stare up at the night sky. She was relieved to find that it was familiar to her. She could still pick out the same constellations that she had noticed that summer above her granda's house.

Ian knew even before he arrived over the hillside that the chanter had moved away from the Faerie Grove. He hadn't expected it would be taken away so quickly, and he panicked as he picked his way carefully into the circle of trees. *What now?* He thought. *Where would they have gone with the chanter? Surely, they wanted to visit the faeries, and there is an entrance here, so why go elsewhere?*

Ian slid off the mare and felt the grass. He could "see" more with his other senses in the darkness than he could with his eyes, and he sensed there had been a scuffle of sorts. Spreading his fingers wide, pressing his palms against the earth, he asked the Darkness around him what the story was. Through images created by the recent outburst of energy that had exploded on this spot less than an hour ago, the old druid learned that the scuffle centered on the chanter. He also sensed that there were two fighting against one, and all three had run off over the hills, headed for the sea.

Good, Ian thought, *that is the direction in which my Clan will be anchored, having just come from the other end of Skye. They will block them from getting any further with my chanter.*

Ian took his mare by the reins and led her along as he

followed what his senses told him was the trail the other three had taken previously. He stopped after several yards.

Curious! There is a fourth who has joined the trail. How does this person fit in? The old man found himself enjoying the puzzle, much like a fox on the prowl for a rabbit.

REUNITED

Isle of Skye, Scotland
Dawn of Lughnasadh

"Wake up! Where is it? I heard ye talking about it. Where is the silver chanter? Who took it?"

Mairi sat up with a start. *So much for staying awake!* Her first thought was to chastise herself. She'd obviously fallen asleep and now was being harshly awakened by a deep voice with a Scottish accent. The sun was peeking through a crack in a large boulder in the distance and she found herself looking at an older living version of the boy in her mother's pictures. He stared down at her with intense green eyes, eyes exactly like her mother's, exactly like her own.

"Who are you?" She braved asking him, though she already was certain of the answer, pulling her wool tartan scarf tightly around her shoulders as she shivered in the wet morning air.

"I might ask ye the same question. But first, we have to find the silver faerie chanter before it's gone."

"Uncle James?" Jamie was sitting up and staring at the towering man with long red-blonde hair hanging past his shoulders, wearing a kilt in the MacLeod tartan pattern, a broad sword tied to his hip.

"I am not sure about the uncle part, but aye, I am James MacLeod and I am hoping that ye are my sister's children. Now get up, we have to find this Danny ye spoke of last night, before someone else discovers ye are here."

"Oh wow! We found you!" Mairi grinned with relief.

"More like I found you, lassie, and thankfully ye are safe. There are many the marauding Highlander and English alike in these parts who would do unkind things to you. Ye move about like a pack of dogs so that anyone within a mile can hear you. Now tell me what has happened that yer bagpipes do not have the silver chanter attached."

Stumbling over each other's words, Mairi and Jamie filled their uncle in on what had happened a mere few hours before. When they explained that Danny was a MacDonald and apparently believed the chanter belonged to him, James nodded his head.

"Aye! Those MacDonalds are a wily clan. Like a fox they will sneak in and take what they should leave alone."

Mairi looked over at her brother, and they frowned, silently asking if they should tell their uncle that they, too, were MacDonalds. Mairi shook her head no.

Ian watched from a distance, sitting in a dip in the grass, while his mare wandered loose down the hill behind him. He was curious to learn what he could before swooping in. *Besides,* he admitted, more honest in his thoughts than he'd be in conversation, *that man's a warrior and I do not like the looks of his broadsword. I'll just watch and see where the chanter has been taken.* He found their story most interesting, though, especially as they spoke a crude form of English.

So they did time travel, after all.

Danny badly needed to stretch his arms and legs. He had squeezed his body into a crevice during the night and the fit was tight. After his two-hour hike from the neighbor's house back to William's, he hadn't been able to run anymore. His lungs had been ready to burst. When he'd noticed a huge rock of some sort ahead of him, he had decided to stop running and hide, in hopes that the daylight would help him find his way back to town.

By morning he was starting to have second thoughts, though. He'd been thinking all night about what he'd done, stealing from Jamie and Mairi. *Maybe I should go back to my cousins and apologize. After all, they're MacDonalds, too...my family...and my friends. Maybe they would have shared the silver faerie chanter with me if I'd outright asked rather than simply taking it.* In the midst of his turmoil, Danny heard someone heavy footed hiking all around him. Someone besides his cousins was searching for him.

He'd stayed hidden during most of the night, not knowing what to do, not knowing who was looking for him, other than his cousins. Besides, he had no idea where they were either. Doubt began to creep in all around him. *What should I do?* Then he heard voices. Mairi and Jamie were talking to someone much older, someone with a deep voice, and it sounded like they were calling him uncle. Overhearing the man's comment putting down the MacDonalds, Danny decided he would hold onto the chanter for now, at least until he figured out what was going on.

The sun's rays began to edge into the crevice, so he peered out of his rocky hiding place. It was then that he realized he had no idea where he was, that this couldn't possibly be William's land anymore. The landscape had completely changed from where he'd been standing last night, watching his cousins under the oak tree.

Where there used to be layer upon layer of mountains and valleys, now there were hills and lakes and what appeared to be the ocean in the distance. *Could we have possibly run that far?* he wondered. But no, he knew the ocean was nearly 40 miles west of William's land. He had a sinking feeling that he had gotten himself mixed up in something far bigger than acquiring an historic silver chanter.

As he hesitated about emerging from his hiding place, a scratching sound behind him, deep in the heart of the rock, frightened him. He crept out of the crack, holding tight to the silver chanter, and made a break for it, hoping the sound of his escape would be hidden by their conversation. He ran down the hillside, not daring to look back for fear his cousins or their uncle would be following him. He saw a stand of trees and made a beeline for it. As soon as he reached the relative safety of the branches and leaves, he stopped to catch his breath.

He couldn't hear any footsteps behind him so he risked a peek up the hill. He saw no one above him, so next he looked down the hill, which continued to the blue sea far below. The water sparkled from the sun as it rose above the mountains and shone on the water. Danny caught his breath.

On the beach he saw a ship, and people dressed in kilts and white robes were coming ashore. They were too far away for him to make out what clan they might belong to, but they certainly were making it harder and harder to convince himself he was still in the 21st century.

His Granny Kate had told him tales of time travel, tales about how his grandfather had once traveled through time with the help of the Faerie Doorways. Danny hadn't really believed his grandmother, but could it be true? Could this be what was happening to him?

"What about you, Uncle James?" Mairi was asking, "How is it that you happen to be out here at the exact time and place Jamie and I show up? Don't misunderstand us. We are grateful and relieved to see you. It's just such an amazing coincidence."

"Tis no coincidence. Every year since my sister disappeared, I've visited this vera glen on all of the eight magical days of the year, sure she would return. I wanted to stay here in the 1700s, and I still do, but I had hoped to see my family from time to time. Surely, they would check in on me, and allow me to visit them, too? After a few years, I stopped really hoping and kept coming out of habit, spending the night under the stars and returning to my wife and bairns by midday to join in the festivities of the Lughnasadh Games."

Deciding to return to the part about his having children later, Mairi was quick to tell him that he had never been forgotten. "Your sister, our mom, she lost all of her powers to make the bagpipes and the necklace work for her when the druid, Ian MacDonald, cursed her as she was leaving. She has always wanted to return to you, and to continue searching for a way to save Gran from life as a cat. She didn't have any way to save either of you and it really depressed her. She had to live her life, find love, have her own family, or go crazy with sorrow that she could do nothing for you. She had to let you both go and focus on herself. She is still powerless, though she does work with herbs and she continues to try to get her powers back, maybe in hopes to rescue you and Gran some day."

As Mairi explained this to James, she realized this was the truth. Her anger at her mother for hiding their faerie connections from her began to dissolve. Her mother had had to live her life, and perhaps letting the tumultuous world of faerie gifts rest, even just for a while, was the only way she could cope with all of the pain that came with those gifts.

Her mother hadn't given up hope, either. Rather, she had shelved it for the years required to raise happy, normal children who would possibly someday enter this world of uncertainty and fear. Her dad dying had been unrelated, yet had pulled her mother out of her peaceful bubble, reminding her that she couldn't run away from tragic events; they were just a part of life. She still had family, her family, and her children deserved to be part of it. Her faerie connections could no longer be kept a secret.

Mairi wrenched herself free of her thoughts and said, "We have to get the chanter back and get to the Faerie Grove before the sun sets and Lughnasadh ends, or we'll be stuck here for the next six weeks, at least."

Mairi was starting to feel the ticking of time, panic rising in her like molten lava in a volcano.

"The sun is up and shining, so let's look around for that dastardly MacDonald first. He has to be here somewhere." They got up and scoured the area all about them.

Ian saw them coming towards his hiding spot, where he'd heard their entire conversation, and he shuffled back down the hill to his mare. *So, these are the grandchildren of William MacLeod, Liam and Mairi's great-grandchildren. I wonder if their powers continue to flow from generation to generation, or if these children rely entirely on the faerie gifts. The girl is wearing the necklace, but they no longer have the chanter. Someone named Danny, a MacDonald, has taken it. He did not pass by me in the dark, so he must be on the other side of this hill. Perfect, that is the way I am going anyway.*

Ian mounted his mare's back and took a circuitous route to the other side of the hill, avoiding the children and their Highland warrior, certain he would find the silver faerie chanter when he got there. He would return to deal with these MacLeod thieves once the chanter was his, and he'd also take the necklace.

Mairi saw no sign of Danny, save crushed grass on the backside of the rock they had slept near during the night. Squinting in the light, Mairi thought she saw a ship, made tiny by the distance, on the shore of the sea below.

"Aye, that will be the MacDonalds' ship. Mostly they live down the other end of Skye, where their clan's holdings are located, so travel by sea is often easiest. They come ashore here to allow their druids the chance to perform their Druid Rites in their Grove along the way. However, I'm afraid the bad news is Danny has probably reached them by now. The good news is, they are surely making their way to the Lughnasadh Games near Castle Dunvegan and we are certain to find a way to reclaim the silver chanter then. Let's make our way to my home and get a bite to eat. Everything will seem better with full bellies."

Mairi did not feel good about postponing the search for the chanter, but tried to trust her Uncle's optimism. *How could things have gone so horribly wrong already? So much for granda's Protection Spell working,* she thought, though a part of her intuited that her uncle was correct in knowing they would all end up at the Lughnasadh Games.

Coming out of her reverie, Mairi noticed they were walking through a field of purple, with high craggy mountains towering over them far in the distance and the ocean a bit closer on the other side of them. *This must be one of the fields of heather that Mom and Gran told me cover the moors of Scotland.* All around them, the golden grass had given way to the little purple flowers, abuzz with the happy humming of bees. Breathing in deep, she smelled a sweet scent, almost like honey, and understood completely why the bees would choose to visit these fields. Gazing all about her, she saw that the landscape was purple for miles and upon closer inspection she noticed there were many birds and animals enjoying the colorful meadow. The birds calling to one another in sharp trills and melodious songs eased the stress she felt from the past night's adventure.

Stopping in her tracks, she spied a little red deer not far off. It was staring at her with its large, honey-colored eyes, looking not at all frightened. She couldn't tear her eyes away, and as they stared at each other, Mairi was suddenly filled with a feeling they needed to hide. As soon as she felt this, the doe broke eye contact and bounded away. Taking heed, Mairi grabbed her brother, who surprisingly didn't protest loudly, and pulled him in the direction of a rock outcropping, hoping her uncle would follow without question. Diving behind the rocks, they heard the heavy-footed marching of a clan on the move.

HIDDEN

Isle of Skye, Scotland
Lughnasadh 8 AM

Ian followed behind Danny, ditching the small horse along the way. He thought about overtaking the young man immediately, but found himself fascinated with how he was dressed. There was something really different about him, so Ian decided to observe him, play with him a little, before he pounced. Ian knew he could retrieve the chanter at any moment. Danny obviously had no power in him or he would have used it by now, was certainly no warrior, and appeared to know absolutely nothing about where he was.

An easy prey, Ian reassured himself, feeling like a spider ensnaring a fly.

Stepping over the threshold, the history buff in Danny was satisfied to see the floor of the vacated hut was indeed packed dirt covered by a layer of straw. *This is called a croft,* he recalled reading in history books. *More proof I'm not in the 21ˢᵗ century anymore. I hope the crofters aren't home.*

A honey scent wafted out the door and he noticed the

purple heather mixed in with the straw on the floor. It didn't quite mask the heavy stench of animal droppings, for all the farm animals came and went as they pleased from the back of the house which was barely separated from the main room by a few wall hangings woven from wool. The smell almost made Danny forget how hungry he was.

Seeing that no one was home, he looked around quickly, searching for anything that would help him disguise his jeans and sweatshirt. He'd almost made a huge mistake by walking up to the Highlanders getting off of their ship while dressed as a complete outlander. He'd caught himself in the knick of time, ducking behind a tree and waiting for them to get a good way ahead before trailing behind them. As they'd passed through a village barren of any people, he'd had the idea to scrounge for clothes or pieces of cloth to cover up his modern outfit.

He'd gone through three huts already, without finding much more than wooden bowls and utensils, and animal droppings. He wondered where everyone was. It was really weird how the huts felt lived in. They were warmer than the morning air outside. Also, he detected the faint scent of porridge beneath the animal odor, and the animals were well fed so not abandoned. He shrugged his shoulders thinking, *not my problem.*

He looked around the hut he was currently in, and spied a plain wooden chest in a corner. He hadn't seen a chest in the other houses, so he quickly went to it. No ornate carvings or metal designs, just plain and simple wood. He was relieved when it opened easily, hopeful it held something that could work as a disguise. A scent of sage and sandalwood wafted up and hit his nose. *Whew! That's really strong,* he thought, waving away the odor with a dirty hand. *Maybe the scent is meant to keep rodents away.* Danny thought he might have read something about that in his history books. There wasn't anything valuable in the chest, nothing like gold or jewels, but there was something better. He pulled out a stiff dingy white fabric and upon shaking it, realized it was probably a druid's robe.

CLUNK!

Danny froze. *What was that?*

The sound came from outside.

Maybe it's an animal, but what if it's a person? Would a whole village really leave their homes completely without protection? Danny pulled the robe over his head, covering up not only his sweatshirt and jeans, but also his backpack with the silver chanter hidden inside. It was a big robe, probably meant for a much larger person, but that was just as well, since it swept down and covered his sneakers, too.

Now he heard voices. Deep voices, slurred voices. At least two different tones, so at least two people. They spoke in Gaelic, and while Danny spoke it a little, taught to him by his Granny Kate who was deeply connected with her Scottish ancestry, he couldn't make out what they were saying so garbled were their words.

Slinking over to the doorway, Danny looked out and saw two men as big as oxen, dressed in dirty kilts in the MacLeod colors, sitting on a couple of large boulders right outside. Their hair was long and greasy, sweeping over their shoulders, their faces unshaven. A breeze blew past carrying the stench of ale.

With a sinking feeling, it dawned on Danny that he was trapped.

"How did ye know to hide, Mairi?" James whispered. "I didn't have a chance to warn ye before ye were already running for the rocks."

Mairi looked at her Uncle, and shook her head. "I don't even know why I'm hiding. I just suddenly became overwhelmed with a knowing that I must hide all of us."

James nodded his head in understanding. "It is the faerie blood in ye, ye kin. It has served me many a time in battle. Well, listen carefully, and ye might realize what yer instincts told ye first."

Mairi listened, and almost felt it before she heard it. A heavy thumping was echoing across the moor, like a hundred giant feet slapping the earth in an uneven tempo. Then she began to hear the creaking of wooden carts and the laughter of men, women, and children. Peering over the rock outcropping, she saw about 50 people following a winding road off in the distance, dressed in matching tartan and carrying all sizes of bundles; some had bagpipes over their shoulders and tucked under their arms. Mixed up in the bunch were several horses, some small black cows and even smaller sheep.

"Who are they? Are they the MacDonalds?" she asked James, hoping this meant they would take back the chanter now.

"Nay, they are Clan Kenzie, making their way to Castle Dunvegan to join in the festivities of today. They are a bit late, though that is nothing unusual when so many people must make their way together. They are allies of MacLeod, so we did no' need to hide after all, but it is best to be safe in these parts, especially with yer not being from here." He waved them to stand up and they continued their walk across the moor, veering off in a slightly different direction than the parade of Highlanders.

Ian watched the two burley MacLeod men drinking

and joking outside the hut he had seen Danny disappear into mere minutes before. Feeling protective of Danny, or rather the chanter, Ian considered attacking the men. He certainly did not want to lose the chanter back to the MacLeod clan just when it was so close to being his again.

Not feeling as strong as he knew he would need to be to take on two young Highland warriors, he leaned into the tree he was peeking out from behind, spread his claw-like hands as wide as old age would allow him to, and felt for the energy that sent the sap coursing through the tree trunk, pulling on that energy until he felt it flow into his own body. Normally, he preferred the energy of the Dark, but the day was too bright to pull from right then, so his second preference was always what he could take from the trees. It would require a good bit of time for Ian to tap into the earth magic coursing up from the roots of the oak, he was still depleted from the long night, so he'd have to hope Danny wouldn't do anything rash in the meantime.

REVELATIONS

Isle of Skye, Scotland
Lughnasadh 9 AM

Over the crest of the hill, Mairi saw several round buildings with straw-covered roofs, tendrils of smoke snaking up and away from each small hut. All around the buildings people, chickens, and small cows and sheep could be seen milling about. The animal calls and shouts of people carried up the hill to their ears, letting them know that this little village was teeming with life. A girl about Mairi's age looked up from her business of shooing chickens away from one of the houses and her face brightened.

"Da!" she called out and began walking towards them, long skirts brushing chickens out of her path as she went.

James introduced them when they met up. "This is my daughter, Anne. Anne, these are yer cousins Mairi and Jamie." Mairi casually looked over the girl in front of them. She was petite, not even as tall as Jamie, with long black hair swept up into a loose bun. Her eyes were bright green and rimmed in long black eyelashes. She had pale skin under streaks of black soot. *Probably from tending a fire,* Mairi guessed. She looked almost nothing like their family, except for her eyes, so Mairi supposed she took after her mother.

Anne gave her dad a puzzled look, then politely curtsied and said in English, "Pleased to meet ye. And how exactly are we cousins?"

"Let's go inside and have a bit of porridge. I can tell ye the tale on our walk to the Lughnasadh festivities," James replied.

Mairi accepted the wooden bowl filled with porridge her cousin Anne handed her and used the wooden spoon to take a bite . . . and nearly spit it out.

It was extremely bland compared to the oatmeal she was used to at home, and Mairi guessed there wasn't much salt used in any of their food. Not wanting to appear rude, or spoiled, Mairi did her best to choke down each bite as she sat outside with the others in the morning sun. She noticed her uncle watching her eat and she smiled politely at him.

"It's no' much to taste, but it will fill yer belly. I expect ye are used to honey or sugar on yer porridge?"

Mairi nodded, relieved he understood her. "Do you think you will ever return home, Uncle James?" she asked.

"Perhaps I will, child, one of these years, at least for a visit. I do miss the ease with which we could sweeten our food." He smiled conspiratorially at her, while Anne continued to look at them all with puzzled expression.

"Ah, Wills. How nice that ye should be able to join us." James spoke to a tall young man with coloring like Mairi's, red hair brushing his shoulders. "This is my son, Wills. He will be competing in the games today, proving how strong he is for all the clan to see."

"Hi Wills! What games are you competing in?" Jamie

asked, practically bouncing with excitement.

Wills barely met any of their eyes, only briefly scanning their faces before focusing on his dirt covered shoes. "Well…" he sighed, as if talking were a burden, each word coming out slow and quiet with a slight stutter. "I-I wi-will be co-competing in the skill of thr-throwing my sp-spear."

"Don't let Wills confuse ye with his quiet demeanor. He is our village's best marksman, able to catch a running rabbit clear across the moors. He is sure to outdo his competition."

Wills blushed bright red from his ankles showing below his kilt, all of the way up to the roots of his hairline, clearly uncomfortable with being the center of attention. Mairi wondered if he would be able to win, based on his being sure to fumble with everyone watching during the competition. She looked around, hoping to think of a new topic so that Wills could relax and eat his porridge he was currently scooping up and plopping back into his bowl in his anxiety.

Mairi spied her cousin Anne watching them curiously. She had the most beautiful coloring, almost as if the fairy tale description of Snow White were based on her. Mairi cautiously smiled at her and asked what she liked to do with her time.

Anne gave her a quizzical smile in return, asking "Do ye mean what do I do all day while my brother is hunting and my da is off battling for the clan? I assure ye, I stay quite busy. I am not a lazy girl like some I have known, ye kin?"

Mairi was confused by her cousin's defensive response. Somehow, she had insulted Anne without meaning to. "I'm sure you are busy. I don't mean to sound rude. I just…" Mairi looked imploringly at her uncle, who appeared slightly amused by it all.

"Anne, yer cousins come from a place that allows for much freedom at yer age. It is the same place I came from, so I remember that I had a lot of time to do what was fun for me rather than what was needed by my family and my village. Ye are one of the few in this village who do both what is fun for ye and what is vera much needed by people. Tell them what ye are talented at."

Anne smiled brightly at her dad, obviously enjoying his sincere compliment. Mairi felt a twinge of jealousy that Anne still had her dad around. Quickly, she brushed aside such feelings, not wanting to let it spoil her day.

Anne turned to her cousins, who stared at her with rapt attention. "Well, like my namesake gran before me, I am a Healer. I have been blessed by the Fair Folk to be able to fix what ails a person, whether it is sickness of body or spirit. No one in our village has been sick for many, many moons since I first came into my abilities at 13 turns of the sun. I suppose it is the mix of faerie blood we MacLeod's are born with and the gift bestowed upon my Grandmother Anne when she was a young girl herself in Ireland. That is how I spend my time, tending to any who might need my attentions."

Mairi was surprised at Anne's candor in speaking so freely of having healing magic. Didn't she worry people would laugh at her? That she wouldn't be believed? But obviously Uncle James had not kept his children in the dark regarding their magical heritage, unlike his sister. Part of Mairi very much wanted to be jealous, while the other part of her, a much bigger part of her, wanted to ask Anne a million questions about all the weird things that had been happening to her in the past several weeks. Glancing over at Jamie, she saw that he was grinning like the Cheshire Cat in *Alice in*

Wonderland. He really was good about taking everything at face value.

"We have an awesome family!" Jamie declared. "I'll be sure to look for you next time I break a bone or get the flu."

Which made Mairi wonder if Anne could have healed her father before the cancer had killed him.

SHOWDOWN

Isle of Skye, Scotland
Lughnasadh 10 AM

Danny sat just inside the hut door, periodically peeking out at the two Highlanders. He had surmised through the few words he made out that they were left behind to guard the village and were not too happy about it. They kept busy all the morning drinking up the barrel of ale strategically placed next to them and now Danny's patience had paid off. They were slumped against each other, shoulder to shoulder, greasy head to greasy head, snoring.

Not losing a minute, Danny slipped the hood of the druid's robe over his head and stepped out of the hut. His stomach growled mercilessly. Unable to resist his hunger, he stopped momentarily to filch a piece of jerky from one man's pouch, which proved to be a mistake.

The Highlander must have felt the tug on his belt, because he lifted his greasy head and opened one pale green eye in his oversized face. "Huh…?"

Awakened by his friend's loud grunting noises, the other Highlander looked up, and seeing Danny in his druid's robes practically frozen to his spot, the Highlander grabbed him, yelling "Filthy druid!"

"Watch it…he migh' have magical tricks up his sleeve."

"Nay, no' this one. He would no' be stealin' me meat if he had his magic."

Their English was heavy with their Scottish accent, but Danny didn't need to be a genius to understand they were angry. He struggled under his captor's meaty fingers, twisting this way and that, trying to loosen the grip so he could make a run for it. He didn't know where he'd run, or even if he could outrun the muscular warriors, but instinct told him to try.

Just then an old man more wrinkled than a lizard's discarded skin, dressed in similar robes as Danny's, and sparking like a sparkler on the 4th of July, stepped out from behind a tree.

"Give the young druid to me," his voice boomed, not at all fitting with his aged appearance.

The warriors must have seen the electricity crackling and spitting from all over the Druid's body just as Danny saw it, because they dropped him like a rag doll onto the ground. The wind was knocked from Danny and he couldn't have stood even if he wanted to. He watched the Highlander's grime-covered sandals back away slowly, and heard their screams as a current of electricity shot across the village and hit them squarely in their chests. Their huge bodies fell to the ground, causing it to shake like an aftershock from a California earthquake. Glancing over his shoulder, Danny could see their chests rising and falling with ragged breaths, so they weren't dead.

Something jabbed Danny under his waist. Slowly reaching past the folds of cloth making up his robes, he felt a baseball-sized rock. Hope coursed through his body. This was a weapon he could use. Standing up slowly, clutching the rock hidden under the overlong sleeve, he looked the old Druid squarely in the face. From the evil intention radiating from his beady eyes, Danny understood he hadn't really been rescued. He knew he would only get one shot, so it better be his best.

As the Druid raised his hands, ablaze and sparking, aiming to blast Danny to the ground, Danny raised his right hand, the sleeve of his robes falling to his elbow, revealing the rock. In one swift movement, he pulled back and flung his hand forward, releasing the rock at just the right moment. The rock hit the old man squarely between his eyes, right on target, knocking him to the ground, electricity zapping out like a switch turned off.

Danny didn't wait around to see if the druid would survive. He took off running and made his way back to the trail where he'd last seen the Highlanders he was following. Thanking his lucky stars that such a large band of men and women, and even children, left many marks for him to follow, Danny easily found his way across the moor.

Ian lay on the ground twitching. The pain between his eyes was nothing compared to the burning fire filling his entire being as the electrical charge of his druidic powers coursed through his body. Still, his anger overwhelming him at losing the silver faerie chanter was worse than all the rest.

LUGHNASADH GAMES

Dunvegan Castle, Isle of Skye
Lughnasadh 11 AM

Mairi and Jamie had helped clean up the breakfast dishes by walking to the community spring, where clear fresh water bubbled up inside a little pool carefully lined by a rock wall, and hauling a bucket of water back to the house. Scrubbing the porridge residue out of the bowls, the remaining water was given to the animals in a trough outside the back door of the house. While she appreciated the sinks and faucets in her house, Mairi thought about how this old way of washing dishes was a much better system than they used in their modern-day homes in which water was used and poured down the drain to be lost at sea for good. She couldn't help thinking what a wasteful society she had grown up in. She had laughed quietly to herself, wondering why she was suddenly caring about the environment.

Now they were all happily trudging over the field of heather again, on their way to the festivities at Dunvegan Castle, little cloths full of hunks of cheese and oatcakes tucked away for lunch. Her uncle was singing a joyous song about threshing wheat and harvesting barley, to which Anne joined in. Mairi realized she'd heard her Granny Kate sing this same song once or twice, then she mused about how their little party of two that had consisted of only herself and her brother had now expanded to a merry band of five in less than half a day, not to mention the groups of other villagers scattered here and there also making their way to the festival.

This was not at all what she had expected when she was getting dressed the night before. She was actually having fun. She heartily agreed when her uncle declared how a swig of mead would be perfect for washing down their oatcakes, though she truly had no idea what he was talking about. She just knew that she felt recharged, ready for anything that might come her way. She was especially ready to take on her Cousin Danny, retrieve the chanter, and finally go visit the faeries. At least one thing had gone according to their plan; she had news of her uncle to bring back to her mom and grandparents when she returned to her own time.

If *we return,* she corrected herself, trying to keep the tiny spark of fear from becoming a bonfire in the pit of her stomach. Time was ticking away and they still needed to reclaim the silver faerie chanter.

As he marched along in his druid robes, surrounded by men, women and children, Danny couldn't believe his luck. He'd caught up with the clan and when one person questioned his presence, he'd explained in halting Gaelic that he was a foreigner apprenticed to the druids who were at the front of the procession. The person gave him an odd look, glanced at what must have looked like a hunched back due to the backpack under his robe, and gave him a wide berth. That was just as well, more space meant fewer questions. Staying near a group of minstrels singing merrily as they marched, the group soon broke into an old folksong and he recognized the words.

Danny was actually happy for the first time since learning about the reality of the silver faerie chanter and becoming obsessed with taking it for his own. He was thrilled to be participating in an ancient song he had been taught by his Granny Kate. It was a song he knew to have to do with the end of summer, which Lughnasadh marked for pagan people, and pagan simply meant "of the country." He was ecstatic at finding himself surrounded by country folk in ancient Scotland, on his way to witnessing a festival he should have only ever been able to read about in books.

He wasn't sure how he felt about actually possessing the silver faerie chanter, though he knew his cousins must be livid with him. For now he decided to simply enjoy himself. *Be here now,* he thoughtfully quoted Ram Dass, a spiritual teacher he'd learned about in the meditation class his Aunt Shaylee had encouraged him to take after expressing anger about his absentee father. *'Now' is a lot of fun, so I'll worry about my cousins later.*

As they came to the end of the song, they crested a hill and Danny caught his first glimpse of Dunvegan Castle. He had studied it off and on over the course of his childhood, having often heard tales at bedtime that his Granny Kate told him. To now see it in person, with hundreds of tartan-clad Highlanders, young and old, filling the moors surrounding it breathed more life into his understanding of Scottish lore than his imagination had ever been able to. For as they marched through the moor to the sound of bagpipes warming up for the noonday competition, there was the castle with the morning sun shining over their shoulders lighting up the towers rising majestically upward into the sky. Battlements connected the towers, upon which were posted the finest

MacLeod Highland warriors dressed in kilts and armed with spears, ready for any trouble that could possibly brew. There was no moat, for the castle was built on a rock rising out of Loch Dunvegan, seawater splashing the base of the cliffs. The only way in was by boat followed by a firmly guarded steep climb up steps carved out of the very stone. Needless to say, they would not be celebrating in Dunvegan Castle, but on the moor looking over the loch.

"We didn't meet your mom. Is she around?" Mairi was walking with Anne, cautious to keep no less than a foot behind Jamie, not daring to risk being separated. The girls had to pick up their skirts as they carefully stepped around horse manure that had dropped in the pathways crisscrossing the moor. Only a small percentage of Highlanders present had horses, and those who did own them had brought them for the upcoming competition of showing off their riding skills.

Anne smiled at Mairi. "She is at the house of her dear friend that has recently birthed her fifth son. With no daughters, her friend needs a woman's help. Anyhow, my own baby sister was only born last winter, so Ma feels she is too little to be brought to the festivities." As she said this, a wind blew in from the loch and stirred up a small flurry of midges, causing Mairi and Anne to gag. Mairi tried to block the midges by covering her face with her tartan scarf, blinking her eyes and clamping her mouth shut as an added precaution.

"I can see why your ma would want to keep the baby away from all these bugs," Mairi said as soon as she could breathe safely again, smacking a midge away from where it had settled on her bare forearm, ready for a meal of her blood. Glancing up, she caught her breath as her attention was drawn to the scene before her.

Looking out over the moorland, with Dunvegan Castle and Loch Dunvegan as a backdrop, the moor was alive with an infectious joy radiating from the hundreds of people gathered there. Women and men dressed in their best clothes, brightly colored tartans and long full skirts of coordinating colors. The MacLeod tartan was seen over and over, its dark blue haze underlining the clan's general feeling of royalty. Mairi appreciated that the tartan she wore was the same as the one her MacLeod relatives wore, making her feel right at home.

Before they could join the revelry, Jamie grabbed Mairi by the scarf and kept her back. "Do you see that group of MacDonald Highlanders arriving over there?" he asked her.

"Yeah, of course I do." *Who could miss them?* She thought sarcastically. They looked to be over 100 people.

"I have a weird feeling when I look at them, a tugging sensation, like something or someone is calling to me. Do you feel it?"

Mairi squinted in the sunlight and concentrated. She tuned out all the merriment going on around her. She felt the heat of the sun on her head, the rush of sea wind at her back, the sound of the seawater lapping against the cliff side below, and the solid earth under her boots. Just as Gran had told her, these elements of nature gave her strength. She sent her thoughts in the direction of the MacDonald group and saw that a lone druid in the back of the line, hunched over from some sort of deformity, swiveled his head in her direction just as if she'd called his name, looking at her with very familiar eyes.

"Danny has arrived. Let's hope he hasn't lost the chanter."

IGNITED
Dunvegan Castle, Isle of Skye
Lughnasadh Midday

Everywhere Mairi turned, there was a feeling of festiveness in the air. Jaunty tunes were being played on bagpipes, girls were kicking up their heels and dancing, boys were laughing and throwing spears at dummies made of hay, and children chased after each other in some original version of tag. Makeshift tents of various tartan blankets were erected here and there, preparing to keep off the noonday sun, and the smell of freshly cooked oatcakes and venison wafted across the moor, mingling with the scent of heather and the sea air.

But all Mairi felt after sighting Danny was cold hard anger.

How dare he take the chanter from us and just disappear? How dare he endanger all of us, even him, by causing us to be stuck in the past? Without thinking it through, she started to push past the people near her to get to Danny before he disappeared again.

Right then, Anne grabbed her hand and pulled her

over to meet a group of her friends, and before Mairi knew it, Danny was out of her sight. She tried not to panic, knowing that they would find him again.

She grabbed Jamie's shoulder and whispered loudly "stay close" as they all stood around admiring their Cousin Wills' ability to hit a dummy some ways off with his spear. Their uncle had not exaggerated about his son.

The hours of the day melted away as they sampled the oatcakes of various sects of the MacLeod clan. Mairi's panic rose increasingly as she realized the sun was steadily following its path across the sky and time was slowly but surely running out. *Where is Danny?* She was filled with hope, which was quickly replaced by cold hard fear as a group of druids swept through the field, sending children running for their mother's skirts, and leaving a smoky-herbal scent wafting in the air behind them. Her sense of urgency was quickly peaking.

Then it happened.

In the midst of watching the horse races, MacLeods, MacDonalds, MacCrimmons, and MacKenzies alike all vying for the title of top horseman, Mairi caught sight of Danny in his hunched-back druid robe. He was a little distance off also watching the races. Mairi could feel the chanter calling to her. Jamie felt it, too, she was sure, because he moved closer to her and his body tensed up. Without a second thought, the two of them moved as one and crossed the racetrack as soon as the last horse passed. Danny's eyes grew big as he saw them heading for him.

"Danny!" Mairi called, feeling as though the ocean spoke through her, adding its boom to her voice. Others must have felt it, for several Highlander druids in the crowd looked over at her. "Do not run away again. You do not know the seriousness of what you are doing." She was angry, but also afraid. She hadn't felt this way except once in her life, when she realized her dad really was going to die. She had been both terrified that he would soon be gone forever, and angry she could do nothing about it. But she'd stuffed those feelings quickly, not wanting their strength to drown out her memories of him, memories full of joy and love. Now she was feeling the same way because she did not want to be stuck back in time, she did not want to lose her mother and her grandparents, not to mention her entire way of life. The anger and fear coursed through her body, and the difference this time was that it made her feel powerful.

Danny sensed her power. He stood rooted to his place. At this very moment, he had to admit he was mixed up in something he most certainly did not understand. His sweet younger cousin who was usually quiet and easy going now appeared to be on fire with some power he had never seen a human being possess, other than the druid he had just battled. *Is she a druid, too? Is she even human?* He asked himself these questions, though he was certain he already knew the answers. The sun hit her red hair in such a way that her head was haloed in a fiery glow, her eyes flashed, and she seemed to grow in stature though he was sure she was still just barely 5'8" as she'd always been. Walking slightly beside her and kind of laughing, Jamie looked ready to tackle Danny if he tried to move.

"We need that chanter back. We cannot return to our time without it. Give it to us now or we are all stuck here forever. I know you want to return home. I know you would not have taken it if you had only talked to us first." Her voice had become calm, soothing. *She's like a Jedi Knight from Star Wars,* he thought. And it was working. Danny wanted to give it back. She was right. He wanted to go home, too… but not yet.

Mairi took a deep breath. She felt shaky, like what was happening was a game of pretend, like she really didn't know what she was doing. And she didn't, not consciously, but she knew instinctively to give herself over to the Elements. Whatever was happening to her, through her, she could see it was working. Danny was reluctantly reaching into his backpack, slowly reaching through the neck of his robe and pulling out the chanter.

Too late, Mairi realized the huge mistake they were all making.

The silver faerie chanter slipped out from under Danny's robe and a druid from the MacDonalds grouped together nearby could be seen whispering to an imposing man standing at his side. Mairi knew the damage had already been done. The MacDonald's eyes squinted as he looked more closely at Danny and Mairi, and she saw comprehension dawn on his face as he clued in to the silver chanter. The Highlander drew his massive sword and Mairi heard her uncle drawing his sword from somewhere behind her.

She did not want this to get bloody, and so she raised her hands up high over her head and drew a bubble of light spun of pure sunshine all around herself, her brother, her cousin, and she hoped, her uncle, too. The Highlander's sword clanged on the bubble as if it had hit solid metal. Jamie must have understood the second chance his sister was giving them for she saw him lunge for the chanter still in Danny's hand. Hastily, he attached the chanter to his bagpipes. Mairi knew he needed time to blow up the pipe bag and still more time to produce the tune needed for their escape. She didn't know how long she could hold the bubble in place, but she would die trying.

Ewan pushed his way through the crowd that was quickly growing larger over by the racetrack. His height and over-large bulk made the task an easy one, and the fact that he was a well-known Druid Leader meant people cowered at the sight of his fiery hair and immense presence. He had felt the draw of barely controlled Energy being taken in and released by someone untrained, and he was going to find out who it was.

He arrived at the center of the circle in time to see a young girl who could have easily been mistaken as his kin, red hair flashing in the sunlight, holding a protective shield around herself, a Highland warrior, and a young man prepping his bagpipes. The sun's rays shone through the bubble of protection and glinted off a silver chanter. Complete understanding came to Ewan in an instant. His first thought was, *Where's my Da?* He looked around the crowd expecting to catch a glimpse of his aged father.

As if in slow motion, Mairi watched the bag inflate, saw the pure hatred in the Highlander's eyes and the druid who stepped beside him raise his hands. She tried to be ready for the blast she anticipated hitting them at any second. In the final instant before she knew her bubble would explode from the impact of the druid's power, she heard the bagpipe music, saw her family move as one to touch her. In a smooth motion, she let the bubble drop, grabbed ahold of Jamie, and intoned under her breath, "To the Faerie Grove." A deep guttural scream from the druid followed them as they escaped.

FAMILY FEUD

Faerie Knoll, Isle of Skye
Lughnasadh 3 PM

In a whirl of darkness, Mairi felt the Lughnasadh festival disappear. There was the usual thump as they landed in the grass, breathless at having avoided danger for the moment. James whooped at having successfully traveled via magic necklace for the first time in over 20 years. Danny, Jamie, and Mairi grinned that they were relatively safe for the moment. However, Mairi had known it before they even landed that she had mistakenly envisioned the rock where they had lost Danny early that morning, not the Faerie Grove. They faced quite a walk ahead of them.

"If we want to make it to the Faerie Grove before we're followed, we best get moving," James urged them along.

Mairi tried to stand up from where she had landed in a clump of grass. Her legs and arms felt rubbery and her head ached. As she slowly rose, she fell back down, dropping her head into her hands, taking in deep breaths of air and trying not to faint.

"What's wrong?" Jamie asked.

"I don't know," Mairi managed to gasp out.

"Yer worn out by yer magic use. Just lay down for a bit and rest. Best to let ye recover than attempt to drag ye back to the Faerie Grove. Eat a little, too. Magic zaps ye of yer energy."

So, they all settled in and started eating their bread and cheese, Mairi sucking in big gulps of water, too. Danny didn't have any food, but softhearted Jamie handed him half of his. Danny was grateful, but could hardly mutter more than a thank you, for all the shame he was feeling inside.

Ian moaned. Gingerly reaching his hand to his forehead, he felt a gnarly lump there. The smell of burnt hair and skin filled the air. Slowly sitting up, he noticed a large rock by his side reminding him of what had happened. Focusing his thoughts, Ian pulled on the earth energy radiating up from the ground, concentrating on pouring it all into healing his aching body. He let out an involuntary groan.

Crawling over to the two greasy Highland warriors stretched out flat on their backs, he carefully pulled strips of dried meat from their pouches and began gumming it, careful to avoid his teeth that were sore from his declining health. Sucking water from his water bag he kept tied to his waist belt, he started to feel well enough to travel.

Looking around, he saw that the warriors had left their horses tied to nearby trees. Using a large boulder as a step to mount the tamer one, Ian began a mad gallop towards the Lughnasadh Games.

The sun was steadily creeping down the hillside into the ocean, so Mairi steeled herself for the walk to the Faerie Grove. But she had a few things to say to Danny first. "That was a dirty trick you played on us, tackling us and taking the chanter!" Mairi jammed her finger into Danny's chest, glaring at him through copper-red eyelashes.

Danny flinched, remembering the power Mairi had displayed at the Lughnasadh games. *Is it my imagination, or has her hair become even redder?* Danny wondered as they started walking over the hills, towards the knoll.

"Why did you do that, anyway?" she asked,

So Danny told Mairi about how he had learned of the silver faerie chanter when he was doing research for a high school essay. He'd realized it must be more than a simple fairy tale their Granny Kate told him at bedtime. When he saw a picture of it in their family heirlooms, then noticed it at her dad's funeral, he had wanted it so badly, as if it were calling out to him. He couldn't stop thinking about it.

"I know what you mean," Jamie chimed in. "I really felt a sense of loss when you took it, and I could feel it calling me across the festival. Maybe that is part of the faerie magic."

Mairi nodded, fingering the necklace. "I feel that from the chanter, too, but more so from this necklace. It must be magic."

Danny continued, "Besides, the chanter belongs in the MacDonald clan, not the MacLeod!" He couldn't help saying it.

Mairi pushed Danny, "I'm your cousin, dummy! Our fathers were brothers. I'm a MacDonald, too!"

She heard a loud gasp behind her and looked over her shoulder to see her Uncle stopped mid-step. *Oh geez! I'd forgotten we hadn't told him about that part of our life.* Turning to face him, hands on her hips, straightening up to make her full height seem even taller, Mairi quickly explained her genealogy to James. "Our dad was a really nice guy and never in a million years believed any of this fairy tale stuff. I guess our Granny Kate told Danny the Celtic fairy tales, because he lived with her for a while, but she rarely told them to Jamie and me, I barely remembered them, so it's all been a big surprise. Mom kept us in the dark, and I'm guessing she didn't care about any of this MacDonald/MacLeod feud pettiness, either, or she wouldn't have married my dad."

"I can see how it might become petty sounding when it is removed from Scotland and a few hundred years have passed," James conceded, "but as ye must know now, it is vera much a real fight in this day and age. Besides, how do ye explain what he," again James indicated in Danny's direction, "did to ye two? He is from your…our time, and he had no problem picking a fight over the chanter. The feud is real to him."

Danny hung his head, kicking a rock dejectedly with his shoulders slumped. "I just got excited that these fairy tales might be real and I wanted to hold the chanter more than anything. I wanted to show my dad that I could be a real-life Indiana Jones, recovering mythical archaeological objects, and maybe, just maybe he'd take notice of me. I never considered you'd let me have anything to do with it if I asked first."

Jamie patted him on the back. He had always looked up to and admired his older cousin. "It's okay, Danny. I think it must be some sort of faerie prank to make humans crave these objects. Besides, we're family. I'm sorry Uncle Adair isn't a better dad, but help us save our Gran and we'll forgive you. Maybe you can have a turn on the bagpipes, too, if you ask nicely." Jamie gave him a teasing smile.

Mairi did not know if she could so readily forgive her cousin, though she sympathized with him about his dad. For now, she had more important things on her mind.

James shook his head incredulously. "Ye are a good person, Jamie, better than me, to be sure. Family is vera important, and I can see that ye three might be the beginning of healing the Clans of Skye." The four of them again started walking toward the Faerie Grove.

Ewan, who was riding wildly across the moor with the MacDonald Druids following closely behind, intercepted Ian's path to the Games. Ewan slowed down and came to a stop next to Ian. "Da! Ye are alive! When I di' no' see ye at the Games, I was certain ye had been killed by that upstart Wild Druid female. Who is she? And how is it that ye are late to the Games?"

"I know nothing of this Wild Druid ye speak of, though I can guess it is the female who arrived in the night. I pursued her companion who had stolen the Silver Faerie Chanter from her, and was about to take it back when he hit me on my forehead with a stone," Ian indicated the lump on his forehead, "causing my powers to turn on me. I have laid unconscious for many hours now."

"There is no time to lose. We are pursuing the very group you speak of. They are off to the Faerie Grove, if I heard her correctly before she whisked all of them away in a bubble of protection. We must get there and stop them, if we are not already too late." Ewan grabbed Ian's reigns and turned his horse's head and they took off, galloping in a cloud of dust to the Faerie Grove.

FAERIE GROVE

Faerie Grove, Isle of Skye
Lughnasadh 4 PM

The walk took longer than expected, for Mairi could not keep a fast pace, but a part of her did not mind for she was lost in seeing the world with a greater sensitivity. The colors seemed more vibrant, the sounds louder, and the smells stronger. The feel of the slightest wind on her cheek had become as tangible as a piece of satin cloth rubbing against her skin. She could hear little critters such as mice and squirrels skittering about collecting seeds for the winter. She heard the call of a far-off cricket.

She noticed a scattering of lights in the wooded area to her left, and found if she stared too long the lights took on the shape of tiny winged creatures, like dragonflies and butterflies with human bodies and entirely made of light. Until Jamie grabbed her hand and pulled her on, she had not noticed she had come to a complete stop. The boys kept looking at her quizzically, but she was so caught up in her enhanced senses she barely noticed. The world was so much more alive to her than ever before. Something had changed inside of her, and Mairi wanted to soak it all in.

As Mairi and her family came closer to the Faerie Grove they had arrived at in the dark of the night before, Mairi saw that it was now occupied by a dozen men and women clothed in long hooded white robes. They stood in a semi-circular form, like a horseshoe shape, under the oak trees. These were not quite the towering oak trees she was familiar with on her Granda's land, but smaller bush-like trees. Still, they gave the Faerie Grove a wild feel, as if no matter how hard humans tried, they could never quite tame it. As she watched from a safe distance, Mairi could distinctly hear a humming sound, like the drone of the bagpipes right before a piper begins to play their song. It was a frightening sound, echoed by so many voices, as though they were angry about something, making the hairs on her neck rise with fear.

She felt several hands pulling her down and Mairi finally saw that the boys were all laying on their stomachs watching the druids, so as not to be seen. "Who are they?" Mairi directed her question at her uncle. "Why are they making that noise?"

"That is Ian MacDonald's Grove of Druids. He is the druid that ye see sitting in the center of the semicircle. He is an old man now, quite powerful, but something seems to have happened to him. He looks to be much weaker." Danny stiffened beside his cousins as he realized exactly who it was James was talking about.

James continued, "That is his son, Ewan MacDonald, standing next to him. The tallest druid there, ye can see his bright red beard shining like fire within his white hood. He is the druid who attacked us back at the festival, and quite possibly the most powerful druid I've ever met."

Mairi shivered as she looked at these two men who

she knew carried a deadly grudge against her family. She doubted it would matter to them that her father was a MacDonald. All they would see in her was her MacLeod and MacCrimmon ancestry. *How are we going to get through these druids and contact the faeries all before the sun goes down and midnight arrives?*

"What are they doing?" Jamie's question interrupted her worrying.

"They are communing with nature, lad." James shrugged his bearish shoulders. "I know little of what the MacDonald druids do, other than to try to steer clear of them for they are a strange lot who are powerful more because of the faith their clan's chief has in them, and the blind eye he turns on them, than because of any magic. Not to deny their magic, of course, which they wield with few rules to bind them."

"Ian is the druid who cursed our mother so that she is unable to use magic anymore. That seems pretty concerning to me," Mairi said.

"Aye, it is. I will not argue with ye about that. Though it appears Ian is no' the one we have to worry about tonight."

They nodded in agreement, for Ian was undeniably weaker and the other druids appeared to be protecting him within their semi-circle. It was his redheaded son that was in charge now.

"They are creating some sort of storm, I think." Danny pointed at the winds picking up in the trees and the swirl of leaves curling off the branches. Sure enough, as the humming got louder, the wind seemed to increase speed, so that soon the branches were beginning to whip wildly back and forth all around the Faerie Grove. The druids' robes and hair did not move, as though protected by a bubble from the roaring of the winds, but Mairi's skirts were billowing about her legs, even as she lay down, and she could see all three of the guys' hair rising and falling in the wind, just as hers whipped about her face.

"I think they sense that you are here." James was shouting now, to be heard over the roaring of the winds. "They have not ever done such a wild ceremony as this in all the years I've watched over this knoll on the pagan holidays."

"We need to get to the entrance of the Faerie Realm now," Mairi shouted back. "Where exactly is it? If Jamie can get a tune going on the bagpipes, we can magic ourselves to where we need to be, as long as we are thinking of exactly where we want to go."

James nodded his understanding, as Danny, Jamie, and Mairi all three looked at him expectantly. He stood and beckoned them to follow him. He ran a little way back to where they had just come from, finding a stand of rocks to hide behind, which blocked the gusts of wind. Mairi and the boys huddled in close, as there was barely enough room for all four of them to find protection. "Did ye notice the tree directly behind Ewan MacDonald, the tallest tree on the knoll?" James asked them.

All three nodded their heads.

"That tree is the guard of the entrance to the Faerie Realm. If ye can get yerselves to behind that tree, ye might be able to get the attention of the Fair Folk and ask permission to speak to the Queen, or the faerie maiden who gifted our family the necklace. I'll create a distraction so that hopefully the druids will leave off their ceremony, giving ye a little time to call the faeries."

"I'll go with you James," offered Danny, trying to show that he really did feel terrible for his earlier actions.

"Nay, ye have to stay with yer cousins or ye might miss yer chance to return to yer own time." Resting his beefy hands on Jamie and Mairi's shoulders, James asked them to pass on a message to his sister and parents. "Tell them I am vera happy. That I have a wife and bairns of my own, around the same ages as ye two, and a wee babe as well. I have truly missed them these past years, and sincerely hope to see them in the near future."

Mairi nodded solemnly. "We'll tell them, and we'll come back. We promise."

"When ye hear the wind stop, ye must be ready and play the bagpipes. Get to the faerie entrance as quickly as ye can. Ye will no' get a second chance." James turned and ran off toward the druids, drawing his sword.

Jamie readied the bagpipes, setting the bag under his arm, pipes over his shoulders. He took a deep breath and began inflating the bag until it was tight like a full balloon. Suddenly, the roaring of the wind ceased, indicating that the winds had stopped. James' distraction was working. Jamie started to play the tune and Mairi held onto both Jamie and Danny's shoulders, picturing the tree as clearly as she could remember it. She felt the familiar tug on her body, and found herself sitting hard on the grassy, leaf-strewn ground, her back against the tree, Jamie and Danny on either side of her.

Danny chanced a look behind him and saw several white robed people chasing after a highlander he could only assume to be James. "Quick! Do whatever it is you need to do!" he shouted to Mairi.

With shaking hands Mairi withdrew the herbs her mother had carefully packed into the little bag she wore tied at her hip. Pulling the drawstrings, she found three faded, dried pink roses, still smelling faintly of their sweet scent, and several sprigs of thyme, giving off a pungent aroma.

Pulling out a small abalone shell, she set it against a grassy hillock directly behind the oak tree. She set the thyme and roses into the natural dish. She also took out of her pouch a Fairy Quartz crystal the size of her palm, sparkling and of a light pink quality, and as gently as her nerves allowed she placed it upon the grass next to the abalone shell. Finally, she set a small clear bowl, the kind her mother often used for serving salt along with a hard-boiled egg, next to the other objects, using her water bottle to fill it with fresh spring water she'd carried from her Granda's land, splashing a little out in her haste.

She sat back with a sigh. "That's it. Now we wait."

"Wait? We have no time to wait. Look!" Danny grabbed her by the shoulders and forcibly turned her to look beyond the oak tree. What she saw terrified her!

Striding toward them, robes billowing about his solid frame, wind whipping through his fiery red hair, as a tornado of wind seemed to follow only him, Ewan MacDonald looked angry enough to kill them. As he stopped, a much frailer Ian MacDonald stepped out from behind him. Mairi could sense that Ian's Energy had returned, the earlier buzzing by the Grove of Druids must have healed him, and in their unity, the two druids were more powerful than she ever imagined.

"*Sa lá atá inniu Beidh mé ar ais go cad a bhaineann leis Mac Donald.*" They shouted in what Mairi guessed was the Gaelic language of Scotland, but she had no idea what they were saying. It was sure to be something full of bitterness and hate, something she probably didn't want to know anyway.

"They say, '*Today I will take back what belongs to Clan Donald,*'" Danny shouted in the growing wind, "and I think they mean it!" Gesturing to the crystal and herbs arranged on the ground, Danny frantically shouted to Mairi, "They'll be here any minute, why isn't it working?"

Turning back to her hastily prepared altar, with her heightened senses she heard a tinkling sound coming from her pouch. Shoving her hand into her pouch, she withdrew the tiny silver bell Gran had told her would be the final ingredient needed to alert the faeries to their desire for an audience with the Queen.

"The bell!" Jamie yelled to her. "You forgot to use the bell!"

Taking a deep breath, trying to ignore the pressure of knowing Danny and Jamie were counting on her to recall what she had been taught the previous month, she cleared her mind of all anxiety. Ringing the bell three times, she intoned *"Oh faeries within the hill, share with me what you will. In this my hour of need, for your understanding I plead. Show me what is currently unseen, grant me audience with your Faerie Queen."*

Stepping back from her altar, she blinked several times. A light had momentarily blinded her, and then there it was. A doorway suddenly appeared in the hillside where none had previously been. A beautiful woman, tall and willowy, with long flowing black hair, her entire body illuminated as though she were lit from within, reached out a thin, perfectly sculpted hand, beckoning. Her skin could have been white alabaster or dark ebony, for all Mairi could see it through the light seemingly radiating from her very being.

In a voice as melodious as the bell Mairi still held in her hand, the faerie said, "Hurry inside! You only have seconds to spare!" Mairi looked into her eyes, an unusual shade of blue tinged with violet, and lost all ability to think, forgetting about her gran's warnings regarding entering the Faerie Realm. She simply did as the faerie's hypnotic voice commanded.

Danny and Jamie started to follow Mairi as she stepped through the doorway into the Faerie Realm, when Danny remembered . . ."Jamie, the *sgian-dubh!*" and Danny sighed with relief when he saw that Jamie understood. Jamie pulled a small, ornate silver knife from his knee-high sock and thrust it into the ground at the entranceway, believing this would enable them to safely return to the world of humans. Danny had read somewhere that this was one of the few known ways for a human to keep their heads clear and escape losing all conscious memory of the human world.

As the portal started to close behind Jamie, Danny saw the look of total frustration on the MacDonald Druid's faces as their chance to regain the silver faerie chanter was taken from them. Danny almost felt bad for them, knowing how strong the desire could be to possess the chanter. Still, considering they would probably be dead, or perhaps trapped in a tree or something equally as frightening if those druids had gotten ahold of them, Danny had very little sympathy. Danny turned to follow his cousins into the complete unknown.

Ian saw his final chance to regain the silver faerie chanter slipping away and, mustering up the last of his renewed Energy, threw himself through the Faerie Door before it closed. Leaning against the tunnel walls, breathing hard, he sank to the cold smooth ground, ignoring the look of total confusion on his son's face as the portal sealed shut. Ian looked down the tunnel, unable to follow the waning light as his faerie mistress led the Wild Druid and her male companions away. He curled up into a ball, calling on the Darkness to renew his energy yet again. He wasn't finished fighting yet.

ESCAPE

The Faerie Realm
Outside of Human Time

The tall faerie woman moved as if she floated, like a bit of milkweed down drifting on a breeze. There was no need for a lantern since a soft glow did indeed shine from her very skin. Her clothing swayed gently as she moved, looking to be made of spider web thread and dyed the deep purple of an iris flower. The floor was shiny like marble, as if hundreds of feet had walked this path throughout time. Mairi could just make out the roots of the trees and plants above ground reaching through the walls and ceiling of the tunnel surrounding them. They whispered to her and a part of her wished to just sit and listen to what the roots might tell her, but there was no such chance. The faerie woman did not speak again, but led them silently deeper and deeper into her earthly dominion below. Mairi shivered in the cold, which seemed to issue from the faerie despite the light she emitted.

They soon broke free from the tunnel, and found themselves on a path that spiraled around and around on the walls of a great cavern. Lights twinkled in the ceiling above, like millions of stars. As Mairi squinted up at them, she swore she saw a shooting star. Though they still wound their way down and around on a solid dirt path, Mairi began to realize they were actually outside. Looking behind her and past her brother and Danny, she could not see the cavern walls above them anymore. She only saw the night sky and the silhouette of trees of all shapes and sizes rising up from the ground far below.

Gran said Faerie Doors lead directly to the Faerie Queen, but this tunnel was long and confusing. Maybe it's meant to mislead humans? Mairi wasn't sure, and was soon distracted from such thoughts as they continued on their way.

Looking down, Mairi saw a beautiful grassy meadow illuminated by the numerous Fair Folk lounging around. Some lay in the branches of the trees, others draped themselves languidly along the banks of a stream, and still others stood in small groups, deep in conversation, their voices floating up like wind-chimes to the humans descending upon them. They were clothed as their faerie guide was, in long flowing dresses and tunics in a multitude of colors as if the flowers of a garden had come to life.

Off to one side under a particularly towering tree, sat a woman with bright red hair down to her waist, a similar shade of red as Mairi's and straight as waterfall. Upon her head, she wore a silver crown made of twisted metal, not unlike the vines of an aged wisteria, a single green jewel dangling from a point resting above the space between her brows. She was clothed in a dress in all the colors of the rainbow shimmering like a prism. She sat upon a moss-covered, flower-strewn throne carved out of solid crystal. At her feet and all around the tree, tiny little faerie folk flitted about like dancing lights, adding to the festive feeling of the glen.

The faerie woman guided her three visitors to stand before the Faerie Queen, for queen she surely was. Bowing slightly first to the regal faerie, their guide then said to the humans, "I introduce our Queen. She is known by many names, all of which are her name, and yet none of them are her True Name. She goes by Aine, or Tanya, or Titania, or Maeve, or any number of designations. Call her the one you like the most and she will answer, but do not ask her what her True Name is for she will not tell you. Even if she did tell you, *you* could not pronounce it."

In saying this last bit, her voice dripped with too sweet of syrup, making Mairi wonder at the faerie's actual intentions.

The Queen murmured, "Thank you, Cali, that will do," sounding like a soft chime in the wind, and the faerie woman who was their guide took her leave.

Mairi attempted a wobbly curtsy, unsure what was expected of her, and knelt down on the grass at the Faerie Queen's feet, grabbing at her brother and cousin's legs to pull them down beside her. As she did so, she was surprised to find that her hand glowed ever so faintly. Watching the boys kneel, she saw Jamie too was glowing softly.

"We should call her Titania," Jamie whispered. "I liked that play by Shakespeare we saw last summer in the park." Mairi and Danny nodded their agreement, both certain they would be too tongue-tied to address the Faerie Queen at all.

"Very well," the Faerie Queen replied with a smile, as though Jamie had addressed her. "Titania I shall be."

Titania rose from her throne and leaned over in front of Mairi. Reaching for her chin, she raised Mairi's eyes to meet her own. Mairi was shocked to see that the Queen's eyes were as green as her own.

"Welcome home, granddaughter."

Danny could not believe what he was seeing and hearing. *The Faerie Queen...I mean Titania...called Mairi granddaughter? And am I really standing in the presence of the Fair Folk?* What had started out as a passion to find the very items that inspired the fairy tales he had grown up hearing, had become a real-life adventure of magic and druids and faeries.

Behind and providing a canopy for the Titania's throne he saw what must be the world's oldest apple tree, bright red apples hanging ripe and low on the long and gnarled limbs, lit up with tiny faeries flitting amongst its branches. Looking all about him at the beautiful flowers and faerie folk beginning to show their true vibrant colors in the dawn of the rising sun, appearing like a garden, he wondered if this was the basis of the most well-known story of all time. Unable to resist, he reached out as if to pluck an apple when a hand smacked his wrist.

"Danny! What are you doing? Don't you know that you do not eat the food of the Faerie Realm? You, of all people, with your studies of fairy lore must know." Mairi was staring incredulously at her cousin. *Can he do nothing right?* Mairi wondered.

"I wasn't! I promise! I only wanted to bring an apple home with me when we leave because it made me think of other stories that I've heard." He whispered the last part, "I don't think I would have eaten it..."

Jamie was standing next to Titania, and she smiled down at him. "I see the Silver Chanter finally made it back into the hands of the rightful family," she said in her musical voice.

Looking pointedly at Danny and Mairi she said, "I always trusted it would."

Mairi and Jamie smiled, and Danny nodded his agreement.

Turning to Titania, Mairi started to ask her about the necklace, but before she could say anything, Titania was embracing them all in a smile like a welcome invitation. Then she announced to everyone within earshot, "Let's give my great-great-ever-so-great grandchildren a welcome like none they've previously ever seen."

Before Mairi could protest that they were in a hurry, music began to play as faeries took up all manner of odd instruments. A song more glorious than all the birds on earth singing in unison began to fill the valley. The faeries that had been lying about the glen took hold of each other's hands and started dancing in groups of two and three in rhythm with the melodious song. In a parade of vibrant colors and flowing fabrics they wound their way over to the clearing on the border of which the Queen's throne stood.

Danny watched in puzzlement as Jamie grinned and began setting up the bagpipes he still held under his arm. *Why is Jamie joining in the festivities?* Not understanding what was rendering them susceptible to the music, Danny pulled the mouthpiece from Jamie, stopping him from inflating the bag.

"No!" insisted Danny, also grabbing hold of Mairi who had begun to join in the revelry along with her brother. "Don't you know that if you start dancing, you may never stop? Why are you under their influence when I am not?"

Titania looked at Danny in amusement. "Dear human child," she called him, though he had already celebrated his 18th birthday, "You are not related to the Faeries of Light as your cousins are, so only you are protected by the little dagger you left at my entrance."

With dawning horror, he grabbed his cousin's shoulders and shook them until reason returned to their eyes. Jamie held his head as if warding off a headache and Mairi looked at Titania with dawning suspicion.

"We don't have time for this! We have to save our gran and return to our time and place before Lughnasadh is over," Mairi exclaimed.

Titania shook her head. "Lughnasadh has already come and gone in your human realm. Do you not see that the sun rose to midday as we spoke?" She gestured to the Eastern horizon and indeed the sun was a golden ball of rays filling the blue sky with a light purer than anything in their modern-day world of grey pollution and chemical enhanced clouds.

Danny was gripped by fear. "We are stuck for the next six weeks?" he asked Mairi. "I have classes starting at UCLA and my mother will think I've disappeared from Northern California, possibly dead."

"You basically have disappeared," Mairi pointed out.

Jamie gave his sister a sour look. Mairi sighed. After all, she understood Danny's panic. Looking to the Faerie Queen, she agreed with Danny, "We do need to get home. Our family will be worried sick. Please, no more tricks. We have to find out what can be done to save our Gran. Can you help us? We've come all this way for your assistance."

"Yes, dear one, for you are so obviously my kin, made evident by your glowing skin, something unique to our kind, and love for a good dance. When your heart answered the call of the faerie music, despite having placed your knife in the entrance of my realm, I was left without a doubt." She spoke kindly to Mairi, reassuring her with her gentle voice. "It is much simpler to help your gran than you may realize."

CHILL

The Faerie Realm
Outside of Human Time

In the cold dark tunnel, Ian leaned against the damp wall regretting misplacing his staff before leaping into the Faerie Realm. Using the wall of the tunnel to steady his walk, he laboriously made his way along the dark tunnel towards the Silver Faerie Chanter and hopefully the necklace, too. *I will be young and without aches as soon as I get my hands on those Faerie Gifts, I'm sure of it.*

How will we ever get home? Mairi wondered.

They were sitting a little way away from the rest of the faerie folk, beside a waterfall that Mairi hadn't noticed on their journey in. The waterfall fell over the crest of the wall of a cliff so high Mairi couldn't see the top, though she leaned back on her arms as she lounged near the stream's edge. She could see eagles and hawks, or some sort of giant birds of prey, circling in the sky overhead. The water crashed into a deep green pool before making its merry way past them as a stream rushing through the Faerie Realm; arched bridges spanning it could be seen all along its way. Mairi and the boys reclined on the soft carpet of grass that covered the banks of the stream, while Titania sat gracefully upon a boulder near the water's edge, shimmering gossamer gown draped all around her.

The Faerie Queen had just finished telling them that she was indeed the faerie who had once fallen in love with a MacLeod chief's son, long ago in what seemed like a barely remembered dream. Now they were finally discussing how she could help them. "You have accomplished the first part of the task required to return your gran to her human form simply by coming to my realm and giving me audience. Next, you must return to your home and choose an area near your house to be a Faerie Door, a shrine to show your alignment with the Fair Folk. For it is the unfortunate circumstance of your grandparents that they ended up living in a time and place where very few humans believe in faeries anymore and that has caused all events which led to Caroline becoming known as Star the Cat. When you do choose an area near your grandparents' home and create a faerie shrine, then your family can visit with the faeries on the eight magical days when the veil between our realms is thinnest. Your mother and grandmother know how to make such a faerie shrine, and I promise, you will see your gran restored almost immediately. But choose wisely, for some spots call more to faeries with malicious intent, what we refer to as the Unseelie Faeries or Sisters of Dark, while other places call to the Seelie Faeries or Sisters of Light."

"How will we know the difference?" Mairi asked.

"I am Queen of the Seelie Court. My faerie sister, Nicnevin, is Queen of the Unseelie Court. I think you will know the difference if you meet her, though I hope you do not. She can be a bit much to deal with and some of her Court can be quite malicious. You've met one of them, my servant Cali is here on...diplomatic business. She is mild mannered for one of her kind."

Mairi dismissed the politics of the faeries before it dampened her mood and allowed her heart to fill with joy at the realization that they might have actually accomplished the task they had set out to do. Her gran returned to human form as well as a message to bring to her family regarding Uncle James, and they still had the silver faerie chanter so as to travel back to their own time and place, even if it would take waiting six weeks for the Autumnal Equinox. Mairi hardly dared believe it might all be true.

Titania rose from her seat on the boulder with the grace of a butterfly fluttering from one flower to the next. Even in the bright sunlight of the day, Mairi could see the iridescent shimmer of prism-like rainbow wings unfurling behind the Faerie Queen's shoulders, both separate from and a part of the glowing light still visible in the light of day, adding to her majestic visage. Gesturing for them to join her, they all rose, Jamie safely tucking his pipes under his arms, Danny hefting his backpack over his shoulder, and Mairi arranging her skirts more comfortably about her legs. Taking Mairi's hand, Titania guided them to a cave opening directly behind the waterfall that Mairi was sure had not been there while they sat talking.

Guiding them through the doorway, for that was surely what the cave was, the boys headed in first. Before Mairi could step through the entrance, Cali materialized as if out of the shadows. "I heard the Queen advising you on building a Faerie Shrine. Might I suggest you build it as near the house as you can, for the sake of your gran's health?"

Glancing over at the dark-haired faerie, Mairi's green

eyes met the other's violet blues and a chill ran up her spine like a North Wind might cause. Mairi shivered in the sudden cold. Cali smiled slightly, "Are you alright, child? Has a cold wind run through you?"

Mairi blinked in surprise, unable to respond.

"Cali, you mustn't toy with them." The Faerie Queen flicked her fingers at the other faerie. Urging Mairi forward, she told her, "Hurry! The tunnel will close soon."

Mairi joined the boys in the tunnel and as they walked away she heard Titania call out, "Safe travels, children. Do return to visit soon."

"It was a pleasure meeting you, Mairi. We *will* meet again soon, I am sure of it," Cali added.

The tinkling sound of the two faerie's voices resonating in her ears, Mairi looked back and saw only solid rock wall behind them. The roots were sticking out of the walls and ceiling, and the floor was as smooth as ever. Though not as bright, Mairi and Jamie gave off a slight glow, which allowed them to see well enough so as not to bump into the walls. As they made their slow ascent through the earth, Mairi noticed the glow of her skin slowly becoming fainter. *I guess it's only strong in the Faerie Realm,* she thought as they made their way through the damp cold tunnel, not at all sure what they would find on the other side.

ROOTS

The Faerie Realm
Outside of Human Time

Walking in heavy silence, pondering what they had just experienced, Mairi's mind drifted to Cali. *Who is she? Should I listen to her and build the shrine close to our house? It makes sense, as Star is so tired all the time, but as a human, Gran should be strong again...I hope.* Mairi shivered all over remembering the cold that blew over her as Cali had spoken to her. *If she's an Unseelie Faerie, why is she with Titania?* Mairi realized she was ready to be free of faeries all together. *They are worse than Tinker Bell, who only kicked and pulled hair. I feel like these real faeries could murder without any more thought than a human stepping on a bug.* She lost herself deeper in thought as she trudged to catch up with the boys.

Jamie turned to Danny, "Do you think it will be Uncle James waiting for us at the exit? It might be fun to spend the next six weeks with my uncle while we wait for the Autumnal Equinox to come around."

Danny shook his head, laughing hesitantly. "Yeah, I'm not so sure it'll be fun. What if it's the MacDonald Druids waiting? I don't think they'll care that we're MacDonalds, too."

SKREEEEEEEECH!

A scraping sound like nails on a blackboard echoed through the tunnel and everyone froze, hearts pounding and palms sweating.

Ian stopped where he was, a few feet behind the one called Mairi, a Wild Druid from his calculations, and the young men who always seemed to obey her. Upon hearing that they were all from the MacDonald clan, his nails had inadvertently scraped the wall as he steadied his walking. *How can that be so? How did MacDonalds get their hands on the silver faerie chanter, and why hadn't they returned it to their clan chief immediately? If they had, the chief would have allowed me to inspect the chanter and all this chasing would be for naught.*

Ian shivered in thinking what all he had been through of late, ending with his wretched time in the tunnels. He had been stumbling for what felt like hours through the twists and turns of the Faerie Tunnels. When he had jumped through the Faerie Door at the Faerie Grove, he had assumed it would immediately open up onto the Faerie Queen's Throne Room. Instead it was a labyrinth of misleading forks and crossways. Yet, here he was, so close to the Silver Faerie Chanter. *Surely, I am stronger than they are. A Wild Druid is untrained, knows nothing of the ancient ways of Druids. And here we are surrounded by Darkness.* Ian's thin lips spread into a wide grin as his hands fed on the Energy surrounding him. His prey was so close!

"What was that noise?" Danny whispered to Mairi and Jamie, gripping tight the rock he'd scooped from the loose soil to his right.

"Prob...probably nothing," Jamie answered. "An underground critter...I think."

Mairi couldn't recall seeing any creatures crawling around the tunnel when they had come in, but that didn't mean there couldn't be some hiding about. *Except my instincts are screaming there's danger nearby. But where can we hide this time?*

Searching, her senses on alert, Mairi whipped around, jumping to the side as she did so, to face the danger she knew lurked behind her. "Who's there?" she called out just as a lightning bolt shot past her down the tunnel, lighting up everything as it passed.

"Ian MacDonald!" Danny shouted, raising his granite weapon above his head, making aim to throw it. But the light flashed out too quickly for him. Realizing Ian was after the Silver Faerie Chanter, he shoved Jamie behind him at the same time Mairi stepped closer to them both. "Can you make a bubble again?" he whispered, "like you did at the Lughnasadh Games?"

"I...I'm trying! I used the sunlight, the ocean, and the wind before. Down here I feel none of those Elements."

Danny gripped his rock tighter. "He's bound to send a bolt again. The second he does, you two scatter. I'm going to try something." They slowly turned in their places, trying to determine where Ian would strike from next.

Ian was enjoying the suspense. *Little mice trapped in a hole, and I'm the snake about to strike.* He finally understood where this family's powers came from, for he could see their slightly glowing bodies, like his Faerie Lady but much fainter. *Unfortunately for them, it makes them easy targets,* he grinned maliciously. He'd toy with them a bit longer before killing them and retrieving both prizes.

Another lightning bolt struck the tunnel ceiling over their heads, and Mairi and Jamie ran away from Ian, in a shower of soil and tree roots. Brushing the bits out of her hair and clothes, she had an idea.

"I know what to do," Mairi told Jamie between panting breaths as they slid against the tunnel wall after turning a corner. "The tree roots, they're my answer." She could see Jamie's glowing head nod, then he shook his head.

"I don't get it."

"The roots, they hold all of the Elements within. They are the highway through which the trees transport all of their nutrients; the oxygen and carbon dioxide,"

"Air!" Jamie whispered with excitement.

"and the chlorophyll,"

"The sun, or Fire , , , and water and earth, of course," Jamie finished.

Mairi "shushed" at Jamie, "I have to concentrate before Ian gets here." She settled her mind and pulled Energy from the Elements and from the Light that exists in trees, slowly feeding fuel to the fear in her stomach, turning it to power.

Danny had seen the lightning bolt leave Ian's hand, but hadn't bothered watching where it had struck, or if his cousins had run like he'd told them to. He'd acted quickly, his hand holding the rock pulling up and back, aiming, he hoped, at the spot the lightning had originated from. He heard a thud and Ian's cold laugh.

"You missssed…" he hissed, but Danny wasn't so sure that was true. The thud had been the rock hitting a human body. It might not matter, though, because he didn't have a second rock, and he'd obviously not knocked Ian out. Turning in what he thought was the direction his cousins had run, he hesitated to move knowing that going the wrong way would get him hopelessly lost.

Heart thumping, palms sweating, Danny peered helplessly into the dark. *Which way?*

Then he saw it, his second chance. He could see his cousins standing ahead of him, their faint glowing bodies magnified by a round, lit bubble. They were beckoning him to hurry!

Danny ran, knowing Ian was somewhere behind him able to strike with lightning at any moment.

Ian rubbed his shoulder where the rock had hit him. He could see the bubble of power protecting his prizes, and he attempted to muster up the last of his strength, regretting his choice to play instead of just grabbing what should already be his. He aimed for the one still unprotected, his shadowy body silhouetted against the light of the Energy Bubble and Ian's final bolt struck between his shoulder blades.

Danny felt the blast and fell, skidding face first along the smooth tunnel floor, stopping at Mairi's feet as he blacked out.

Mairi expanded the Energy Bubble to encompass Danny's still form. Jamie knelt and shook Danny's shoulder, then put his hand on Danny's back. Mairi could see it rise and fall, and she breathed a sigh of relief. Jamie looked up at her with fear in his eyes, "How do we get out of here?"

Mairi took a deep breath and as she slowly let it out she turned her thoughts inward. *What is my Energy telling me to do? What are my instincts saying? This is so hard!* Mairi shook her head to clear it. *Oh! I've got it!* She visualized a red energy, the color of the Root Chakra she recalled from Gran's teachings about the Celtic Chakras that spiral through the bodies of animals and humans, and sent it shooting out of her protective bubble straight at Ian. Hopeful that he wouldn't expect such an attack since she'd never done it before, she banked on the element of surprise.

The red light enveloped the old druid, lighting up his entire body, showcasing the look of shock in his eyes. An image flashed into her mind of a caterpillar wrapping itself in a cocoon and then melting into a puddle before reforming as a butterfly. She heard Ian scream in pain, and then there was total silence.

Did I actually just melt a human being? Shuddering, she decided she would never know, dismissing her concern considering he had been determined to kill them.

Remembering that her cousin still lay on the cold tunnel floor, barely alive, she refocused her attention on him. This time she visualized a green energy, the color of the Heart Chakra, surrounding Danny's body. Drawing again from the trees above, she saw that energy manifest as a halo of green light encompassing him. He groaned and within seconds rolled over and blinked his eyes open. Mairi dropped the protective bubble with a sigh.

"Come on, Jamie. Help me support him. We have to get out of here." Together they pulled him up and wrapped his arms around their shoulders, struggling to walk in unison. Somehow, miraculously, Mairi still had energy to move her feet.

After an unknowable number of hours later, the bedraggled trio turned yet another corner, and Mairi saw daylight streaming through the tunnel entrance. Shifting Danny's weight, she told Jamie to help her sit him against the wall so she could see what they were about to face. Taking a deep breath and bracing herself for whatever was to come her way, she slowly poked her head out of the Faerie Door. What she saw was not at all what she had expected would be waiting for them.

HOMECOMING

Harris, California
Time Unknown

Mairi, Jamie, and Danny stepped out of a large hollow in the base of a giant oak tree. Spread out before them wasn't the Faerie Grove of Scotland, but the Oak Knoll on William MacLeod's property. The familiar view of mountains and valleys for miles as the crow flies with no ocean in sight immediately told them they were back in California. There was no way to tell what the date was, though Mairi guessed it was summer from the dry heat and golden grass. *The real question is whether it was the next day or years later?*

The next question quickly followed the first. *Will we be in time to save Gran?* The thought weighed heavily on Mairi's mind.

But the sense of relief at not facing the fury of angry druids was enough to give them a new burst of energy. With one glance at each other, they all hobbled as fast as they could down the mountainside toward home. When their eyes caught sight of the deeply rutted driveway, they began shouting and whooping. Completely worn out, all they could do was resume silently trudging along.

Mairi wanted to run with complete abandon, she was so happy to be back on her Granda's property, but she was pretty certain she would only make it if she kept a slow steady pace. She was just happy knowing Granda's house, his mini MacLeod castle, was at the end of the trek. Despite the clunky boots that were definitely giving her blisters, she fairly floated over the dips and rises in the mountainside on her cushion of joy.

She caught sight of the house and all three began calling for their family again. The front door flung open and Shaylee came running down the steps, Granda taking lengthy strides behind her. They met on the bridge spanning the nearly dry streambed, catching each other in a group bear hug.

Mairi pulled back first. "Where's Star?" The cat was nowhere in sight.

"It's not good," Shaylee said, and Mairi saw Granda's hair was sticking out in all directions and his eyes were blood shot.

"Let's go inside," Mairi said with a heavy sigh, heading slowly toward the porch steps. "We have good news. I just hope we're not too late."

That night, sitting around the kitchen table, mugs of peppermint tea in their hands, bathed and dressed in clean clothes, Mairi slowly stirred in the honey as she let the knowledge sink in that it was now August 15th, two weeks after they had left. *Time really does pass differently in the Faerie Realm! But, it could have been worse. Two weeks isn't really that long.* Her poor mother had thought they were stuck in the past for six weeks or forever, she didn't know which, and had been a wreck, evident by the dark circles under her eyes and her greasy, unkempt hair.

Now they were all sitting around the kitchen table, Star wrapped in a warm towel on Granda's lap. They wore identical wide-eyed expressions as Jamie regaled his elders with tales of their adventure. *He's inherited Gran's talent for storytelling,* Mairi thought, a bit proud of him.

When he had finished explaining what the Faerie Queen had told them they needed to do, they all began right away with designing the Faerie Shrine they would build in Gran's honor. They couldn't wait to get started as Star's end was definitely catching up to her.

FAERIE SHRINE

Harris, California
August 22nd, present year

Mairi sat back on her heels, wiping the sweat from her brow. *Will this really work in time?* It had been one week since she had returned to the present. She would be taking the bus back to San Diego with her mom and brother in a little over another week, with barely a day left before the start of school. Danny had already left for his first year at UCLA and would be signing up for his classes today. He had promised to share with her and Jamie all that he learned about Faerie Lore from now on and how it might relate to their families. Mairi realized how good it felt to be a team with him and Jamie.

Looking around at the little Faerie Shrine she and her mom had been working on that week, she had to admit it wasn't as lovely as the Faerie Realm had been. Nothing ever would be for her heightened senses had begun to fade as soon as she had returned to the present time. She held tight to the memory of being able to hear every creature's movement, smell every minor scent, and even to see what most humans only ever dreamed of seeing. On the one hand, it was good not to be inundated by so many sounds, smells, and sights all at once. On the other, she had felt powerful, like a super hero, something she hadn't felt since before her dad had died and she was still surfing.

Still, the shrine was as beautiful and as full of every detail they could think of. They had chosen a little natural alcove across the stream that flanked the other side of the house, in the opposite direction of the path leading to the driveway. A small tan oak tree made a canopy overhead, and underneath they had planted several types of mosses, ferns and flowering shade plants. They had chosen this spot because it was easier to walk to and water than the Oak Knoll up higher on the mountain. It was much closer to the house and simpler for her aging grandparents to visit on a regular basis. To make the walk easier, she had carefully made jewel studded stepping stones leading from the front porch, meandering through the herb garden that was beginning to flourish, and heading over the stream. Her brother and Danny had helped Granda carefully build a wooden bridge made from the branches of pine trees to span the narrow stream, stripping the bark off to expose the smooth white wood beneath.

Star was currently lying in Granda's lap as they lay in a hammock hanging between two nearby trees, overseeing their progress on the Faerie Shrine. Mairi had just gotten back to the shrine after fetching several items under the watchful eye of her mom. She smoothed down a bit of moss directly under the tree where she rested an abalone shell, larger and more colorful than the one she'd left in ancient Scotland. She filled the shell with sprigs of thyme, mint, and rosemary, the petals of several types of roses, and a large sparkling Fairy Quartz, this one a shade of lavender. Then she put down the gorgeous glass bowl she had used for potato salad on the 4th of July so long ago. Going to the barely trickling stream with a cup, Mairi made several trips back and forth to fill the bowl full of fresh water. The final touch was the little chime bells Mairi had picked out at the Farmer's Market on her last trip to town, a gift for the faeries.

A cold breeze blew past and a sharp tinkling sound was heard. Mairi shivered, remember Cali's cold smile. Something about this shrine didn't feel quite right, but Mairi shook the feeling off as nerves. So much was at stake. She was truly looking forward to getting a genuine hug from her human-Gran. Looking over at her cat-Gran, she smiled warmly at her and received a weak feline grin back. At that moment, directly above Star, a red light flashed and the chime sounded. Mairi shivered again, wondering if she should be worried about the Unseelie Faeries coming to this shrine.

DREAMING

Harris, California
August 29th, present year

The moon had reached full and was shining bright through Mairi's window. It illuminated her room with its soft silver glow. Another week had passed and still Gran hadn't changed back to her human form. Mairi's patience worn thin, her anxiety growing, they had pored over every book they found on the subject of faerie lore, but they didn't find anything beyond faeries loving to be honored by a shrine. Mairi would be leaving in another day and she was getting angry. She wanted so badly to see her Gran's situation resolved. *After all we've been through? Star won't last much longer! Is there really nothing else we can do to help her?* With that question burning a hole in her mind, Mairi fell into a fitful sleep.

Mairi dreamed that their neighbor, Helena, was visiting them. She was dressed all in velvet layers in shades of browns and woodland green. She still had her purple streak of hair in her grey, and was adorned with silver and precious stone jewelry. She was bustling around the kitchen talking to Gran, just as if she knew all about Gran's curse to be a cat. Mairi cautiously made her way into the kitchen, knowing she was moving in a dream. Helena turned and looked at Mairi.

As she turned, a deer with antlers walked up behind Helena and stood by her side. Mairi stared into the deer's eyes and she saw the deer was beginning to shimmer and transform. She stood up on her hind legs, her forelegs shrinking and reforming into long graceful arms tipped with elegant hands, her hind legs becoming human. Her muzzle shrank back and her face formed into a beautiful woman with long brown hair, little braids interspersed with twigs and moss tucked here and there, deer antlers still rising up from the crown of her head. Her eyes were honey-colored and round. She was now clothed all in suede-like fabric, in shades of earthy browns and forest greens. Mairi realized it was only this deer woman alone with her now, all else had faded away, and they stood in the Oak Knoll bathed in moonlight.

"Who are you?" Mairi heard herself whisper.

"I am Elen of the Ways," the deer woman said in the soft tones one would expect a nearly silent deer to use. "I am the Protector of Travelers, and I have a message for you."

The deer woman reached out her hands, running them through Mairi's hair on either side of her head, gently cupping her face. Her touch was soft and comforting, like a favorite baby blanket. Mairi felt safe.

"Child, you stand on the threshold of so much, yet time is running out. Your first task of many is to bring your Gran here, before the full moon begins to wane. This is where the Faerie Shrine is meant to be, this is where she will be healed."

"Is this the message you have been trying to tell me all along? Why didn't you just tell me when I first got here?"

Mairi was shocked by her own boldness, but the questions burst forth, unchecked, her temper rising.

"Gently, my dear one." The Goddess dropped her hands from Mairi's face, taking her hands instead. "All events in our lives happen when and how they are meant to. All that we endure teaches us a lesson we need to learn, no matter how difficult that lesson may be. My messages can only be delivered when the time is right, once certain events have taken place. Before now you were not ready, you would not have believed the importance of what I am saying. This is my first of many messages to you, but now you must go! You are needed and your time is limited. Your threshold is moving on."

All around Mairi, the world shimmered and blinked out, taking the deer woman with it. Mairi was alone in the dark.

TRANSFORMATIONS

Harris, California
August 29th, present year

Mairi blinked her eyes open and lay staring at the fading light from the setting full moon. Dawn would come soon. Mairi sat up. *A threshold! The time when magic is its strongest is when night turns to day!* The farther into day and beyond dawn that time ticked off, the less the magic would likely work. With the bonus of a full moon on the threshold of waning, their time was ripe.

Mairi jumped out of bed and pulled on her sheep-lined boots. Not bothering to take off her pajamas, she pulled on a heavy sweater over everything.

"Get up! Everyone, get up! I know what to do!" She shouted through the silent house, pulling open her bedroom door as she shouted again, "Mom, Jamie, Gran, Granda! Wake up! We have to change Gran back NOW!"

She nearly stepped on Star who sat outside her door. "I had a dream that you knew what to do. I was just coming to ask you what it was." She purred loudly as she wobbled back on weakened legs to Granda's open door. Mairi could hear her talking to Granda to urge him to move quickly.

Mairi ran downstairs, taking the steps two at a time in her haste. She saw her mom pulling on her hiking boots and a jacket over her sweatshirt and pants. "Bring your blanket," Mairi told her, intuition telling her it might be needed. Her mom nodded and wrapped it around her shoulders.

As Mairi ran to Jamie's room, she could hear her granda coming down the stairs. "Jamie, hurry! Grab your backpack," she called as she snatched a small bowl made of clay and a bouquet of flowers from the dining table.

Her mom came up next to her and handed her a bell anklet that she had always worn to parties for as long as Mairi could remember, and a pair of crystal earrings. "Will these do?" Mairi grinned at her and nodded.

Jamie was groaning as he pulled his sweatshirt on, stumbling out his door in dirty blue jeans and untied shoes. "This better be important."

Mairi ignored him and pulled open the front door, "This way, before the sun fully rises." Shaylee and Jamie followed, and Granda came behind carrying Star.

Completely breathless from their dash up the hill, they stumbled onto the relative flat of the Oak Knoll. Mairi went over to the giant oak tree that had been their doorway out of the Faerie Realm and set the bowl on the moss growing at its base. She beckoned to Jamie to come over and she pulled open his backpack, grabbing his water bottle she knew would be full since her brother, like a good Boy Scout, was always prepared for an emergency. Carefully pouring the water into the bowl, she sprinkled the flower petals in the water and all around on the ground. Hooking her mom's crystal earrings over the side of the bowl, she lifted the anklet from her pocket and gently shook it so that a soft tinkling sound could be heard in the predawn silence. She circled the anklet around the base of the bowl and sat back on the wet ground to wait.

The first rays of the sun stretched out across the sky, darkness rimmed by fiery orange and mountain silhouettes now in shades of purple. In response, birds everywhere took up their songs. Whistles and chirps could be heard coming from the meadow grasses and high in the trees.

As Mairi let out the breath she realized she was holding, she heard a gasp behind her. Turning to her left, she saw the cause of the gasp. Star the cat was glowing golden like the sunrays. As she watched, Gran's legs stretched and grew into human legs and arms, bare skinned and almost as white as the fur that once covered them. The fur on her head grew long, still fluffy and soft, reaching down to what was now a human waist. Star's sweet feline face became the elegant features of an older Gran similar to the woman in the pictures, though not as old as expected for her skin was barely wrinkled.

Shaylee ran forward and wrapped her mother in the blanket she had brought, a tartan wool cloth good for keeping the cold at bay. Granda, who fell to his knees and wrapped his wife in their first human embrace in more than two decades, quickly followed Shaylee. Mairi and Jamie rushed over, too, amazed that Gran was finally returned to her human form.

FULL CIRCLE

California
August 30th, present year

Mairi looked out the bus window, watching the morning sunlight glint off the blue green river. It meandered like an eel far below the bridge they were crossing from one Northern California cliff to the next. She and her brother were taking the bus home even though Jamie had backed her up in begging their mother to let them use the necklace. Shaylee had remained firm in her decision that some things would remain normal, like taking a 19-hour bus ride rather than a 10-second magic trip. Mairi had grumbled, but knew her mother could be stubborn so didn't bother arguing further. Besides, she was so exhausted from the day before, the dash up the mountain to the Oak Knoll, her Gran's transformation, and the excited celebration all the rest of the day, that Mairi actually liked the idea of not arriving home quickly where chores and school most definitely waited for her.

The redwood trees of the grove they snaked through on Highway 101 reached up high above the frame of the large bus windows, so high that Mairi could not see the tops. It dawned on her that she had not once that summer visited the redwood groves nestled so near her grandparents' mountain community. She lapsed into a happy daydream of taking a walk there with Gran, perhaps next summer, or sooner if they could.

Thinking of her gran, her mind raced through the events of the summer. It was hard to believe all that she had experienced since her last bus ride, over two months ago. Hard to believe how much her life had changed since she stole the necklace, mostly for the better she supposed. Now she had grandparents and an uncle and cousins she had previously known nothing about. She had faerie kin and magic, and the promise of more adventures.

Nothing could have made this summer better, except the impossible…if only her dad had been there with them. The hole in her heart left by the loss of her dad felt smaller, even if just for that moment. In a rare instance of vulnerability, she laid her head on her mother's shoulder and put her hand in her brother's, and drifted into a peaceful sleep, enjoying the warm sunlight on her cheek, happy to have her family by her side.

ACKNOWLEDGMENTS

Thank you to my Aunt Ann for her honest critiques and for reading several versions in the beginning when, I now realize, they must have been awful and not even a genre she likes. Thank you to my mom, Sue, for reading every version and letting me drone on and on and on for several years as I talked about my characters as if they were my friends. Her endless support is no doubt why I actually finished this book. Thank you to all of my early readers, Neda and Aden, April and Kaitlyn, Darcy and Hayden, Aunt Lillian, Cousin Jane, and Julie. Thank you to everyone from my novel writing classes at San Diego Writers, Ink for encouragement, to my amazing friends Raina, Marina, and Isis for input on my cover design, as well as to my later readers who critiqued for content, Emilia and Lily, and for a final copy edit, Marnie. To my husband, Curtis, who's quiet reassurance was more uplifting than he'll probably ever know. To my children, Jayden and Avalon, and my niece, Jazmyne, thank you for listening and offering suggestions here and there to help my young characters feel authentic. Finally, thank you to anyone and everyone who let me talk incessantly about "my book." My enthusiasm had to have grated on your nerves from time to time. There are too many people to name, but if you remember a time when I talked to you about "my book," then I am thankful to you for listening.

Coming Soon

**Celtic Magic
Book 2**

The Witch's Knot

Celtic Magic

Be wary the gifts the faeries may give,
We know not how they influence the life we live.

The Witch's Knot

Autumn is a time for change
Covering the earth with blankets of leaves
Underground the dead are bustling
Following the stories a faerie weaves.

Author Bio

H R Conklin grew up in the rural mountains of Northern California where her mother gardened and her father played the bagpipes, as well as spending long hours in the theater where her parents were a dancer and an actor, which undoubtedly led to her overactive imagination and love for nature. She currently lives in San Diego with her husband, two children, three dogs, and one cat. She teaches kindergarten at a public Waldorf charter school in which she tells many fairy tales to the children, and makes up stories in her spare time.

Connect with H R Conklin on her website, Facebook, or Instagram under Wild Rose Stories

Please leave a review on Amazon.com.

slàinte mhath
Scottish Gaelic for "good health"

Made in the USA
San Bernardino, CA
23 January 2018